As the top-secret uncovers the evil traitor in its ranks, **A YEAR OF LOVING DANGEROUSLY concludes....**

"Jonah"

The mysterious man behind the SPEAR agency is about to come out of hiding and do combat with his greatest nemesis....

But first, the world-weary agent had a debt of the heart to pay. And so he traveled to see the one woman he had always loved—the woman he had left behind—but had never forgotten....

Cara Justice

Age had only made this blue-eyed beauty even more lovely....

She had never thought she would see him again, yet suddenly, there before her, stood the man she had fallen in love with when she was just sixteen. The father of her child and the soldier who had stolen her heart. Dare she hope their happily-ever-after had finally arrived?

"Simon"

He would have his revenge, even at the cost of revealing himself to his foe....

Simon was preparing for his greatest battle yet— facing down the one man he could never forgive. The elusive "Jonah," a man he knew better than anyone—even himself. A man he was determined to destroy—even if he died in the process....

Dear Reader,

The excitement continues in Intimate Moments. First of all,
this month brings the emotional and exciting conclusion of
A YEAR OF LOVING DANGEROUSLY. In *Familiar Stranger,*
Sharon Sala presents the final confrontation with the archvillain
known as Simon—and you'll finally find out who he really is.
You'll also be there as Jonah revisits the woman he's never
forgotten and decides it's finally time to make some important
changes in his life.

Also this month, welcome back Candace Camp to the
Intimate Moments lineup. Formerly known as Kristin James,
this multitalented author offers a *Hard-Headed Texan* who
lives in A LITTLE TOWN IN TEXAS, which will enthrall
readers everywhere. Paula Detmer Riggs returns with
Daddy with a Badge, another installment in her popular
MATERNITY ROW miniseries—and next month she's back
with *Born a Hero,* the lead book in our new Intimate Moments
continuity, FIRSTBORN SONS. Complete the month with
Moonglow, Texas, by Mary McBride, Linda Castillo's
Cops and...Lovers? and new author Susan Vaughan's debut
book, *Dangerous Attraction.*

By the way, don't forget to check out our Silhouette Makes
You a Star contest on the back of every book.

We hope to see you next month, too, when not only will
FIRSTBORN SONS be making its bow, but we'll also be bringing
you a brand-new TALL, DARK AND DANGEROUS title from
award-winning Suzanne Brockmann. For now...enjoy!

Leslie J. Wainger
Executive Senior Editor

Please address questions and book requests to:
Silhouette Reader Service
U.S.: 3010 Walden Ave., P.O. Box 1325, Buffalo, NY 14269
Canadian: P.O. Box 609, Fort Erie, Ont. L2A 5X3

Sharon Sala
Familiar Stranger

Silhouette®

INTIMATE MOMENTS™

Published by Silhouette Books

America's Publisher of Contemporary Romance

Special thanks and acknowledgment are given
to Sharon Sala for her contribution
to the A Year of Loving Dangerously series.

 SILHOUETTE BOOKS

ISBN 0-373-27152-2

FAMILIAR STRANGER

Copyright © 2001 by Harlequin Books S.A.

This edition published by arrangement with Harlequin Books S.A.

® and TM are trademarks of Harlequin Books S.A., used under license.
Trademarks indicated with ® are registered in the United States Patent
and Trademark Office, the Canadian Trade Marks Office and in other
countries.

Visit Silhouette at www.eHarlequin.com

Printed in U.S.A.

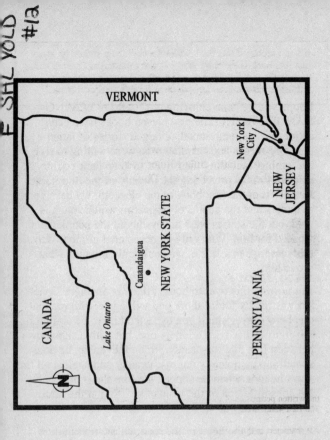

Dear Reader,

I hope you've been enjoying A YEAR OF LOVING DANGEROUSLY. The past eleven books have been action-packed, emotionally charged stories of larger-than-life heroes and heroines who were willing to risk everything, including their lives, to keep their country safe, as well as protecting the identity of the inimitable Jonah. From the first book to the eleventh, we have come to understand the depths of respect in which Jonah is held, but the stories were always about the people who worked for him. With only an occasional glimpse into this secretive man's life, we could only imagine what drove him.

But now, in this twelfth book, *Familiar Stranger*, Jonah's story is finally told. I think you will agree with me that this hero is everything you expected him to be and more. His journey has been a lonely one, but with a showdown between him and the deadly Simon inevitable, he does something completely out of character and against all the vows he took when he slipped into the shoes of Jonah. He goes in search of the woman he lost and the family he's never known.

As you read, the heart of the man will be revealed, as will Simon's identity. And even then, you won't know—until the very last pages—how A YEAR OF LOVING DANGEROUSLY will end.

I love to hear from my readers and can be reached at P.O. Box 127, Henryetta, OK, 74437, or online c/o www.eHarlequin.com.

Sharon Sala

Chapter 1

Rain thumped against the small, thatched roof like soggy bullets. The familiar sound of an incoming Huey rocked the air as it passed overhead, but Private David Wilson was deaf to everything but the panic.

Blood...so much blood. Don't look at Frank. Don't think about what he's done...what he made you do. Destroy the evidence before it's too late.

The scent of gasoline was everywhere now. On the walls, on the bodies, saturating the money that his brother, Frank, had been willing to die for.

Stupid. Stupid. Stupid. Money for guns. Brother for brother. Honor for sale. Stupid. Stupid. Stupid.

Match. Need a match. Don't look at Frank. Just think about what has to be done.

Jonah rolled from his belly to his back and kicked in his sleep, unconsciously sending his covers to the foot of the bed. Even though the second-story window beside his bed was open, there was little breeze stirring. It was un-

seasonably warm for the Colorado mountains this time of
year, but the sweat on his body wasn't from the heat of
the night. It was from the hell in his dream. And even in
that dream, he still couldn't control his own warning.

*He looked. And saw the dead gunrunners…and the
money, now saturated with rain and mud and gasoline…and the blood pooling beneath his brother's body.*

A muscle twitched near Jonah's mouth, a reflex to the
scream echoing inside his mind as the match was struck.
A word slipped from between his lips, too faint to be
heard, although it hardly mattered. He'd been alone for so
many years he wouldn't have known how to share his
thoughts if he'd had the chance.

In the space of one breath, the dream jumped from 1974
and Vietnam to two weeks ago in New York City, bringing
with it the same sense of desperation and leaving Jonah
writhing in torment.

*From the air, New York City appeared as a vast but
inanimate object, with only a small cluster of land and
trees they called Central Park embedded within the mass
of concrete and steel.*

*He banked the chopper toward the unwinding ribbon
that was the East River, and as he did, his heart began to
pound. Only a few more minutes and this hell would come
to an end.*

*Below him was a dark blanket of land peppered with
thousands and thousands of lights. Almost there. With the
desperation in Del Rogers's voice still ringing in his head,
all he could think was, no more. Too many innocents have
been caught in this crazy man's revenge to bring me down.
Please, God, just let Maggie and her baby still be alive.
Let us get them out of all this still breathing and kicking.*

Unconsciously, Jonah's hands curled into fists, as he relived the descent of the black stealth helicopter he was

piloting, all the while knowing that Simon was holding a woman and child between himself and destiny.

A faint breeze came through the open windows, blowing across his nude body, but Jonah was too deeply asleep to appreciate the sensation. The muscles in his legs twitched as he relived landing the chopper.

In the landing lights, the fear on Maggie's face was vivid, overwhelming Jonah with a renewed sense of guilt.

The cowardly son of a bitch, using innocent people just to get to me.

The force of wind from the descending helicopter whipped Maggie's hair and clothes and sent a shower of grit and dust into the air around them. He saw her trying to use her body as a shield for the hysterical baby in her arms, but the man holding her hostage gave her a yank, making sure she still stood between him and the guns aimed in his direction.

As the helicopter landed, Jonah could only imagine what was going through Maggie's mind—all this hell—all the danger to her family—and for a man she didn't even know. He slid open a door in the side of the chopper and flashed a bright light in Simon's face.

In that moment, Jonah's mind shut down. Before his senses could wrap around the truth of what he was seeing, Simon's body jerked. He had been shot by Del Rogers.

After that, everything seemed to be happening in slow motion.

SPEAR agents firing from surrounding rooftops.

Simon taking another bullet.

The play of emotions moving across Simon's face—a face that was aged with hate as well as passing years, bearing scars both old and new.

The impact of the bullet as the shot tore through Simon's body.

The desperate lunge Simon made toward the East River in a last-ditch effort to escape.

The way the water parted to let him in.

The knot of dismay in Jonah's belly when he realized that Simon was gone.

Jonah woke with a grunt and sat straight up in bed. It had been two weeks, and he still hadn't gotten over the shock of seeing Simon's face. The guilt of all these years—of thinking he had killed his brother—had been for nothing.

"Ah, God…Frank. I thought you were dead."

He shook his head and then massaged the tension in the back of his neck. As he did, the powerful muscles in his shoulders bunched and rolled. The misery of these nightmare-filled nights was getting to him. He needed to work it off, but not in the weight room, as he normally did. He wanted the air against his skin and the ground beneath his feet. He needed to run until he set his muscles on fire.

It was 5:10 A.M. as he rolled out of bed and strode to the bathroom. Even the shock of cold water on his face was not enough to wash away the horror of what he'd been dreaming. With a curse on his lips, he strode into his bedroom, moving through the darkness with the confidence of an animal that well knew its lair.

Every motion was deliberate as he dressed—grabbing a pair of shorts and a clean T-shirt from the top drawer of the dresser, then lacing his running shoes and fastening the holster of a small-caliber handgun at the waistband of his shorts. Five minutes later he paused at the kitchen table, fingering the single page of a letter he'd received less than twenty-four hours ago. Although the room was too dark to read the words again, he didn't need to read them to remember.

I know who you are. Your time has come. I'll be in touch. Frank.

Jonah shuddered. Ghosts. He'd never believed in them until now. He dropped the letter and moved onto the deck. Daybreak was less than an hour away, but he didn't need light by which to see. He stretched a couple of times to ease tense muscles, then he stepped off the deck and began to walk toward the trees. Within moments, he'd moved to a jog, and by the time he disappeared into the tree line, he was running, only now there were no demons to outrun. He had a face and a name to go with it and only a short time left before the inevitable confrontation. Only God knew how it would end, and in a way, it almost didn't matter.

Almost.

He wanted this over. All of it. Being Jonah. Hiding secrets. Telling lies. Just over. He wasn't the first man to give up his identity for the good of his country and he wouldn't be the last. But he'd given up more than an identity, and that was what dug at him in the wee hours of the mornings when sleep eluded him.

He'd given up Cara.

Unconsciously, he increased his speed as the memory of her face crept into his mind. So pretty. So young. And they'd been so much in love. Looking back, he would say crazy in love.

He ducked on the path to avoid a low-hanging branch and swiped his arm across his forehead, catching the sweat before it ran in his eyes. His calves were starting to burn. The pain felt good—a reminder that he was more than just a machine for Uncle Sam.

Cara.

My God, what had he been thinking? They were only sixteen years old and he'd begged her to run away with him. What had he thought they'd do? Better yet, where in hell would they have gone? The fact that she'd pleaded with him to wait until they were out of college said something for the theory that girls matured faster than boys. In their case, she certainly had. She'd known what he'd refused to consider, and because they'd fought and then been too stubborn to admit they were wrong, their lives had turned upside down.

A large bird flew across his line of vision, and he could tell by the absence of sound at its passing that it was an owl, probably on its way home from a night of hunting.

If only he'd had the sense to go home after their fight, but no, he'd had to show the world—and maybe himself—that he was a man. And what better way to do that than to go fight a war?

His older brother, Frank, had signed up months earlier and was already somewhere in the jungles of Vietnam. The family had gotten one letter from him in all that time, and their mother had cried herself to sleep when it came. But that hadn't occurred to David then. All he'd wanted to do was prove that he was man enough for Cara to love.

When he told her he'd enlisted, he hadn't expected her to like it, but he'd expected her to wait for him to come back. Instead, she'd cried hysterically, claiming that he'd chosen the army over her. Unable to undo all the choices he'd made, he got on the bus and never came back, although at first, that hadn't been his plan.

He'd written to her religiously, but to his dismay she never replied. Over a year and a half later and a world away in Saigon, it had all come undone. Receiving a package containing all of his letters unopened was rough, but it was the two accompanying newspaper clippings that nearly killed him. One was the announcement of her wedding, the second the birth of her first child.

He knew Cara, and he'd done the math. The baby was his. He had a daughter back home in the state of New York, and someone else was going to raise her.

After that, short of turning the gun on himself, he'd tried

to die. So many times. In so many ways. It should have been simple. Everyone else around him was dying in combat, but it was as if he'd become immortal. Nothing could hurt him.

Then he'd discovered Frank's treason, and bloodshed had followed. After that, he'd quit on everything, including himself. Just before the war was over, he was recruited by SPEAR. By then, giving up David Wilson was simple. His parents were dead. Cara had given her life and their child to another man. A man who slept with her and laughed with her and raised the baby David had put in her belly.

And David had left her alone—until now. With no way to know what the future would hold, he needed to make peace with his past. Cara was a widow these past three years. Their child was grown. Hell, he was a grandfather and had never set eyes on his own daughter. It, by God, wasn't fair.

Daybreak was hovering on the horizon by the time he reached the edge of the cliff. His heart was still pounding from the run, his clothes dripping with sweat as he lowered himself down into a sitting position on the lip of a rock, as he had so many, many times before.

The air was beginning to stir, promising a stiff breeze before the day was out. He sat with back straight and legs folded, his hands resting lightly on his knees, staring at the crack of light appearing over the mountain. The sky was changing now, wrapping itself in pale, dusty blues intermingled with threads of hot pink and gold.

As he watched, the anger in him slowly stilled. He'd seen just such a sunrise many times since he'd come to this place, but it never failed to instill in him a feeling of awe—a gentle and vibrant reminder of Who was really in charge. The vista blurred and he told himself it was nothing but sweat in his eyes.

Moments later, the sun made itself known—the first rays

catching and then holding in the silver wings of hair at his temples. With a deep, heartfelt sigh, he stood. It was time to go home. But not just to the cabin. Thanks to the chaos Frank Wilson had created, his days as Jonah had to be over. His guess was, the President was probably already in the process of choosing his successor, but would wait until his formal request for retirement. And before that came, he had the final showdown with Frank. The way he saw it, he owed it to himself to make peace with his past, and to do that, he had to become David Wilson one last time and see Cara—the girl he had left behind.

Finger Lakes Region, New York State

Cara Justice swatted at a bee that kept pilfering about her flowers as she knelt at the side of the flower bed.

"Get back, you little beggar. Just let me get these weeds out of the bed and then you can have at the blossoms."

The bee, of course, didn't answer, and Cara, of course, expected none. But it felt good to be talking aloud, even if there was no one to hear. She tossed aside the last handful of weeds and then stood, brushing off the knees of her slacks and straightening the collar of her shirt. The day was warm, but not unbearably so. She stood for a moment, surveying the landscape of her backyard, and smiled. She loved this time of year. Everything was new and green, flowers in varying stages of buds and blooms, birds nesting.

Renewal.

That's what it was. Everything was new all over again. *Except me,* she thought, and then thought of her youth and sighed. Those had been sad times and nothing she would ever want to relive. She'd suffered, endured and prevailed. After that, she'd made herself always look forward, never dwelling on the past. Truth be told, she didn't want to be young again. It had hurt too much the first time around.

Turning fifty had been a plateau she'd welcomed. Her oldest daughter, Bethany, who lived just down the road, was grown and married, as were her two youngest children, Tyler and Valerie, although they lived out of state.

She bent to pick up her hoe, and as she did, her blond chin-length hair brushed the sides or her face. She straightened, tossing her head to get it out of her eyes, and made a mental note next time she came out to tie it all back. As she started toward the gardening shed, a stiff breeze came out of nowhere, molding her clothes to her body and momentarily outlining her slender, willowy build. From a distance, she could easily have passed for a young, thirty-something woman. It wasn't until one looked closer that the tiny wrinkles at the corners of her eyes and the small laugh lines framing her mouth were evident. Her stomach growled as she put up the hoe and tossed her gloves in the basket. She glanced at her watch, surprised that noontime had come and gone.

As she started toward the back door, she heard the sounds of an approaching car. It couldn't be Bethany. She and her family were on vacation and weren't due back for several days. Maybe it was the mailman with a package, she thought, and hurried toward the front of the house, anxious to catch him before he left.

It wasn't until she rounded the corner of the house and saw the tail end of a dark sedan that she knew it wasn't the mailman. She paused in the shade beneath the cluster of maple trees and watched as a tall, middle-aged man emerged from the driver's side of the car. His shoulders were broad, his belly flat beneath his white polo shirt. He walked with a military bearing—head back, chin up. His hair was short and dark, but winged with silver above his ears. In reflex, she touched her own hair, aware that the same silver threads lay there among the taffy-colored strands, only not as evident as those on the man.

He didn't see her at first, and so she allowed herself to stare, trying to think why he seemed so familiar. She was certain she'd never seen him before. She would definitely have remembered. And then the stranger suddenly stopped and turned, as if sensing her scrutiny. She waited for him to speak.

David didn't have to look at the map to Cara's home that he'd downloaded from the Internet. It was burned into his memory. Even though he knew how to get to her house, he felt lost. As Jonah, he'd done something unheard of by seeking out any part of his past.

But it wasn't as if he'd just walked off the job. There was enough equipment in the trunk of his car to connect him with everything from spy satellites to the President of the United States, should the need arise. For all intents and purposes, he was still in charge of SPEAR, but in his heart, he was already pulling away.

Frank had set the ball rolling in this direction the day he'd kidnapped Easton Kirby's son. After the last incident with Maggie and her baby, David had mentally called it quits. There would be no more people assigned to risk their lives on his behalf. Not for an issue that was technically personal. The President knew David's feelings on this, and although David had not said a word about looking for Cara, he made sure the President knew things were going to change.

As he came around a curve, his heart started to pound. He was almost there. He began slowing down, then turned the steering wheel, guided the car into a long, graveled drive and pulled up to the house. He killed the engine and then sat for a moment, absorbing the structure.

It was a long, rambling two-story brick home with a porch that ran half the length of the house. A chimney rose from the center of the roof, evidence of warm fires on cold winter nights. Ancient trees threw large patterns of shade upon the lawn while flowers in bloom abounded everywhere.

He sighed. It looked so beautifully ordinary. Would a woman who lived in a home like this be able to accept what he was going to say? Then he took a deep breath and got out of the car. Hesitation would gain him nothing. Centering his sunglasses comfortably on the bridge of his nose, he started toward the house.

More than halfway up the walk, he caught a movement from the corner of his eye and paused, then turned.

God in heaven, it was her—standing beneath a cluster of maples with a curious look on her face. Once he'd seen her, his feet moved of their own accord. When he was only yards away, he said her name, and as he did, he saw confusion and then panic as it registered on her face.

"Cara."

She gasped, then in spite of the heat, shivered.

He took a step toward her, and then another. Cara started to shake.

"Cara, don't be afraid."

"No," Cara moaned, and covered her face. "No ghosts. No ghosts. I don't believe in ghosts."

Suddenly his voice was right beside her. She opened her eyes.

"I'm not a ghost."

"David?"

His stomach knotted. After all these years, hearing his name from her lips was more painful than he would have believed.

Before he could answer her, she shook her head in vehement denial.

"You're not David. David is dead."

This was harder than he'd imagined. "Cara... I'm sorry...so sorry."

He reached for her hand. When he touched her, she shuddered once, then her eyes rolled back in her head.

He caught her before she fell.

"Damn, damn, damn," he muttered, as he carried her unconscious body to the shade of the porch.

Choosing the nearest chair, he sat down, cradling her carefully as he looked at her face, trying to find the girl that he'd known in the woman he held in his lap, but she was gone.

It wasn't until her eyelids began to flutter and he saw the clear, pure blue of her eyes that he found the girl he'd left behind.

"Are you all right?" he asked.

Her hands cupped his face—her eyes wide with disbelief.

"David? Is it really you?"

A car drove past on the road beyond the house, and David looked up, suddenly aware of how public their reunion had become.

"Let's go inside. We need to talk," he said, and started to carry her inside when she slid out of his lap and threw her arms around his neck.

"How? Why? Did you—"

He put a finger across her lips, momentarily silencing her next question.

"Inside…please?"

Cara grabbed him by the hand and led him inside the house. The moment they entered the hallway, she shut the door behind them then stood, staring at his face with her hands pressed to her mouth to keep from crying.

David ran a shaky hand through his hair, then gave her a tentative smile.

"I don't know quite where to start," he said. "Do you want to—"

Tears rolled down her face, silencing whatever he'd been about to say.

"Oh, honey, don't. You know I never could stand to see you cry."

And then her hands were on his shirt, moving frantically across the breadth of his chest, then up the muscular column of his throat, then tracing the outline of his features. He grabbed her fingers, trying to put some distance between them so he could think. But there had already been forty years of distance, and for Cara, it was forty years too much.

His name was just a whisper on her lips as she wrapped her arms around his neck. Before he could think, she'd kissed him—a tentative foray that went from testing ground status to an all-out explosion. It was instinct that made him pull her against his body, but it was need that kept her there.

"If this is a dream, I don't want to wake," Cara muttered, and then pulled his shirt out of the waistband of his slacks.

His stomach flattened as he inhaled sharply. The feel of her fingernails against his skin was an aphrodisiac he wouldn't have expected. Then her arms were around his waist as she lifted her lips for his kiss. David was broadsided by the sexual tension erupting between them. He'd planned for everything—except this.

"Cara...God, Cara, we shouldn't be—"

"Since when did shouldn't become part of your vocabulary?" she asked.

She caught him off guard, and he laughed. And the moment the sound came out of his throat, he wanted to cry. He couldn't remember the last time he'd known joy. His eyes narrowed hungrily as he began pulling at her clothes, undoing buttons and shoving aside fabric. Her hands were on him, as well. Somewhere between one moment and the next, his shirt was on the floor and his slacks were undone. He lifted her off her feet and then spun around, pinning her between his body and the wall. Her arms were around his neck, her legs around his waist and she threw back her head and laughed when he slammed into her.

One hard, desperate thrust followed another and another, as if they were trying to destroy all the bad memories with this sexual act. Somewhere between one breath and the next, it began to change—turning into a dance between lovers.

Cara's eyes were closed, her lower lip caught between her teeth as she followed the rhythm of his body and was taken by surprise by the force of her climax. While she was still riding the high, David spilled himself within her in what seemed like endless, shuddering thrusts.

The silence that came after was as abrupt as their mating had been. David's hands were slick with sweat as he eased her down, and when she moved away and started rearranging her clothes, David followed suit. He could tell that she was as shaken by what they'd done as he, and was afraid she'd withdraw in embarrassment before he had a chance to explain. He touched her shoulder, and when she turned, he cupped her face in his hands.

"Look at me," he said.

Cara hesitated, then lifted her head, meeting his gaze straight on. Again, disbelief came and went as she stared at him. Then she touched the swollen edges of her mouth, as if needing the reminder of pain to assure her what had happened was real.

"I see you," she said. "Oh, David, there are so many things I have to tell you. After you left, I found out I was pregnant. We have a—"

"I know," he said. "Bethany."

A look of shock came and went on her face and then her eyes narrowed sharply.

"You knew we had a daughter?"

He nodded.

The timbre of her voice rose a notch. "You knew and you still didn't come back?"

David felt as if he'd been sucker punched. He should have seen this coming, and yet after what they'd just done...

"It wasn't like—"

"No. Wait. Let's start this meeting all over again."

The anger in her voice was blatantly apparent now, and he knew there was no going back.

"David Lee Wilson, just where the hell have you been?"

Chapter 2

"Cara, please…can we do this somewhere else?"

She made no attempt to hide her pain. "Maybe we should adjourn to the bedroom to talk, since we just had sex in my hall."

David inhaled slowly, using every mental skill he had to remain calm.

For Cara, his silence was stronger than any denial he might have made. Courtesy demanded she apologize. She lifted her chin.

"I'm sorry. That was uncalled for. What happened just now was more my fault than yours. If you don't mind, I'd like to change my clothes. The guest bathroom is just down the hall if you'd like to…uh…I'm just going upstairs now and…"

"Ssh," he said softly, and lifted a lock of her hair with one finger, gently pushing it into place. "Go do what you have to do. I'll be here when you get back."

The tenderness in his voice was her undoing. Tears filled her eyes, but she refused to let them go.

"You'll pardon me if I have doubts about that," she said. "I seem to remember telling you the same thing about forty years ago and look what happened."

She walked away, leaving him with nothing but a cold, hard truth. He had walked out on her—twice. Once when she wouldn't run away with him and then again when he left for Vietnam. He headed for the bathroom, feeling a lot less optimism than he had when he walked in the door with her earlier.

Cara barely made it to her bedroom before she started to cry—huge, gulping sobs that shattered her all the way to her soul.

Tearing off her clothes as she went, she staggered into the shower and then turned the water on full force, standing beneath the stinging spray until her mind was numb and her skin was burning.

One minute led to another and then another until she lost all track of time. The adrenaline rush of making love to a man she'd long thought dead was fading, leaving her shaken and weak. If it hadn't been for the slight discomfort between her legs, she could have made herself believe it was nothing more than a dream.

She flinched as the water began to run cold and reached down and turned off the faucets. She pushed back the curtains only to find David sitting on a small stool by the door.

He handed her a towel.

"I got worried."

She clutched it in front of her nudity like a shield, and as she did, realized any show of modesty was like closing the barn door after the horse had escaped.

"If you'll give me a few moments…"

He stood up and quietly closed the door, leaving her alone to finish drying.

Cara's hands began to shake as she swiped erratically

at the moisture clinging to her body. It wasn't until she was completely dry that she realized her clothes were in the other room, with him. She grabbed her bathrobe from a hook on the back of the door and quickly put it on, wrapping and tying it firmly before making another appearance. To her relief, he was nowhere in sight.

As she began to dress, she glanced at the clock. It was almost three. It had been just after one when she'd come around the corner of the house. No wonder he'd come looking for her. He probably thought she'd gone to her room and slit her wrists.

She snorted lightly as the thought came and went. If ever there had been a day when that thought had crossed her mind, it was long since over. She'd survived a lot more than this with a hell of a lot less reason. Except for their child. After she'd known about Bethany, everything had changed. David Wilson might have walked out on her, but he'd left a piece of himself behind that he'd never get back. With that thought in mind, she gave herself the once-over in the mirror, nodding in satisfaction at the simplistic style of her clothes. No need dressing like this was any kind of a celebration, because it felt more like a wake. But as she started down the stairs to face the ghost from her past, she had to accept the fact that she didn't want to bury him again.

David was lost in thought, staring at the array of family pictures displayed on the mantel and trying not to resent the picture of the short, stocky man with his arms around Cara. Ray Justice. They had been laughing when the picture was taken. He took a deep breath, making himself accept the reality of her life. She'd done just fine without him. Maybe being here was another selfish act on his part and he should never have come back. Before his thoughts could go further, he heard her footsteps in the hall and turned to face his accuser.

She saw him by the mantel. Her gaze slid from his face to the pictures behind him, and she realized what he'd been doing.

"She's beautiful," David said.

Cara's lips trembled, but she nodded. "She has your coloring. All that pretty dark hair and your eyes."

"But she has your smile."

Cara caught back a sob, determined not to fall apart again.

"Oh, David…where have you been? We were told you were dead, you know."

"Yes, I know."

Cara tried not to stare as she sat down on the sofa, but it was difficult not to do so. Her memories encompassed a young, gangly sixteen-year-old boy, not this powerful, secretive man.

"Won't you please sit?" she said, as she seated herself on the sofa.

"I think better standing."

She sighed and then smoothed her hands down the legs of her navy slacks.

"I couldn't form a rational thought right now if my life depended on it," she said.

David shoved his hands in the pockets of his slacks.

"I know this is going to be difficult for you to understand, but you've got to believe me when I tell you that what I did, I did *for* you, not *to* you."

Cara's eyes teared again, but she remained firmly in her seat.

"Letting me think you were dead was doing me a favor?" Her voice started to shake. "Even if I didn't matter to you anymore, how could you father a child and then ignore her existence?"

"No…no…not that. Never that."

"Then explain," Cara begged. "Make me understand."

He took his hands out of his pockets as he began to pace, and Cara couldn't help but stare at the animal grace of his movements. And then he started to talk and she became lost in the sound of his voice.

"It began with the letters."

"What letters?"

"The letters I wrote to you."

"I didn't receive any letters."

"Yes, I know...at least, I knew after a while, but before I found out, I kept wondering why you didn't answer mine. There were dozens and dozens. I wrote almost every day for about three months and then as often as I could after that."

She stiffened. "I don't believe you."

He strode to a chair and picked up a packet he'd gotten from his car while she had been dressing.

"See for yourself. I carried the damn things all over Nam after they came back. Half a dozen times I thought about chucking them, but I couldn't bring myself to get rid of them. Even though you hadn't opened them, they were the last link I had to you."

Cara's brows knitted as she dumped the contents of the packet into her lap.

"That's not all of them," David said. "But enough for you to know I'm telling the truth."

As she turned them over, she started to shake. The evidence was there before her eyes. Water-stained papers. Ancient postmarks. All addressed to Cara Weber and all unopened. But it was the two newspaper clippings, yellowed with age, that startled her. One was of her wedding, the other an announcement of her baby's birth.

"Where did you get these?"

"Your parents sent them to me, along with all of the letters I'd written you."

She gasped.

"The message was plain," David said. "I had no place in your life anymore. You had a husband and a child." He tried to smile, but the pain of saying what he'd lived with all these years made it impossible. "Only I knew the child was mine. I knew you would never have cheated on me before, and the baby came too soon after your wedding."

"But David...why let everyone think you were dead? I would never have refused you the right to know and love your own child."

"I know, but you have to understand. It was hell over there and Frank died about a month after I got the package. After that, I guess I pretty much went out of my head. I tried so many damn ways to get myself killed, but it didn't work. I volunteered for mission after mission, and each one should have been my last. When my tour of duty was up, I reenlisted. I was there when Saigon fell."

Tears slid down Cara's face as she sat with her hands clenched tightly in her lap.

"Why didn't you come home then? Why did you let me...let everyone...think you were dead?"

He shrugged. "I don't know. Hell...I felt dead, I guess I was just waiting for my body to catch up with my mind. Only thing was, Uncle Sam beat me to it."

"I don't understand."

He hesitated, trying to figure out exactly what he could say without giving too much away.

"I can't tell you everything," he said. "But I got recruited by a Special Forces unit and became involved in some covert missions for the government. One thing led to another and now, let's just say that my years with Uncle Sam are coming to an end."

"Are you telling me you became a spy?"

"Don't ask me anything more, honey...please. I've already said more than I should have."

"My God," Cara muttered. She stared down at the un-opened letters in her lap and then covered her face with her hands.

David dropped to his knees and took her hands in his.

"Cara?"

Forced to look at him, she realized that, for the first time, she was really seeing the man—and his secrets—and his scars.

"Why did you come back? Why now, after all these years?"

He hesitated again, still carefully choosing his answers.

"Because I needed to make peace with myself and with you. I needed to look you in the face and tell you that when I left for Vietnam, I had every intention of coming back and making a life with you. I couldn't go to my grave knowing you still believed I'd walked out on you, leaving you pregnant to raise our baby on your own. I swear to God, Cara, I would never have done that to you. I loved you."

"What do you mean, go to your grave? Are you ill?"

He slid into the seat beside her, reaching for her hands.

"No, no, I didn't mean it like that. I'm fine."

Cara looked down at his hands, so gently worrying the knuckles of her fingers, wondering if it was safe to give so much of herself away. And then she shoved the worry away. They'd already lost too many precious years. What-ever he had to give her, she was willing to take.

"What are your plans?" she asked. "I mean…can you stay awhile? Maybe a few days? I want to show you things…and oh, David, you have to stay and meet Beth-any. She and her family are on vacation, but they'll be back at the end of the week. Five or six days. You can stay that long…can't you?"

He heard himself answering and knew he was making a mistake, but there was no way he was going to lose her again, at least not yet. There was every reason to believe that his final showdown with Frank could be his last. He didn't want to give Cara false hope, but on the other hand, he couldn't deny himself this little bit of heaven.

"Yes. I'll stay. At least for a while."

For the first time in a very long while, Cara felt a sense of anticipation.

"Are you hungry? I was coming in the house to make myself some lunch when I heard you arrive."

The lilt in her voice only deepened his guilt, but he found himself agreeing. "That sounds good. I can't remember when I last shared a meal with anyone."

Cara pulled out of his embrace. "Can't remember when you last shared a meal? My God, David, what kind of life *have* you been living?"

"You don't want to know."

It was the dripping faucet in this excuse for a kitchen that finally sent Frank over the edge. He picked up a pan and began hammering on the fixture until it broke off in the sink. Water shot up like a geyser, spraying the ceiling and cabinets alike. A string of virulent curses filled the air as he reached for the shut-off valve beneath the sink. Finally, the water ceased to flow and Frank was left with a bigger mess than before he'd started. But it wasn't the condition of his decrepit hideout that was pushing his buttons. It was the fact that, once again, he had failed to reach his goal. The water pooled around his pant legs as he leaned back against the cabinets and closed his eyes. He'd been close, so close.

He'd seen the stealth chopper coming in and knew in his bones it was David. Who else would have access to such state-of-the-art military equipment but the infamous Jonah?

As he thought of David, the muscles in his wounded

shoulder gave a twinge and he shifted, easing his back to a more comfortable position against the cabinets. It was nothing but a flesh wound. He'd had worse. And the wound on his ear was almost well, too, although it would never be the same. Then he ran his hands through his hair in mute frustration, absently fingering the ancient burn scars on the side of his face. Hell, nothing had been the same since the day his own brother tried to burn him alive.

Disgusted with the mess in which he was standing, he went to the phone to call the manager to fix the sink. It didn't occur to him that, like the sink, all of his troubles stemmed from something he'd done, rather than something that had been done to him. Afterward, he strode into the bedroom to change his clothes, absently stepping on a cockroach as he went. As he crossed the threshold, he caught a glimpse of himself in the cracked and dusty mirror across the room and froze. In that moment, he saw himself as others saw him, a tall and aging man with a glass eye and a bitter expression. His gray, thinning hair was brushed back, baring his scarred face for anyone who chose to look. Oddly enough, the look seemed to appeal to a certain type of woman, although he rarely took advantage of the fact. He still mourned his beloved Martha, his wife of so many years.

As he thought of her, pain shafted. He turned away, moving to the closet to get a fresh change of clothes. As soon as his shoulder was better, he was going after David himself. No more trying to get to him through the agents who worked under him. He was tired of this game. He wanted it over.

He dressed quickly, his mind shifting from one scenario to another, imagining the pleasure of watching the life drain out of David's body. There was no future for him beyond that fact. His daughter had ceased to exist for him when she'd defected to the other side by falling in love with one of the agents. If only Martha was still alive. She'd been his reason for living. Then he blanked out the thought. There would be time later to wallow in memories. Right now, he had murder on his mind.

Night had come when Cara wasn't looking. One minute she was cleaning up their supper dishes and tidying the living room and the next thing she knew it was dark. The idea of sleeping under the same roof with David Wilson was almost frightening. She'd known the boy, but she didn't know this dark, brooding man. Then she reminded herself that his persona hadn't bothered her enough to stop her from making love to him in her hall. Surely they could sleep beneath the same roof without incident. It wasn't like he was going to murder her in her bed.

And the moment she thought it, her sanity took a hike. He'd all but said he was a spy. Spies killed people. Then she shook off the thought. He'd also been a soldier, and they killed people, too. It didn't make them heinous. It made them heroes.

Having settled that in her mind, she began to rearrange the magazines on the coffee table, unaware that David was watching her from the doorway. It wasn't until she straightened and started to leave that she saw him standing in the shadows.

"Oh! David! You startled me."

"Sorry. I didn't mean to."

"Was there something you needed?" she asked.

Yes, my life back...with you. "Not really. I was just watching you, thinking how very beautiful you are."

"I'm a middle-aged grandmother," she muttered, and gave the coffee table a final swipe with her dust cloth.

"With a damned fine body and a face that could still break a heart," he added, and then walked into the room and took the dust cloth out of her hands. "We need to talk."

Her heart fluttered, then settled back into a normal rhythm as she reminded herself there was no need to be nervous. The man was the father of her child. But when he took her by the hand and pulled her close to the light, she felt naked all over again beneath his gaze.

"I frighten you, don't I?" he asked.

Cara blushed then sighed. Finally, she nodded. "A little."

"My life has been ugly, I'll admit, but I would die before I'd hurt you."

The tenderness in his words was shattering. Before she knew it, her hands were on his chest, her face tilted toward the light—and him.

"I didn't mean it like that," she said quickly. "I wasn't thinking physical harm. It's just that I've been alone for almost three years now and just starting to learn to live without the sound of someone else's voice. It's hard to become accustomed to loneliness when you've shared your life with another."

"I wouldn't know."

Again, his answer pulled at her emotions.

"What I'm trying to say is…you were my first love, David. I gave the truest and best part of myself to you."

He groaned and started to take her in his arms when she stopped him.

"No…wait…let me finish." She took a deep breath. "The only thing that kept me going after you left was knowing that I carried your child. My husband was a good man. He loved Bethany as if she was his own and never made a difference between his affections for her and our other two children." She ducked her head and then made herself look at him. "But I'm ashamed to say that I never gave him what I should have because I'd already given it to you. Dead or alive, you had my heart. Now he's dead and you're back and I'm afraid. I'm afraid to get to know the man you've become. I'm afraid I'll love him as much as I loved the boy.'' Her voice trailed off into a whisper. ''And I'm afraid that if I do, I won't get over losing you again. So…what I guess I'm asking is, why did you really come? Was it just to assuage what you perceived as guilt, or were you looking for something more?''

He wanted to assure her, but he couldn't lie. As long as Frank was loose, his life wasn't worth a damn.

''I'd be lying if I said I'd only come to say hello. But there are a lot of loose ends to my past that have to be tied, and until that happens, I don't have the luxury of making plans.''

Cara felt the blood draining from her face. That wasn't what she expected to hear.

''That sounds fatal,'' she said, trying to fake a laugh.

He didn't answer, and the laugh became a sob.

''My God…tell me I'm wrong.''

''I can't make promises…but if I could, then I'd be giving you fair warning that I wanted back in your life.''

Her voice trembled. ''How far?''

''As far as you'd let me go.''

''Ah…David…you always were a hard sell,'' she said, and then wrapped her arms around his neck.

The weight of her body against his chest was a gift.

''So, are you saying it's enough?''

She shook her head. ''No, I'm not saying that, but I am saying that I'll take what you're willing to give. I asked for too much the first time and lost you. I'm not willing to make that mistake again.''

He wrapped his arms around her, pulling her close.

''God…woman, you don't know how many years I've dreamed of this.''

She pulled back to look at him. ''Oh, but yes, I do. And

while I would like the luxury of being wooed and courted, I'm not willing to waste our time on the ritual.''

''What are you saying?''

''I want to fall asleep in your arms and wake up the same way. I want to laugh with you and cook for you and play with you. I don't want to think about loose ends. Whatever time you have to give me will have to be enough.''

He tunneled his fingers through her hair, taking her kiss without asking, ripping her emotions to shreds with the anguish on his face.

''I don't deserve this,'' he said.

''No, you don't,'' she said. ''But I do.''

He laughed softly, then swept her off her feet and into his arms.

''Are you going to make love to me?'' she asked.

''Hell, yes,'' he muttered.

She sighed. ''It's about time.''

''If you don't mind,'' David whispered, nuzzling the side of her neck, ''I'd rather do this in a bed this time.''

''Down the hall, third door on the right.''

As he carried her there, he had to remind himself that this wasn't a dream. Cara was really in his arms.

When they reached Cara's room, he set her down by her bed and kissed her. Tentatively, then gently, then with a low, muffled groan.

Cara tangled her arms around his neck, clutching him desperately. When he began to take off her clothes, her knees went weak. This was happening, she knew, but it was all so surreal. She couldn't count the number of times in her life when she'd imagined such a scene. David striding through the door and sweeping her into his arms and then carrying her off into the sunset. The fantasy had lasted through her twenties and her thirties, and somewhere around the middle of her forties, she'd given up on fantasies.

Now this was happening and it wasn't a dream.

It wasn't a fantasy.

It was David—a rock-solid, flesh-and-blood man who wanted her as much as she wanted him.

When he began pulling off her clothes, then his, her pulse accelerated. Seconds later, she was flat on her back in the middle of her bed and he was hovering above her.

"You are so very beautiful," David whispered, and then rolled over onto his side and began tracing the contours of her body with one hand, fingering the curve of her chin, cupping the shape of a breast, mapping the plains of her belly, then testing the juncture between her thighs.

Cara's heart was pounding, her mouth slack with desire. She wanted to touch him, too, to test the strength of his muscles against the tenderness of his gaze, but she was too distracted by what he was doing.

"David?"

He shook his head and leaned over her, taking license with everything that he chose while leaving her breathless and aching for more.

One minute passed and then another and another and the coil that had been winding within Cara's belly began to throb. She moaned, then moaned again. This time louder. This time longer.

David's head was pounding as the blood rushed through his veins. The need to be inside her was strong, but he was waiting for that breaking point of coming undone.

Then he heard her gasp and saw her eyes lose all focus. When she clutched at his arms, his name a prayer on her lips, he made his move.

"David...oh...oh...please."

He was above her and inside her before she took her next breath. Her climax shook him, coming within three strokes of entry, and it was all he could do not to follow. But when she started to cry in soft, happy sobs, he couldn't hold himself back. The joy of knowing he'd given her this pleasure was an aphrodisiac he couldn't control. He rode the feeling with all the strength he could muster, and when it was over, thought he'd died in her arms.

Cara woke abruptly, as mothers always do when sensing something wasn't right in their world. Only this time, it wasn't the high-pitched wail of a frightened child that woke her, it was the man beside her. She lay motionless, listening to the labored rhythm of his breathing, and fought an urge to cry. His skin was clammy and he kept muttering something she couldn't understand. She raised up on one elbow, staring intently into the shadowed contours of his face, then let her gaze drift down his body. She'd seen the scars. Bullet holes. A shrapnel wound. A thick, ropy scar along the back of his leg. Dear Lord, what had happened to him? What hell was he reliving in his dreams?

Suddenly, he sat straight up in bed and she fell back in surprise.

"David?"

At the sound of her voice, his body went limp.

"I forgot where I was," he said.

"You were dreaming."

"Yes."

"Can I get you something? A glass of water? Some aspirin?"

He crawled out of bed and walked across the room to where his suitcase was lying.

"Where are you going?" she asked, as she watched him dig a pair of shorts from the case.

"I need to run it off," he said shortly. "I'll be fine. Go back to sleep."

"Run what off, David?"

He turned then, nothing but a mass of shadow and shape on the other side of the room, but the tone of his voice was image enough.

"The past."

"But David, you can't run away from the past."

"I know, but I can damn well wear it out. Now go back to sleep. I'll let myself in when I come back."

"You'll need a key," she said, and started to get up.

"No, I won't."

Then he was gone.

She lay there for a moment, absorbing the last thing he'd said and then started to tremble. What kind of man had she let into her bed?

Chapter 3

David ran without thought, focusing only on the impact of foot to ground and the mind-numbing relief that exhaustion always brought. Leaving Cara had seemed cowardly, especially after he'd come all this way to see her. But he was too ashamed to let her see his weaknesses— to admit that something as innocuous as a nightmare could undo him to this extent.

When he'd first run into the woods behind her house, he'd gone without a destination other than to forget. But a short time later, when he realized he had no idea where he was, he paused in a clearing and looked at the sky, reading the heavens like road map. The North Star was a constant that he quickly sought out. Once he found it, he realigned himself with the world and wished it was as simple to do that in his own life. By the time he'd outrun the demons, he had begun to circle back and was less than a mile from her home. Now it was simply a matter of getting there before exhaustion hit.

He came out of the trees, his steps dragging, his feet numb and burning. As he started up the gentle slope behind her house, he looked up and then stopped.

Lights.

She'd turned on the lights so he could see to come home.

There had been so many times in his life when he had not allowed himself the luxury of shedding a tear. He had no way of knowing that the simple act of lighting his way home was all it would take. But now...

He shuddered, then swallowed around a lump in his throat. Not once since he'd begun this lonely journey that had become his life had he had someone to come home to.

Dear God, if only he did belong here—to Cara and what was left of her world. He needed it—deserved it. He'd given up so damned much. Surely he would be allowed some joy on this earth before his days were over. He took a deep breath and then shook off the thoughts. As long as the showdown with Frank still loomed, he couldn't allow himself to dwell on the future. He threw back his shoulders and started to walk.

Cara saw him come out of the trees. Her shoulders sagged with a relief she wouldn't voice. He paused at the bottom of the hill, and although she couldn't see his features, she was struck by the stillness of his posture, as if he'd become a part of the scenery. Then he started toward her, his steps slow and dragging.

She stood up from the chair in which she'd been sitting, then stayed within the shadows, struggling with the urge to run to him. Still uncertain where she fit into his life, she watched, waiting to take her cue from him.

David felt her presence before he saw her, and when she stepped out of the shadows to the edge of the porch, a weight lifted from his chest. This was just like a dream he'd had so many times before. Coming home to find this woman awaiting his arrival was nothing short of a miracle.

"Cara."

"Are you okay?"

"Yes."

"I made some coffee. There are fresh towels and a washcloth in the bathroom." She hesitated, then added, "Do you need anything else?"

He swallowed around a lump in his throat. "Just you."

"I've been here all the time."

"I know. I'm the one who's been lost."

She walked off the porch and took him by the hand.

"Then welcome home, my darling," she said softly, and led him inside.

David went silently, knowing that simple act had done more toward saving his sanity than anything else she could have ever done.

When he came out of the shower it was close to four in the morning. The lights were out in the rest of the house, with only a small ginger jar lamp lighting the area beside Cara's bed. He stood in the doorway, watching her sleep. So still. So beautiful.

He wondered how many times Ray Justice had done this very same thing, maybe in this very same place—watching his wife in their bed. Jealousy burned low in his gut but he shoved it aside. There was nothing left to be jealous about. The man was dead, and he was here.

But there was Frank.

The possibility existed that he might never have another chance to do this—to stand within the quiet of a home and watch the woman he loved as she slept. This time, it was regret that drew him to the bed. He pulled back the covers and slipped in beside her, selfishly taking everything she had to offer now.

When she sighed and turned, snuggling her cheek against his chest, his arms tightened around her.

God...don't let this end.

Then he closed his eyes and let exhaustion claim him.

David smelled coffee and rolled over in surprise. Most of his adult life had hinged on being cognizant of his surroundings, even in his sleep, and yet Cara had arisen from this bed and dressed without him knowing it. And from the scents wafting down the hallway, she'd been up for some time. Not only did he smell coffee, but if he wasn't mistaken, also bacon and the aroma of baking bread. He rolled out of bed and grabbed a clean pair of shorts and a shirt, unwilling to waste another moment of this day. After a quick trip to the bathroom to brush his teeth and comb his hair, he padded barefoot down the hall. The television was on in the living room and he stopped, taking a moment to listen to the announcer.

"Talks between the Irish Republican Army and Great Britain have come to a halt. Reports from unnamed sources tell us that the recent bombing in Trafalgar Square has been attributed to a renegade faction of the IRA and that until this has been sorted out, negotiations will cease."

"Damn," David muttered, and made himself a mental note to check on the status of the situation. When the announcer continued, he lingered another moment, although he was torn between his duty to SPEAR and his longing to be with Cara.

"On the local front, hit-and-run robberies are continuing within a three-county area of upstate New York. Just last night, a liquor store in Three Corners was held up, and the clerk on duty was shot and robbed of more than six thousand dollars. The woman, a thirty-four-year-old

Asian mother of two, is still in surgery. More on her condition later.''

David sighed, sorry for the woman and her family, but his focus had to be on the larger picture. Even though it was on a limited basis, terrorism had already made its mark in the United States. It was part of his job to make sure it didn't escalate.

When the station broke for commercial, he turned to other issues—namely breakfast with Cara.

When he entered the kitchen, Cara was washing her hands at the sink. He walked up behind her, slipped his arms around her waist and nuzzled the back of her neck.

Cara gasped with surprise.

"David! You startled me," she said, then she leaned back against him and closed her eyes as his hands moved up her belly to her breasts.

"Then we both got a surprise this morning," he said, as he turned her in his arms and kissed the smile on her lips.

"How so?" Cara asked.

"I never heard you get up."

She shrugged. "I was trying to be quiet. You were sleeping so soundly I thought you must need the rest."

"That's beside the point," David said. "There were lots of days and nights I went without sleep and I still stayed alert. It made the difference in my ever seeing another sunrise."

She cupped his face with her hands. "Yes, but that was when you were in danger, right?"

"Yes."

"So…subconsciously, you knew there was nothing here to fear. End of story. Now come sit down. Breakfast is almost done."

She was right, and the answer was so simple, he didn't know why it hadn't occurred to him first. Maybe he'd spent too much of his life in hiding to be able to do this normal-guy stuff.

"Need any help?" he asked.

"No, but thanks."

He took a seat, thinking he couldn't remember the last time he sat down to a meal with flowers on the table. Then he saw the basket of hot blueberry muffins and his heart skipped a beat. He felt Cara's hand on the back of his neck.

He looked at her. She was smiling.

"You remembered," he said softly.

"How could I forget," Cara said, and then brushed a brief kiss across his mouth. "We had breakfast together at Flanders' Deli the morning you left for basic training. I was so mad at you and I still came to say goodbye."

David sighed, unwilling to think about the negative aspects of their parting. "It was blueberry muffins with some kind of sugary stuff on top."

"Streusel. It's called streusel."

David touched the corner of her mouth. "You had it stuck right here."

Cara smiled. "And you removed it with your tongue. Caused quite a scene there in the deli, as I recall." Then she frowned. "Someone told my parents. When I got home, there was the proverbial hell to pay."

"Sorry," David said.

"I'm not. Even though they've been gone for several years, after knowing what they did to us, David, I don't think I can ever forgive them."

"Holding on to grudges isn't healthy," he said, thinking of Frank. "Let's just focus on here and now."

Cara sensed he was alluding to more than what her parents had done, because that dark look was back in his eyes. Determined not to talk about anything negative, she handed him a muffin and made herself smile.

"Start on that while I get the rest of our food."

The bread was warm against his palm, and when he broke it open, the scent of sugar and blueberries made him feel like a kid of sixteen all over again. Ignoring the butter and jam, he took a big bite, savoring the taste as well as the thought behind it.

"What do you think?" Cara asked as she set a plate of bacon and scrambled eggs at his place.

He swallowed. "I think Ray Justice was a damned lucky man."

At first, the mention of her deceased husband was startling, until she began to accept the compliment in the manner in which it had been made. She smiled.

"Why, David...what a genuinely dear thing to say."

He arched an eyebrow. "I have my moments."

She laughed and then went to get her own food, leaving David with the sound of her laughter echoing in his ears and the knowledge that whatever happened later, he'd been right in coming.

They finished their meal in near silence, each absorbed in the simple wonder of sharing food. For Cara, the whole experience seemed surreal. Day before yesterday, David Wilson was a heartache from her past, and now he was sitting in her house, at her table, eating the food that she'd prepared. But this David was nothing like the boy who'd left her behind. He was hard and secretive and rarely smiled. She wanted her old David back. Not only that, she wanted more—so much more. But she kept remembering an old saying about being careful of what you wished for. Her life was settled. If he stayed, could she live with a man with so many secrets—a man who had to wear himself out physically to be able to rest? She sighed. God help them both, because she had never wanted anything so much in her life and she was afraid she wouldn't be up to the task.

David got up to pour himself another cup of coffee.

"Want a refill?" he asked.

"No, I've had enough."

Her words wrapped around his senses, reminding him that he would never have enough of her. The smile he'd been wearing stopped at the corner of his mouth as he sat the cup down on the counter, unfilled. Then he walked across the room, pulled her up from her chair and into his arms.

"You sure?" he asked, his voice husky with promise.

She smiled. "Maybe I was a little hasty."

"If you come back to the bedroom with me, we can take all the time you need to decide."

A shiver of longing rolled through her as she slid her arms around his neck.

"The way I'm feeling right now, it won't take any time at all."

A rare smile broke the somberness of his face as he scooped her up in his arms.

"I *can* walk," she said, as he carried her down the hall.

He laid her on the bed and then crawled on top of her, straddling her legs. There was a gleam in his eye as he began to undress her.

"Tell me that again afterward," he said.

Breath caught in the back of her throat as his hands tugged her shirt from the waistband of her slacks. From where she was lying, he seemed indomitable. And then he leaned forward and centered his mouth across her lips. She moaned.

He leaned even closer, his mouth against her ear as he whispered something dark and promising that sent her sense of self into a tailspin. Could she do something like that—even with a man she loved?

Clothes came off, flying in every direction.

Her slacks.

His shorts.

Her bra.

His shirt.

When there was nothing left between them but his promises, he turned her over on her stomach.

Cara shivered as his hands encircled her ankles. After that, nothing in her life would ever be the same.

Cara stepped out of the shower to find David waiting on her. She smiled slowly, gazing her fill of his strong, naked body and the look in his eyes.

David returned her grin as he wrapped her in a towel. "What?" he asked.

"It would have been an absolute tragedy if I'd lived my whole life without experiencing that."

The corner of his mouth tilted, but not much. "That, as you call it, is one of the most interesting pages of the Kama Sutra."

"Oh? And here I thought you'd learned that from some Mata Hari type during your world travels."

"Hell, honey, it wasn't a James Bond type of life, I can tell you that. I could count the number of women I've slept with in the last twenty years on one hand and have fingers left over."

"Oh, I wasn't speaking from jealousy," Cara said. "Quite the reverse. I was going to suggest that if I'm ever with you and you see any of those women again, please introduce me."

"Why?"

"I want to thank them for whatever they added to your expertise."

His eyes widened in surprise and then he threw back his head and laughed as he swung her off her feet.

Cara wrapped her arms around his neck, grinning at his delight.

"God, woman, you unman me," he said, as he set her on her feet.

"Not for too long, I hope. Now let me get dressed. I can't stay naked all day."

"Why not?"

Her grin widened. "Because I have things to do."

He frowned. "What kind of things?"

She shrugged. "Normal, everyday things, like picking up some clothes from the cleaners, buying groceries, washing the car. You know…just stuff."

David followed her into the bedroom and sat on the bed as she began to dress. He didn't want to admit that he *didn't* know. *Stuff* hadn't been on his agenda since the day he'd left for Vietnam.

"Can I come?"

Cara turned, surprised by the hesitant tone in his voice. "Of course you can. I expected you to."

"Is there a dress code for this kind of *stuff?*"

She started to laugh and then realized he was serious. Her hands fisted as she struggled to keep the anger out of her voice.

"I keep wanting to ask exactly what the hell the United States government did to you in the name of peace, but I'm afraid of the answer. You can wear shorts or any kind of pants. Jeans…slacks, whatever you like. A shirt of any kind is fine with me. There's this great little restaurant where we can have lunch." She frowned, then added, "Actually, it's more like a tearoom, but the dress code is casual."

"Okay," David said, and took a pair of chinos from a hanger, then stood for a moment, choosing a shirt that would match.

Cara paused, watching the play of muscles across his back. Her gaze fell on the multitude of scars on his body as it had so many times before. Suddenly blinded by tears, she turned before he could see them and began digging through a dresser drawer.

It occurred to her then that she'd taken her freedom for granted, never considering the countless men who sacrificed on a daily basis so that she would never live in fear. She turned abruptly.

"David."

"Yeah?" he muttered, as he bent over to tie his shoe.

"Thank you."

He looked up. "For what?"

"For the years you spent in the service of this country. For the nights you didn't sleep and the pain—"

He stood and put his forefinger in the center of her mouth, gently stopping what she'd been about to say.

"You don't have to say this," he said.

"Yes...actually I do," Cara said. "I spent a lot of years feeling sorry for myself because my life didn't work out the way I'd planned. And then I see you, like this, and what you suffered while I was warm and safe and—"

Her voice broke and she looked away.

David's expression was shuttered. How did he respond to a brutal truth?

"Come here, honey. It's okay."

"No," she muttered. "It will never be okay."

"It's almost over," he said.

She frowned. "That's not the first time you've alluded to unfinished business. What is it, David? Why can't you tell me?"

He tried to grin. "You know the old spy joke. If I told you, then I'd have to kill you, and we both know I couldn't do that. So..."

Cara turned away, muttering something beneath her breath as she finished dressing.

David arched an eyebrow as he smiled. "Those are pretty salty words for such a pretty lady."

She purposefully ignored him, which made him smile even more. This woman was a far cry from the girl he'd left behind. He was falling in love all over again.

"I'll finish dressing now," he said.

She almost glared. "Are you making fun of me?"

"No, ma'am."

She sighed. "Yes, you are."

"What would it take for you to change the subject?" he asked.

She lifted her chin, refusing to smile. "I'm going to the living room. When you're ready, I will be waiting." Then she marched out of the bedroom, leaving him on his own.

David hesitated briefly, then grabbed his wallet and keys before following her exit. This might be new and uncharted territory for him, but damned if he wasn't looking forward to it.

Tearoom, indeed.

Two hours and a half dozen errands later, they walked into the restaurant. Almost immediately, Cara saw people she knew. They waved a hello, and she could tell by the looks on their faces that their curiosity was raised by the man at her side.

Earlier, she'd almost lost his company when she had gone into the hair salon to pick up a bottle of her favorite shampoo. One of the stylists had flirted, which he'd calmly ignored, but when the shampoo girl came by and pinched his behind, Cara thought he was going to bolt. Cara had calmly told the girl to go molest someone else, which had made everyone laugh, including David. After that, the rest of the morning had been fairly innocuous. But now there was this. She glanced at David, judging his expression. To her surprise, he was looking at her.

"What do you think?" Cara asked.

"It smells good in here," he said.

She smiled. "The food tastes as good as it smells."

"Then I think you made the right choice, and I think those people at the table near the window are trying to get your attention."

Cara sighed. "Yes, I know. What do I do…about you, I mean?"

An eyebrow arched. "What do you want to do…about me, I mean?"

She grinned. "One thing has certainly changed since I first knew you. You have a wicked sense of humor. Now be serious. Is it, uh, safe to introduce you as David or should I—"

David slid his hand along the length of her spine and gave her a gentle push in their direction.

"I am who I am. If it was dangerous for me to surface, I damn sure wouldn't have brought it to you."

She looked startled, and he realized she hadn't considered that aspect of his life having a negative impact on hers.

"Cara! Dear! How wonderful to see you."

Cara smiled. Obviously they'd stood too long at the door waiting to be seated. Her friend Debra Shay had been too curious to wait.

"Good to see you, too," Cara said.

"Well…aren't you going to introduce me?" Debra asked, and then glanced coyly at David.

Cara smiled. "If you promise not to pinch him on the backside, I will."

Debra giggled and patted David's arm in commiseration. "Oh, no! You must have been at Ream's Salon. That Janis female is lethal around good-looking men."

David smiled. "I'll take that as a compliment," he said smoothly. "I'm David Wilson. It's a pleasure to meet one of Cara's friends."

"David, this is Debra Shay," Cara said. "Ray worked with her husband, Roy."

David nodded congenially while thinking that he felt like he was playing a part. Normal chit-chat, ordinary people, having lunch in a tearoom in Chiltingham, New York. It was a far cry from subterfuge and espionage. And then the hostess arrived and the moment ended.

"I'm sorry for the delay," she said. "Please follow me."

"Nice to meet you," Debra gushed, giggling again as David and Cara were shown to their table.

David seated Cara, then took the chair beside her. As soon as the hostess left, he took Cara's hand.

"That wasn't so bad, was it?"

She made herself smile. "No."

"Why do I feel like there's a *but* just waiting to come out?"

She sighed. "Because there is."

"Then what?"

"This doesn't feel real."

He started to smile, which was the last thing Cara would have expected him to do.

"What's so funny?" she asked.

"I'd forgotten that we used to think alike."

"What do you mean?"

"Just a few moments ago I was thinking the very same thing. I feel like I'm acting a part and any minute now someone is going to yell cut and I'm going to turn back into—"

He caught himself before he said the word *Jonah* and looked away, but the message was clear. Cara put her hands over his and gave them a squeeze.

"It's all right, darling," she said quietly. "If you're uncomfortable, we can go home. I'll make us some sandwiches and we can—"

"Hell, no. I'm not fragile, just out of practice," he said, and then handed her a menu. "Now, tell me what's good."

The smile on her face was worth every uncomfortable moment he'd had thus far. When she bent her head to study the menu, he watched her changing expression as devoutly as he'd watched the sunrises over the Rockies. He didn't know how this journey was going to end, but he would never be sorry he'd made it.

"How hungry are you?" Cara asked.

He blinked. Telling her the truth about what he really hungered for would probably embarrass her, but when she started to blush, he figured she'd just read his mind.

A small grin tilted the right side of his mouth, then as quickly disappeared.

He leaned across the table until their foreheads were almost touching. "I'm starving," he said softly

Her blush heightened. "Just don't lick the corner of my mouth again until there's a really good reason."

His eyes glittered warmly as he sat back in his chair. "You're safe for now," he promised. "Now, since you're the expert here, why don't you order for me?"

"Really?"

"I think I'm secure enough as a man to let a woman order for me without feeling threatened. Besides, I'm curious as to what you think might appeal to me."

"What if you don't like it?"

He thought of the times he'd eaten grubs and insects to survive and decided against mentioning it.

"I'll still eat it."

She beamed. "My kind of man."

The teasing disappeared from his eyes. "Sweetheart, I was always your man."

Unprepared for the gentleness in his voice, Cara's eyes teared, but she blinked them away.

"Just for that, you're going to get their famous dessert, too," she said.

"What's that?"

She grinned. "Cake. It's called Better Than Sex."

David thought she was putting him on until she pointed to the dessert portion of the menu.

"No way," he muttered, wondering what else had changed in this world while he'd been hiding behind the generations of Jonahs who'd gone before him.

"Oh, yes, and when you've finished your meal, I'll prove it," Cara said.

At this point, David's sense of justice got the best of him. He'd never had a bite of food in his life that was better than making love to Cara—not even when he'd been starving.

"You just do that," he whispered. "And I'll be a really good boy and eat everything on my plate, but when we get home, I'm going to prove to you that there isn't anything better than sex, especially when it's with the right person."

"May I take your order?"

Startled, Cara looked up. The waitress was grinning—proof that she'd overheard, at the very least, the last thing David just said. Cara glared at David and then rolled her eyes. This would be all over the tearoom before they'd been served their first dish.

The waitress waited, her pen poised above her pad.

Refusing to look at David, Cara gave their order. As soon as the waitress was gone, Cara glanced up, but he seemed preoccupied with a couple across the room. She turned to look and then sighed. It was Ben and Katie Murphy and their new baby girl. Probably their first outing since the baby's arrival last month. She looked at David again. The pain in his eyes was unmistakable. Despite the fact that everyone in the room would see and put their own interpretation on the action, she reached for his hand.

Startled by her touch, David blinked, then turned his focus to Cara.

"I'm sorry," she said softly.

He sighed. So she'd read his mind again. So what else was new?

"You have nothing to be sorry for," he said briefly.

"Don't, David."

"Don't what?"

"Don't deny your feelings...not to me."

"Okay then. What do you want to hear first?" he asked, his voice barely above a whisper. "That I envy that young couple the life ahead of them, or that I want things I know I can never have?"

"I can't give you back your youth, but I can give you a daughter...and grandchildren." She held her breath, afraid to say the rest of it—that she would be his wife if he wanted it.

David made himself smile, unaware that the action never reached his eyes.

"You've already done that," he said. "And I can only hope that they will forgive me as quickly as you have."

"There's nothing to forgive," Cara said, refusing to admit her disappointment that he had mentioned nothing about the future of their relationship. "When they get to know you, they will love you."

Before David could answer, he saw a woman approaching their table. From the look on her face, the curiosity was eating her up. He gave Cara a nod and then braced himself, thankful he was sitting down. This one looked as if she wouldn't settle for a simple pinch on the behind.

"Ooh, Cara, who's this big hunk and where have you been keeping him?"

Cara flinched and David saw it, identifying the woman as someone other than a friend. Whoever she was, she'd just become his enemy, too.

"Macie, I thought you were in Reno."

"I just got back, and look, I'm a free woman again."
She wiggled the empty fingers on her left hand as proof.

"I'm sorry to hear that," Cara said.

"Don't be! I don't know what I was thinking when I
married that Glen Harvey."

"That he owned his daddy's business?" Cara muttered,
too low for anyone but David to hear.

"Well," Macie said. "Aren't you going to introduce
me?"

It was the way Macie Harvey leaned over, displaying
her more than ample charms in David's face, that pushed
Cara's buttons. That plus the fact her husband, Ray, had
confessed to having a brief affair with Macie between husbands three and four. Although she had finally forgiven
Ray, she had never confronted the woman. Suddenly, now
seemed like the perfect time to yank her chain.

She turned in her seat, giving Macie a beatific smile.

"Macie, this is David Wilson. He's not only my childhood sweetheart, but also Bethany's father. David, Macie
Harvey. Elizabeth Taylor has nothing on our Macie for
shedding husbands. I believe Glen was number seven...or
was it eight?"

David was surprised but secretly pleased that she'd admitted their relationship. He stood and held out his hand.

"Mrs. Harvey, my condolences on your recent divorce,
but as I'm sure you must know, time *does* heal all wounds,
except those that kill you, of course."

Macie blinked. She didn't know whether to be insulted
first, or run to spread this juicy bit of news. She opted for
the news.

"Yes...well...thank you, I'm sure," she said, giving
Cara a fierce glare.

Cara returned the look, still wearing her smile. Macie
was the first to look away.

"I'd better get back to my table," Macie said. "I think my order has arrived."

"Enjoy," Cara said.

Cara's eyes were glittering as she turned to David.

"Cara, honey?"

"What?"

"Remind me never to make you mad."

She started to grin. "Why?"

"Because you shed blood better without weapons than anyone I've ever seen."

She tossed her head and then smiled primly. "Thank you. It's part of the gift of being a woman."

"Old enemies are often the most difficult to dispatch," David added, thinking of Frank.

"She had an affair with Ray. They thought I didn't know."

David's heart twisted. So many things she'd had to endure, and all because he hadn't come home. This time, he was the one reaching for her hand.

"This time, it's me who's saying I'm sorry."

She shrugged. "You didn't do it. You have nothing to apologize for."

"Oh, but you're wrong," he said softly. "It's what I didn't do that has caused the most hurt."

Before she could answer, their food arrived and the tension of the moment dissipated.

"Hot beef sandwich and tuna salad, coming up," the waitress said, setting the hot plate of thinly sliced roast beef on toast points with thick brown gravy in front of David and the plate of cold tuna salad on lettuce in front of Cara. "Eat hearty, folks, but remember to save some room. You don't want to forget that dessert."

David laughed.

It filtered through Cara's anger, leaving her weak and

breathless. It had been so long since she'd heard that re-markable sound.

"This looks great," David said. "I don't remember the last time I had this."

He dug in with relish, rolling his eyes in appreciation.

Cara smiled and tucked into her own food, all the while thinking about cake and sex with the marvelous man at her right.

Chapter 4

Frank Wilson slammed the phone down in disgust. So far, no amount of money had been able to buy him any pertinent information on where his baby brother had gone. David had disappeared as thoroughly as he had when he'd first come back from Vietnam. He frowned as he stared across the room. He didn't like not knowing where his enemies were. It left him defenseless, and he didn't like being weak.

Abruptly, he strode to the window overlooking the street below. East L.A. was an easy place to get lost in. Cash bought anonymity here. Identification was unnecessary for renting rooms or cars if enough money changed hands. Despite all that, the fact that he was still in the United States was dangerous. He'd messed with Uncle Sam's elite, and even though he'd gotten away, he'd ruffled far too many feathers to think they'd brushed him off.

His frown deepened as he absently stared at the people on the street below. There were too damned many people in this world and not a one of them knew their hand from their ass. The longer he thought about it, the more convinced he became that that was what was wrong with his plans. No more trying to get to David through other people. He'd taken eleven runs at the man and come up empty-handed every time. The next time it happened, it would be himself and David—face to face.

Next time.

In frustration, he suddenly slammed his fist against the window ledge, and in doing so, jarred his shoulder, sending a barrage of pain up his neck and to the back of his head. What if there was no next time?

Cursing the infirmity that caused him pain, he turned away from the window and moved to the bed to lie down, telling himself that he would find David. It would happen—when he was ready. He had no desire to face him again until his gunshot wounds weren't so tender. Another day or so and he'd be raring to go.

He closed his eyes, letting his thoughts drift. Outside, the squeal of a police siren came and went, while down the hall, he could hear a man cursing and a woman's shrill cries for help. He rolled over on his good shoulder and pulled the pillow over his head. Crazy. The world had gone crazy. Within a few minutes, he was snoring. Sometime later, he began to dream.

"Frankie, go find your brother and tell him supper is ready."

Ten-year-old Frankie Wilson rolled his eyes, then peeked over the kitchen counter to the pies cooling on the rack near the sink.

"Okay, Ma, and can I have seconds on dessert?"

"If you eat good."

"I will," Frankie said, exiting the kitchen on the run.

He jumped off the porch and ran around the holly bushes toward the side of the house where his six-year-old brother, Davie, had been playing. But when he got there, the yard was empty.

"Dumb kid," he muttered, thinking of the dessert awaiting him inside. "Hey, Davie! Supper!"

No one answered and no little kid came running. He began to circle the house, thinking that Davie must have moved to the shade tree in front. But when he got there, his little brother was nowhere in sight.

"Hey, Davie! Davie!"

No answer. He frowned. Frankie Wilson considered himself almost grown, but Davie was just a kid, and he knew better than to leave the yard without permission.

He jogged toward the sidewalk, and as he did he heard the unmistakable cry of someone in pain. A few feet farther, he rounded the lilac bush and saw his little brother sitting on the curb, holding his knee. His bicycle with training wheels was lying on its side in the street.

"Hey, kid, what happened?" Frankie asked, as he knelt in front of Davie.

Davie sniffed loudly, then wiped a dirty hand beneath his nose.

"I fell and skinned my knee," he said.

Frankie looked. Sure enough, the kid was missing a good chunk of skin and bleeding all over his shoes.

"You weren't supposed to be in the street. If Ma finds out, she'll whip your butt."

Davie's eyes widened. Not only had his brother used the B word, but he was right about their mother. She would whip him for riding his bike in the street.

"Don't tell on me, Frankie. I don't want a whipping."

Frankie sighed. Being a big brother carried a lot of responsibilities. He patted Davie on the head and then helped him to his feet.

"Come on, kid. I'll get your bike in the yard and Ma will just think you fell off there, okay?"

Davie nodded. "Okay." Then he smiled through his tears. "Thanks, Frankie, you're the best brother ever."

"Yeah, I know," Frankie said. "Now hurry. Supper is ready and we got cherry pie for dessert."

A car backfired and a motorcycle revved before taking off, leaving a single trail of rubber behind on the L.A. street. Frank jerked in his sleep, but he didn't awake. Instead, the sound shifted his dream from childhood to Vietnam.

David came out of nowhere. The stupid little bastard. He was going to mess everything up. Then Frank's shock turned to panic when he realized the gunrunners were reaching for their weapons.

"Don't!" he yelled. "He's my brother."

"Get rid of him," one of them snapped, "or we'll do it for you."

Before he could react, David stepped between them, yanking the money out of Frank's hands and throwing it on the ground.

"What the hell do you think you're doing?" Frank yelled.

"Saving your stupid ass," David said. "Now let's get out of here."

"What's going on?" the gunrunner asked.

Frank spun, his eyes blazing with anger. "Leave this to me," he said, and shoved David aside as he reached for the money.

But the kid stepped on his fingers, stopping his intent. After that, everything became a blur. Before he knew it, both of the gunrunners were dead and David was staring at him as if he'd never seen him before.

Time blurred the memories of what came next. All Frank could remember was pointing a gun in his brother's face and then pulling the trigger. After that, he remembered coming to on the floor of the hut, smelling gasoline and feeling the heat of the fire against his face. He'd crawled through fire, living with one purpose only, and that was to make David pay for what he'd done. Over the years, Frank had chosen to forget that he was the one to fire the first shot. His entire purpose for living was revenge.

And that same revenge had kept him alive in Vietnam, hiding in an empty village under the nose of the Vietcong until he was healed, then smuggling himself into Indonesia and stowing away on a freighter bound for New Zealand. He strangled the man who helped him on board, stole his identity, then hid in the hold among the freight until they docked weeks later. Within a year, he was working the opal mines in Australia and saving every penny he could get his hands on. Through every tough, hungry day and night of his life, one thing had kept him going—the knowledge that some day he would find David Wilson, and when he did, he would kill him.

Finally, Frank slipped into a deep, dreamless sleep. As he did, he rolled onto his back, his arms flung out. Asleep, his scars gave him a look of vulnerability, but they were deceiving. He'd gone into this vendetta with nothing to lose. His beloved Martha was dead and his only child, like his brother, had turned into a traitor. There was nothing helpless about Frank Wilson, and everything to fear.

It was three in the morning when the nightmares started. Cara woke abruptly, her senses on an all-out alert. David was still asleep, but curled up in a ball with his back to her. The muscles in his arms were jerking, and every now and then he would kick, as if fighting off an invisible foe. She reached for the lamp, quickly turning it on and illuminating their corner of the room with a soft, yellow glow. A thin film of sweat covered his skin, and the sheet that had been over his body was twisted around his ankles.

Cara got up from the bed, untwisted the sheet and pulled

it up to his waist before crawling in beside him. Then she spooned herself against the curve of his back, slid an arm around his waist and held on.

He moaned.

"Ssh, David, ssh. Everything is all right, darling. Everything is all right."

The softness of her voice seemed to penetrate his subconscious. He stiffened momentarily and then ever so slowly began to relax.

Cara pulled herself closer against him, and as she did, he turned over and pillowed his cheek against her breasts. His face was streaked with sweat, his features twisted into a grimace. As she looked, she felt like crying. Instead, she held him close. Only after she heard the even tenor of his breathing did she close her eyes.

David was no longer the fearless young man who'd first gone off to war, convinced of his immortality. This man who'd come back to her had been forged in hellfire and was holding himself together by nothing more than sheer will. He was hard to the point of brittle, and his smiles were far too rare for her peace of mind. He existed by day and suffered by night. And her rage for the injuries he'd sustained grew with each passing day. The only thing she had to give him was her love. She prayed it would be enough.

Dawn finally broke, bathing the couple in the warm fingers of light slipping through the curtains. David was the first to stir, and as he did, he realized that something of a miracle had occurred. He'd slept the entire night through without waking up. And then he felt Cara's arms around him and realized she must have held him while he slept. A great wave of peace fell over him, leaving him weak and humbled. Dear God—he didn't deserve this woman, but he wasn't going to give her up. Not now. Not when he'd finally found a reason to live again.

He shifted slightly so that he could see her. The morning light was soft, shadowing the fine lines that time had etched on her face. So beautiful. She was so very, very beautiful. He thought of Frank and knew that he couldn't put off their meeting too much longer. If Frank had even an inkling of Cara's importance in David's life, he would kill her just to see David weep.

He shuddered, and as he did, her arms instinctively tightened around him. Even in her sleep, she seemed to sense his despair.

He raised up on one elbow. She opened her eyes. For a moment, it was as if they'd seen into each other's soul. Then David cupped her face and kissed her. She sighed as he levered himself above her body. He kissed her again. She shifted, making room for him to come in. He took her there, in the early morning light with her hair in tangles and love in her eyes.

By mid-morning, Cara was in the kitchen packing a picnic lunch while David was rummaging in the storage shed out back, looking for Ray's fishing equipment. Despite his claim to the opposite, Cara suspected it had been years since he'd done something as innocuous as fishing, especially for fun.

The day was warm with a line of white puffy clouds in the distance, the wind almost nonexistent, making it a perfect day to go to the lake. She was putting the last of the sandwiches into the cooler when the doorbell rang. She wiped her hands and then frowned as it began to ring again. Someone was certainly insistent. She hurried through the house, peeked through the window before answering the door and then groaned.

It was Harry Belton.

He'd been trying to court her for more than a year now. She didn't know how much plainer she could be without being terribly rude, but she wasn't interested. Masking her irritation, she opened the door.

"Cara! How are you, dear?"

"Harold?"

"I know I should have called, but I was in the neighborhood and couldn't bring myself to leave without saying hello."

She frowned. He was lying, and they both knew it.

"You really should have called," she said. "I was just going out."

Ignoring the hint she had just given him to make a graceful exit, he stepped inside the door and then peered over her shoulder.

"I see by the car in the driveway that you have company. I hope I'm not intruding."

"Actually, that's what I was trying to—"

"There's the silliest rumor going around Chiltingham that there's a stranger staying in your house."

Cara's eyes flashed angrily, although she maintained her calm.

"No. There's no stranger staying in my house," she said.

He smiled and put his hands on her shoulders. "There now! I knew when Macie said it that she was just telling tales. Even though Ray has been gone these three years, you just aren't the kind of woman to—"

Cara watched his eyes widen and his mouth drop. The fact that he'd forgotten what he was saying told her that David must have come in the house.

Harold glared at her, and the tone of his voice changed from happy to accusing.

"I thought you said you were alone."

"No. I didn't say I was alone. I said there wasn't a strange man in my house. David isn't a stranger."

Harold's face turned a dark, ugly red, his eyes narrowing angrily.

"If I hadn't seen this with my own eyes, I would never have believed it."

Suddenly, David was standing at her back, his voice dark and full of unleashed anger.

"You've never seen a fishing pole?" David asked, and then thrust a rod and reel in Harold's face. "Then here, take a real good look before I shove it right up your—"

Cara stifled a grin as Harold dropped the rod and bolted for the door. Only after he was on the porch with the screen door between them did he stop and turn. It was a mistake, because David was right behind him. Now the only person still in the house was Cara.

"Don't touch me!" Harold screeched.

"Don't ever raise your voice to her again, do you hear me?" David asked.

There was a look in the man's eyes that Harold seemed afraid to challenge. He nodded.

David continued. "And you better hope I don't hear one denigrating word being said about Cara Justice or I'm coming after you."

"But what if I'm not the one who said it?" Harold muttered.

"Then I suggest you pray."

"My word!" Harold gasped, and bolted for the car, leaving dust and gravel in the air behind him as he drove away.

Cara came outside and slipped her hand in the crook of David's arm.

"My hero."

David looked at her and then shrugged. "He ticked me off."

She smiled. "I could tell."

"Are you mad at me?" he asked, suddenly aware that he might have run off someone she actually cared for.

She laughed. "For getting rid of Hasty Harold? No way!"

"Hasty Harold?"

"It's an unfortunate nickname, but one he's certainly earned. He's the first man on the doorstep when a woman gets divorced and the first one to express his sympathy when there's a new widow in town. I've been fighting off his advances for three years now. Thanks to you, I think I've just seen the last of the pest."

"You're welcome," he said, and then slipped his arm around her shoulders. "Are we still going fishing?"

"Oh, yes," Cara said. "I wouldn't miss this trip with you for anything. Let's load up before we have any more uninvited visitors."

They were on their way within the hour, and for David, everything seemed surreal. He had the love of his life at his side, a picnic lunch in a cooler in the back of Cara's SUV, along with a couple of fishing poles and tackle. The sky was a pale blue-white with a few scattered clouds upon the horizon. All they needed to finish the postcard image was a couple of kids screaming in the back seat and a dog poking his head out the window. He glanced over at Cara, who was talking about something that had happened in her past. He was so fascinated by the fact that he was actually here in the moment that he lost track of what she was saying. Suddenly, a shiver of foreboding ran up his spine. The day was almost too perfect. He shrugged it off as a hangover from the life he'd just given up and concentrated on his driving and the directions Cara was giving him to the lake.

"Look!" Cara cried, as they came around a bend in the road.

It was a magnificent buck, momentarily spellbound by their oncoming vehicle.

"Wow, a sixteen pointer," David said, admiring the rack of antlers on the animal's head.

Cara was scrambling in the glove box when the buck suddenly came to itself and bounded into the surrounding woods.

"Darn it," she muttered. "I was going to take a picture."

"You brought a camera?"

She nodded, holding up a compact 35mm camera with a telescoping lense. Her expression of joy suddenly stilled, as if she was afraid of his reaction.

"What's wrong?" David asked.

"Nothing."

He frowned and then pulled off to the side of the road and turned to face her.

"That look on your face is not nothing," he said. "Talk to me."

She looked away, afraid he would read what was in her heart. "It's no big deal. I just wanted to take a few pictures to remember this day."

It wasn't what she said but what she omitted that hit him like the proverbial rock. God. It was just like before. She didn't trust he would come back and was making memories for the day that he would leave. What hurt him the most was that he couldn't promise to return. He could say he wanted to. But that didn't mean he would live through his confrontation with Frank.

It was at that moment he made up his mind to quit thinking negatively. He, by God, *was* going to come back and he *was* going to spend the rest of his life with her. He brushed the side of her cheek with the back of his hand, then gave the lobe of her ear a gentle tug.

"That's good. We can look back on them when we're

old and gray and remember that I was the one who caught the most fish.''

Cara turned her head, saw the challenge in his eyes, and in spite of her fears made herself smile. Two could play at this game of pretend.

"The most fish? You're already telling me this is going to be a competition in which you're going to win and you haven't even wet your hook?''

He grinned as he pulled onto the road. "So I like a little challenge now and then. What's so wrong with that?''

"Absolutely nothing," she said. "And I'm going to add a little something to the pot, okay?''

"Why not? I know how to be a good sport. Name your something.''

"The loser has to clean the fish.''

He wrinkled his nose. "I don't know. I don't want you hurting yourself.''

She laughed. "My word! The utter gall of the man. Not only have you announced yourself winner before the game even starts, but you're already concerning yourself with my inability to clean a fish.''

"Not *a* fish, my darling woman. Lots and lots of fish.''

"Fine. I accept your challenge.''

He nodded in satisfaction. "Good. Now…is this the turnoff you told me to take, or do we take the second one posted on that sign?''

"This is it," Cara said, pointing toward a narrow black-top road leading off to the right of the highway. "Caribou Lake, dead ahead.''

It was late afternoon before Cara showed signs of wearing out. They'd shared a picnic and taken pictures and reminisced about so many people that David's head was flooded with things he had spent years trying to forget.

To his delight, she'd caught the most fish, and her pride

had been obvious. His claim to fame for the day was that he'd caught the smallest, which she had promptly recorded for posterity with a demand for a pose. Laughing, he'd held up the four-inch fish on the line, measuring it with his thumb and forefinger for the camera as she snapped the shot.

He glanced at her again, as he had so often during the day, smiling about the smear of dirt on her forehead and the faint hint of sunburn on her reddening nose and cheeks.

"Don't you think it's time to call it quits?" he asked.

She looked at him, her eyes snapping with challenge.

"Only if you're the one who's saying uncle."

"Then uncle...and aunt, and cousin Joe, and Uncle Bob, and whatever the hell else it takes for you to admit you're as tired as I am."

She grinned. "All right then, just one more cast and I'm yours."

"Now you're talking," he said, and then watched as she made a perfect cast into the lake.

"Good one," he said. "Where did you learn to fish like this?"

"My son, Tyler. He demanded his time between ballet lessons and cheerleading practices."

David nodded, wondering where Ray Justice had been during those years. So far, Cara rarely mentioned his presence in their everyday lives. Then her next comment answered his question without being asked.

"Ray was always working," she said. "Someone had to do the guy stuff with our son." Slowly, she reeled in the line, skillfully playing the lure in the water as she talked. "I got pretty good at it, too. In fact, there for a while, spending the night at Tyler's house was all the rage because his mom wasn't squeamish about worms."

David grinned.

Suddenly, Cara's line jerked.

"I've got one!" she shouted, and began backing up as she reeled.

The pole was bending, the line quivering and taut. When it was less than five feet from the shore, they could see the shadowy shape of the fish beneath the water.

"It's a big one," she squealed. "Just look at him fight."

David glanced toward the water just as she took another turn on the reel. In that moment, the fish slipped the hook. The tension went from constant to nothing and the hook came up and out of the water like a pronged bullet, heading straight for Cara's face.

David reacted without thinking, spinning between her and the missile, then flinching in pain when the hook set itself deep within his back.

Still blinking from an impact that never happened, Cara saw David reaching over his shoulder, feeling his way around the wound. When he removed his hand, it came away bloody.

"David?"

"It's in my back," he said. "If I had a pair of needle-nosed pliers, I could pull it out."

"Oh, my God," she moaned, and made him turn around. "I saw it coming and just froze. If it hadn't been for you, it would have been in my face."

"It's nothing," he said. "Lord knows I've had worse. Now go look for the pliers, will you?"

"I will not," she stated firmly, and took a pocketknife out of her tackle box and quickly cut the line. "We're going to the emergency room. You're going to have that taken out like a decent human being, not ripped out of your flesh like some barbarian."

"But I am a barbarian," he muttered.

"Not in my world, you're not."

"Damn it, Cara, it's a little bitty hook."

"That's imbedded in your back," she retorted.

He glared.

She frowned.

He sighed.

She began gathering up their things.

"Give me those," David said, taking the heaviest of their gear out of her hands. "I'm not crippled."

"No, just difficult," she said, and then started to cry.

"God...don't do that," David said, as he followed her to the car.

"I have to," Cara said.

"Why?"

"Because I'm a woman and because if I don't cry, I might say something stupid. Trust me. It's better if I cry."

In spite of the burning pain in his back, he had to grin.

When they reached the SUV, she opened the back door and slid the rods inside.

"Is this something I should start getting used to?" David asked.

Her cheeks were streaked with tears, her eyes still brimming, but she managed a weak smile as she took the tackle boxes from him and put them in the floorboard behind the front seat.

"What? You mean crying?" she asked.

"Um...that and being bossed around."

This time her smile was genuine. "Was I bossing?"

"Oh, yeah."

"How did you feel about it?"

He grinned back. "Scared?"

"Oh, right," she muttered, and held out her hand. "May I please have the car keys?"

"And you're driving, too? Dang, Cara, I'm not dying."

"Do you know where the hospital is?"

"Oh."

"That's what I thought. The keys, please."

He handed them to her without further argument and got into the passenger side.

"What about the fish that we caught?" he asked.

"Drat," Cara muttered, as she realized she'd left her stringer of fish in the water. "Wait a minute. I'll be right back."

David watched her sprinting toward the lake, her long, slender legs making quick work of the distance. When she reached the shore, he saw her kneel and lift the stringer out of the water. But to his surprise, she didn't bring it to the car. Instead, she gently removed each one and released them into the lake.

When she got to the car, she tossed the empty stringer into the back seat with the rest of the tackle and brushed her hands on the seat of her pants.

"So, I'm not going to have to clean them after all," David said.

She looked at the bloodstained portion of his shirt and the hook still protruding from his back, and her eyes filled with sympathetic pain.

"I just realized how the fish must have felt when they bit the bait. I thought it was only fair that I let them go."

David's heart twisted. Her empathy for suffering was humbling. He thought of all his years in the military and then his years with SPEAR and wondered, if she knew what he'd done in the name of freedom, would she still be as sympathetic to his pain?

Chapter 5

They walked into the emergency room, still arguing. The nurse at the admitting desk looked up, saw the blood on the man's shirt as well as some of the same spots on Cara's arms.

"Cara! My word! What on earth is going on? Are you hurt?"

"I'm not, but he is," Cara said. "He's got a fishhook in his back."

"Goodness gracious," the nurse said. "Come this way. We'll get that taken care of immediately."

In a town as small as Chiltingham, it stood to reason Cara would be recognized, but for David, a man who'd spent most of his adult life pretending to be someone else, it was a bit disconcerting.

"How did this happen?" Frances said, as she reached for a pair of scissors and began cutting David's shirt down the middle of the back.

"I liked that shirt," David muttered.

"You can buy another one," Cara said. "Now quit fussing and let her do her thing."

David wanted to glare, but the damned hook was really starting to throb. If he had to give up a good T-shirt, then so be it. Anything to get a little relief from the pain.

"There now," Frances said. "I'm going to get Dr. Edwards. I'll be right back."

Cara bit her lower lip. Now that the shirt was gone, she could actually see how deep the hook had gone.

"If that had hit my eye, it would have blinded me. I can't believe you just stepped in front of it like that."

"It was reflex," David said. "It didn't amount to anything much."

"It's much to me," she muttered through tightly clenched teeth. "If I say you're a hero, then you're a hero."

At that point, a tall, skinny man who looked to be on the far side of sixty walked up to the side of the examination table where David was sitting. If it wasn't for the white lab coat he was wearing over a Grateful Dead T-shirt and jeans, David would have doubted the man's authenticity. This, he supposed, would be Doctor Edwards.

"Well, now, Cara, who do we have here?" he asked, looking at Cara instead of the man on the examining table.

David frowned. They were acting as if he was dumb, as well as bloody.

"My name is David Wilson," he said, answering for himself.

"He's my friend," Cara said. "And if he hadn't moved as quickly as he did, that hook would have been in my face, not his back."

Now Marvin Edwards looked at David, looking past the bloody condition of his clothes to the anger on his face and offered his hand.

"Then on behalf of the residents of Chiltingham, let me

be the one to thank you. Cara is a much beloved member of this community and it seems you have averted a tragedy. I like to fish myself, and know how these things can happen. One minute a fish is on the hook and the next it's not. Those hooks can come flying, especially if there is a lot of tension on the line. How did you react so quickly?''

David wasn't in the mood to explain that it had been the same instinct he'd had a thousand times before in the jungles of Vietnam.

Knowing a sniper was hidden somewhere up a tree.

Knowing there were booby traps on the trail up ahead although nothing could be seen.

Knowing that the smiling old man who appeared on the trail in front of him was holding an unpinned hand grenade beneath the sheaves of rice.

It was an ingrained sense to survive. Or in this instance, to protect.

''I don't know. I just did,'' he said.

Marvin Edwards smiled, satisfied with David's reticent attitude. He could respect that. There were plenty of times when he didn't much want to talk. Unfortunately, in his line of work, he didn't have the luxury of clamming up.

With the shirt off his patient's back, Marvin ran his fingers across the multitude of scars on David's body without comment, then waved at Frances.

''Get me a syringe, Frances. We're going to need to deaden this area first.''

The nurse busied herself at a nearby table while David fidgeted beneath Cara's worried gaze.

''Look,'' David said. ''Trust me, Doc, this is nothing. I've been hurt enough times in my life to know the difference.''

''Then humor me so I can humor our friend Cara Justice. What do you say?''

David grimaced. ''Fine. Look and dig. It's just a hook.''

Marvin Edwards grinned. "Look and dig? I spent all those years and all that money on medical school just so I could look and dig?"

The older man's sarcasm almost made David grin. "Sorry. Figure of speech."

"Apology accepted," Marvin said, as he closed the curtain around the examining table and took the syringe the nurse handed him.

"Here goes nothing. Please don't move."

David sighed, barely aware when the doctor shoved the needle into his back, but he winked at Cara, who looked as if she was going to cry.

"Honey, why don't you go find a bathroom and wash that blood off your hands?"

"Are you saying you don't want me here?" she asked.

"No. I'm saying you don't need to be here. You're going to cry again and it's really not a big deal, okay?"

"Promise?"

"I promise."

"I'll be right back," she said.

"I figured that."

She slipped out of the curtained area, leaving the two men alone.

"So...David, is it?"

David nodded.

"Exactly what line of business are you in?"

"I'm semi-retired," David said.

"Um, I see. But before...what did you do?"

David didn't respond.

Marvin Edwards glanced up. The expression on the man's face was closed, so he tried another topic.

"Are you just visiting, or planning to stay?" he asked, as he reached for a small scalpel.

David didn't answer.

Marvin grunted. So the man wasn't a talker. That was all right with him.

"This might sting a little," he said, as he made the first cut. "Frances, swab that for me, will you?"

The nurse caught the instant flow of blood as he lifted the scalpel from David's flesh.

He made another small cut and then laid down the scalpel and picked up an instrument that looked to David a whole lot like the damned needle-nosed pliers he'd wanted in the first place. With a couple of tugs and one small sideways twist, the hook came out.

"That's got it," Marvin said. "Flood it with disinfectant, Frances, then I'll stitch it up."

David felt cold fluid running down his back, but nothing more. That would come later, when the shot wore off.

In between stitches, the doctor watched David's face, absently noting the military-straight set to his shoulders and an unflinching stare. It reminded him of a drill sergeant he'd known and hated.

"Who are you?" he asked.

David sighed. How the hell did he answer that one? Then he remembered what Cara had done yesterday and took his cue from her.

"David Wilson."

"I knew Cara and her husband for years. I never heard either of them mention you before."

"I don't doubt that," David said.

This wasn't the answer Marvin was looking for.

"Look, I'm not being nosy." Then he sighed. "Well, yes, maybe I am, a bit. Cara's a widow. Sometimes widows can be very vulnerable. I would not like to see—"

David took a deep breath and jumped in with both feet. "Do you know Cara's daughter Bethany?"

"Sure do. I delivered all three of her children."

"I'm Bethany's father."

Marvin Edwards's jaw dropped, but only momentarily.

"I'm sorry. I never heard them mention—"

"They thought I was dead."

"For all these years?"

David shrugged. "It seemed like a good idea at the time."

Suddenly, Marvin Edwards began to see things in a different light. The horrific scars on this man. The secrets. The military bearing of a man who was supposed to be dead. His gaze sharpened.

"I was a medic in Nam," Marvin said softly.

David shifted. "You must have been pretty young."

"Yes, a lot of us went in too young, didn't we?"

David resisted an urge to look around lest they be overheard. And then he realized it no longer mattered. Lots of people were veterans, which is exactly what he'd become. Finally, he nodded.

"So, did you die on your own, or did Uncle Sam help you?"

Again, David was surprised by the man's perceptions.

"It's no longer a factor in my life," David said.

"You planning to stick around?"

David sighed. "I would like nothing better." He refused to acknowledge, even to himself, that there was still a huge obstacle between him and a normal life.

Marvin grinned and held out his hand. "Then, welcome home, soldier."

David knew he was shaking the doctor's hand, but he couldn't feel it. He could tell that the man was still talking, because he could see his lips moving, but he couldn't hear what was being said. All sound had faded except Marvin Edwards's last words. He'd never thought of himself as a man without a country, because he'd given a good portion of his life in helping keep it safe, but it was true. Until this moment, David Wilson had never truly come home from Vietnam. The emotion of it all almost nailed him. His hands were shaking as the doctor continued to talk.

"So," Marvin said, as he took his last stitch. "Do you golf?"

It was the most benign question David had been asked in over forty years, and he didn't know how to answer it. Coping with the innocence of everyday life was more difficult than he would have believed.

"No. Can't say that I do."

"Shame," Marvin said. "I'm always looking for a buddy to play the front nine."

"I thought doctors were supposed to be notorious for their eighteen-hole games," David said.

Marvin shrugged. "Not doctors in towns this size. We're always on call and it seems as if I always get paged before I get to the back nine."

Before David could respond, Cara returned.

"Is he okay?" she asked.

"Ask me," David muttered. "I'm the one to whom he shoved a knife in the back."

Cara blinked, then grinned as Marvin Edwards calmly ignored David's petulance and answered.

"Right as rain," Marvin said. "And he'll be just as pretty as he was before. My stitches are as good as my grannie's quilting stitches were."

David resisted the urge to roll his eyes. Quilting stitches? Have mercy.

Marvin Edwards put a small bandage over the stitches and then gave David a thump on the thigh. "Don't forget what I said about that golf."

David nodded. "I remember…I remember everything you said." He hesitated, and then impulsively shook the doctor's hand. "And I thank you."

"For what?" Marvin asked.

The words "welcome home, soldier" were still ringing

in his ears, but he couldn't bring himself to admit how much they'd meant. Instead, he just shrugged.

"For everything."

"You'll get my bill," Marvin said, and handed him a prescription for pain pills.

"What's that?" David asked.

"Something for the pain."

"I won't need it," David said.

Marvin Edwards arched an eyebrow, purposefully letting his gaze linger on the big scar on David's chest.

"Oh, right, what was I thinking?"

Cara ignored them both and took the prescription from David before he could protest.

"We'll get it filled at the drive-through pharmacy," she said.

"Better yet, take these instead," Marvin said, and handed Cara some pharmaceutical samples from a drawer.

"Thank you, Dr. Edwards."

"You're welcome," he said, than waved a finger in David's face. "Mind that woman, you hear me, boy?"

David didn't answer, but a smile teased the corners of his mouth as they left the hospital.

"I'm still driving," Cara said.

David didn't argue.

"I like that," Cara said.

"Like what?" David asked, as she started the car.

"That smile on your face. You should wear it more often."

David thought about waking up beside Cara each morning and sleeping beside her each night. Of buying groceries and getting haircuts and playing golf with a friend. Yes, it would be easy to smile about a life like that.

"You think?" he asked, and gave her a wink.

"Yes, I think. Now make yourself comfortable, darling. We're going straight home."

Home.

God. His fingers curled in his lap as Cara accelerated the car.

Frank stood before the bathroom mirror, adjusting his wig and running his fingers over the mustache he'd affected, testing its position. Everything seemed stable enough. He straightened the collar of his white Gucci shirt, checked one last time to make sure it was tucked neatly into his navy blue slacks, then picked up the sunglasses from the back of the commode and slipped them on before looking up.

Perfect! The man in the mirror was a stranger.

He grinned, and as he did, the movement puckered the burn scars on the side of his face, giving him a slightly demonic expression. If she'd still been alive, his own mother would not have recognized him.

Frank was a master at disguise. It had kept him alive all these years without detection. He had no reason to suppose it would fail him now. The wound on his shoulder was almost well. Only now and then did he feel a real twinge of pain. The fact that he was missing most of the top half of one ear was hidden nicely by the hairstyle of the wig.

Convinced that all was well, he strode out of the bathroom, picked up the suitcase he'd packed last night and then paused at the door, giving the apartment a final look. Satisfied that he'd left nothing of himself behind, he opened the door and walked out. No more roach motel. It was time to move up and on, which meant once again changing his persona.

When he passed through the lobby, he tossed the room key on the desk and kept on walking. The clerk didn't bother to look up, which was just as well, because he wouldn't have recognized the man as the former resident of room 413.

Frank was on the street less than a minute before hailing an empty cab.

"Where to, buddy?" the cab driver asked.

"LAX, and step on it," he said. "I've got a flight to catch."

David lay on his side on the bed. At Cara's insistence, he was supposed to be resting, but in truth, he had a lot of thinking to do. Before he'd come, his expectations of seeing Cara had not included a future. All he'd wanted to do was see her—ask her forgiveness—and if possible make a place for himself within his daughter's life. Not as a father, of course. He didn't deserve that much consideration. But he wanted to know her—and he wanted her to know him. That had been the apex of his dream. Making love to Cara within minutes of his arrival would never have occurred to him, not even in his wildest imagination. But it had happened and he had accepted the fact that she'd been making love to the boy he'd been, not the man that he'd become. However, that didn't account for the other times since, or the fact that Cara had openly admitted she wanted him to stay. And he wanted to, desperately so. He wasn't going to lose her again.

Somehow, he had to find a way to stop Frank for good without losing his life in the process. Frustrated with the mess he was in, he rolled over on his back, wincing slightly as the pressure caused a slight pain, then he closed his eyes. In spite of himself, the pain pills were having their way.

He didn't know how long he'd been sleeping when the phone rang. He woke abruptly, waiting for Cara to answer, but she didn't. On the fourth ring, he thought he heard water running from the faucet outside and realized she must not be in the house. He reached for the phone and answered as it rang again.

"Justice residence."

There was a soft gasp on the other end of the line and then a young woman's voice, hesitant and suddenly anxious.

"Who's speaking, please?"

David hesitated briefly, then opted for minimal introduction.

"This is David."

"Um...David, this is Bethany. Is my mother there?"

David stood abruptly, his heart pounding against his chest. All he could think was, *My God, I am hearing my daughter's voice.*

"Hello? Are you still there?" Bethany asked.

David felt like crying. Instead, he took a deep breath and then exhaled slowly, making himself focus.

"Sorry. Yes, I'm here, and so is your mother, but I think she's outside. Do you want to wait while I check and see?"

"Yes, please," she said.

David didn't want to break the connection, but was not about to explain his reluctance.

"Okay. You'll hang on?"

"Yes."

He hurried through the house and then ran into Cara as she was coming in the back door.

David held up the phone. "It's Bethany. She wants to talk to you."

Cara's eyes widened. She could tell from the stricken look on David's face that he had been sideswiped by the call.

"You didn't say anything about who you are?" she asked, keeping her voice low.

He shook his head.

Even though she wanted to tell Bethany everything

about David's arrival, it wasn't news to be told over a phone.

"Hello? Bethany?"

"Mom, are you all right?"

Cara rolled her eyes at David, who was pushing her toward a chair.

"Yes, I'm fine, sweetheart. How's the vacation going?"

Now David was the one rolling his eyes at her as she struggled to make conversation.

Cara made a face at him, and they both smiled.

"So...Mom?"

"Yes?"

Cara heard an exasperated sigh and knew Bethany wasn't anywhere near satisfied with what she'd been told.

"Who is David?"

Cara looked at the man sitting across the kitchen table from her.

"He's a friend."

Bethany snorted. "I've never heard you or Dad mention anyone by the name of David. When did you meet him?"

"Years ago," Cara said. "Enough about me. How's the vacation? Are the kids having fun?"

This time Cara could hear noise in the background and deduced that the rest of Bethany's family was just returning to the hotel room.

"Yes, they're having a ball. Actually, we're all having a wonderful time. We've got to come here again and when we do, you have to come with us. You would love Disney World as well as Epcot Center."

Cara smiled. "I'm glad everything is going well."

Bethany continued, "I didn't really have a reason to call other than to say hello and to tell you we'll be home Sunday. I think our plane lands around two in the afternoon. We should be home before dark. We'll talk more then."

"I can't wait to hear all about the trip," Cara said. "Oh,

by the way…when you get home, we need to talk. It's important."

David flinched. Just the thought of facing his daughter and trying to explain why he'd absented himself from her life made him sick to his stomach.

"Mother! It's about the man who answered the phone, isn't it? I knew it! You haven't been out with a man since Dad died. Who is he? Is this serious?" Then she shrieked. "It can't be serious. We've only been gone for eight days. Please tell me you've known him longer than eight days!"

"Much longer than that," Cara said. "Now calm down. We'll talk when you get home."

"How much longer?" Bethany asked. "Weeks? Months?"

"Years, darling. Years and years. Now have a safe trip home and call me when you get in."

"Mother, you're not telling me what I want to hear."

"I love you, Bethany. Take care and give my love to Tom and the girls."

"Mother! Don't you dare hang up until you—"

Cara calmly punched the off button and then laid the phone down on the table beside her.

"Our daughter is in a panic," Cara said.

"Why? Because I'm here?"

Cara nodded.

"Are you okay with this, because if my being here is going to cause you trouble, then I'll leave. I won't want to, but I'll do it for you."

Cara got up from her chair and sat in David's lap. Relief hit him fast and hard as she wound her arms around his neck, careful not to touch his stitches.

"If you weren't wounded…"

He grinned. "It's not fatal," he said, as he began unbuttoning her shirt.

"But your stitches…"

"Are not in the way," David said, finishing her sentence for her.

She grinned. "That's not what I was going to say and you know it."

He stood up and then grabbed her hand, giving it a tug.

"Today, I was a hero, remember? No one gave me the keys to the city, so I'm taking you instead."

He didn't have to ask her twice. In spite of her better judgment, she let him pick her up in his arms and carry her all the way to her bed.

"We seem to be doing an awful lot of this lately," Cara said.

David paused in the act of removing his shirt, his eyes dancing with mischief.

"What? Undressing?"

She blushed. "No. Well, yes, but not that specifically."

David tossed his shirt and then reached for his belt.

"Are you referring to the fact that I keep taking you to bed?"

She arched an eyebrow. "You know exactly what I mean."

"Ah...well then," David said, removing his right shoe. "I look at it this way. I have forty years of making up to do and not a long time to do it, so if I'm ever going to catch up..."

She laughed and threw a pillow at him.

He dodged it neatly then kicked off his other shoe, shed the rest of his clothes and pounced.

Cara was still laughing when he slid into her body. The laugh turned into a groan and then a sigh. After that, it was downhill all the way.

Later, as they lay quietly in each other's arms, talking and savoring the pleasure of what had just happened, Cara could feel David starting to withdraw. She raised up on one elbow, looking at him.

"Is something wrong?" she asked.

He started not to answer, then sighed. "Not with you...or with us. It's just that I need to...uh...check in at the office."

"Of course," she said, and reached for the phone. "Please feel free to use my phone anytime you need. I'll get dressed and give you some privacy."

David grabbed her arm, stilling her intent.

"Thank you, Cara, more than I can say. But I can't use your phone."

"Why? I don't—" Understanding dawned. "Oh."

He kissed the side of her face. "It's all right. I have everything I need in the trunk of my car. However, it will take a while to set up and I don't want you to think—"

This time, she was the one to silence him.

"David. Enough. You don't explain to me. You do what you have to do and just stay in one piece. I'll be satisfied with that, all right?"

He smiled. "Thank you, baby."

"Use any room in this house that you need. I have plenty of things I need to do outside. Just let me know when you're through."

David thought about it and then shook his head.

"No. I don't want to bring any part of that life into this house, and I don't need to necessarily be inside. I think I'll drive back toward the lake."

She nodded, frowning as she tried to picture a place at the lake where he could stay unobserved.

"You remember where we turned to go to the landing?"

He nodded.

"If you skip that turn and take the next one instead, it will take you to a very wooded area of the lake. There aren't any campsites or boat docks there. I think they have plans to develop it, but so far nothing has been done."

David smiled. "Sounds perfect."

Cara looked pleased. "Good, and while you're gone, I'm going to do some laundry. Do you have anything you need washed?"

"No, baby, but thanks," David said, and gave her a quick kiss before he rolled out of bed and headed for the bathroom.

When he came out a few minutes later, Cara was already gone. By the time he dressed and left the house, he'd left more than Cara behind. David Wilson wasn't the man who got into the rental car and drove away toward the lake. It was Jonah.

By the time he reached the area that Cara had mentioned, he had completely refocused. There was nothing in his head but duty. In less than thirty minutes, he had everything set up and running. With a laptop and modem, some prototype chips in his Global Positioning System and a couple of other gadgets from technical research that had yet to be named, he had logged into his site and retrieved his messages.

Within an hour, he had two agents en route to Illinois to investigate death threats against the President, another dispatched to the border between Mexico and Texas and had restructured a list of agents on foreign soil to insure their identities stayed anonymous.

Out of curiosity, he checked a site reserved for personal messages between him and the White House. To his relief, there were none. He checked another site, hoping that there was some sort of message on there that had been intercepted from Frank, but again, there was nothing.

Convinced that he'd done all he could do, he logged off, packed the stuff back in the trunk and then strolled to the edge of the lake.

The day was calm, the water so still it looked like glass. Only the smallest of ripples could be seen as the water lapped at the shore. He stood for a while, absorbing the peacefulness of the day while mentally letting go of Jonah before he returned to Cara.

A trio of gulls circled high over his head. Curious, he watched for a while, thinking that they were quite a distance from the sea. Probably blown here with the last storm to pass through and just stayed—so symbolic of the path his own life had taken.

He'd set out on one path and had been war-tossed into another. And, instead of finding his way back home, like the gulls, he'd stayed. Had it been a mistake? If he'd come back after the war, what kind of a husband and father would he have been? He thought of the hell he'd lived with, thinking he'd not only killed his own brother but had hidden the truth about Frank being a traitor. In that moment, he accepted his life without regret. He would have been hell to live with, would have ruined whatever chances he and Cara might have had for a happy life, and they would have been divorced before they were thirty.

He sighed, remembering something his mother had said, that things always happened for a reason. It wasn't always easy to understand, but that with time, understanding always came. She'd been right. Now, looking back on what he'd done and his mental state at the time, he'd done the best thing for both of them.

The water beckoned.

Impulsively, he shed his clothes where he stood and then walked into the water until he was up to his chest and then started to swim. The water was cool against the heat of his skin. He swam until his car was little more than a black speck beneath the trees before he turned and went back. By the time he emerged from the lake, he was tired but renewed.

Within a very few minutes, he was dry enough to put on his clothes. As he walked to his car, he began to smile. It had been a long time since he'd done anything so innocent as skinny-dip. Maybe he was actually getting the hang of being a normal guy, after all.

By the time he got to Cara's house, it was mid-afternoon. When he drove up and parked, she looked up from the flower beds in front of her house and waved, but then continued to weed. He had no way of knowing how many prayers she'd sent up in his name, or that she'd cried more than once, fearing he would not return. All he saw was a woman confident within her life, waving a hello.

"Looks like you've been busy," he said, tweaking the end of her sun-stained nose. "You're about to get a sunburn, honey."

She rocked on her heels and put the back of her arm against her cheeks and nose, only then feeling the emanating heat.

"Ooh, you're right," she said. "And I forgot to put on sunscreen before I came out." She stood, dusting off her gloves and pushing her hair away from her face. "I've done enough anyway. Let's go inside. Are you hungry?"

He realized that he was.

"Yes, starving."

She smiled. "Good. How about a ham and cheese sandwich?"

"How about two?"

She laughed. "I think that can be arranged."

She went inside, leaving the door ajar for him to follow. As he stepped over the threshold, he sighed.

David Wilson was home.

Chapter 6

Sundown had long since come and gone. The evening had passed with remarkable simplicity. It was as if the time David had spent away from the house had somehow settled some of the turmoil he'd brought with him. They'd watched television together like a couple who'd been married for years. David sat with an open book in his lap, sometimes reading, other times watching the program in broadcast, while Cara shelled some peas she'd bought from a nearby truck farm.

The gentleness of the evening had rolled over into their bedtime. Now, Cara lay naked beneath David's gaze. The love she felt for him was there in her eyes for him to see. All he had to do was look. Silently she watched as he undressed beside the bed. He moved in the darkness as if he had lived here all his life. She could tell he was far more comfortable within the shadows than the light.

"David."

He dropped the shirt he'd just taken off and turned.

"Yes?"

"That bullet scar on your back."

"What about it?"

"How did you get it?"

He frowned. "I thought you wanted to make love."

"I do, but I also want to know who I'm making love to and there is a huge gap between the boy who went off to war and the man you are today."

"If you knew, you wouldn't want me in your house, let alone your bed."

The defeat in his voice surprised her. She got up on her knees and then pulled him down onto the bed beside her.

"That's not true," she said. "I didn't ask because I feel a need to judge you. I asked for the same reasons I see in your eyes when Ray's name is mentioned."

David pulled her into his arms and pressed her cheek against his chest.

"It's not jealously, baby, I swear," David said.

"I know, but we lost so many years...wonderful years we could have spent together. I just have this overwhelming urge to fill myself up with your life. Maybe because it's the only way I have left to share it."

David bowed his head, pressing a soft kiss against her cheek, and then eased her back onto the pillow.

"If I talk, will you promise to lie still?"

She sighed. "Are you turning down my rather blatant request?"

He grinned. "Not by a long shot...just postponing it a bit."

She made a face.

He tweaked her nose. "Okay, you wanted to know about the scar on my shoulder?"

"Yes, please."

He thought of the searing pain from Frank's gun, spinning him around and knocking him off his feet.

"Vietnam."

"And the one on the side of your neck?"

"Afghanistan. Don't ask me why I was there."

"What about the long scar on the back of your right leg?"

"Disagreement with a sniper in Beirut. He ran out of bullets and I jumped him. I didn't know he had a knife."

Cara's eyes were huge, her lips slack with shock. He was telling these horrors in such a calm voice, and she felt like throwing up. She laid her hand on the sickle-shaped scar above his heart.

"And this one?"

He hesitated, and suddenly Cara put her hand on his mouth before he could answer. "I don't think I want to know."

"Now you're getting the picture. They don't matter anymore, baby. That part of my life is almost over."

Cara looked away and then closed her eyes.

David could tell she was fighting tears. He cupped her cheek gently, then kissed the side of her face.

"What, honey? Don't shut me out now."

"Oh, God, David. Don't you understand? It's the *almost* that undoes me." She ran a finger along the surface of the old scars. "I can live with these. It's the ones you have yet to receive that scare me most."

There was nothing he could really say that would reassure her and still be truthful. And he wasn't lying to Cara—not ever again.

"Look at it this way," he said. "I was always outnumbered and survived. This time it's only one man."

"Why do you have to do this alone? Aren't there people you can call on? Isn't there anyone in authority who will stand beside you?"

David hesitated. "It's not that. It's just that the man wants me and only me. He's spent the better part of a year

trying to destroy me and damned near took a huge chunk
of national security and my best agents along with him.
We can't afford...no...*I* can't afford to waste any more
time. He has to be stopped.'' His voice changed to a deep,
warning growl. "How much do you value your life and
the lives of your children and grandchildren?''

Cara's mouth parted, her lips slack with shock.

"If he knew about you...about Bethany and her family...their lives wouldn't be worth dirt. In the past eleven
months, he's kidnapped, lied, stolen and killed, and all in
the name of trying to get to me. I am resigning from my
post because I can't let another person fight what was ul-
timately my battle from the start.''

"Dear God, David, what manner of man is he? Why
you? What did you ever do to him to make him hate you
this way?''

Silence hung between them, shrouded in secrets and
guilt. He preferred not to answer, but if they were ever
going to have a chance at any kind of a future, she had to
know part of the past.

"He's a man gone crazy. It started years ago in Vietnam. He shot at me. I shot back. In fact, I thought I had
killed him.''

"Who is he, David? What kind of man hates like that?''

"You know the old saying about blood being thicker
than water? Well, hate within a family is just as strong.''

Cara frowned. "I don't understand. Your parents are
dead. Your brother died in Vietnam. Who else is—''

Even though the room was in darkness, she saw enough
of his expression to realize what he'd been trying not to
say.

"Oh...my...God. Please tell me it's not what I'm thinking. Frank's dead...isn't he?''

His silence rocked the room.

She inhaled sharply. "What can you tell me?''

"Nothing that will make any sense."

Her gaze went straight to the scar on his shoulder. She touched it in disbelief.

"He did this, didn't he?"

David nodded.

She started to cry.

"We all tried to kill you, didn't we, darling? Deception. Lies. Betrayals. My God, you must have thought there was no one on your side. Not even me."

"Don't say that," he muttered, and took her in his arms. "I never once blamed you. You did what you had to do."

"I will forever blame my parents for the lies they told me about you."

"And they did what they thought was right, too. Let it go, Cara. I'm here now."

She buried her face against the curve of his neck. "I'm scared."

His arms tightened around her. "I'm scared, too, but not *of* Frank...only what he can do if he isn't stopped. You understand, don't you?"

Her voice was shaking, her face streaked with tears. "Yes, as much as I hate to admit it, I do. I promise I won't talk about this again. We have now and we have each other. And when you come back, we'll have the rest of our lives."

Now David felt like crying. Instead, he laid her down and began to kiss her. Gently at first and then with desperation, until they were lost in the passion.

After a day of traveling in his new disguise, Frank Wilson was comfortable in his skin as he tossed a handful of bills onto the counter, picked up the sacks containing his new wardrobe and sauntered out of the Denver, Colorado store. The day was almost balmy. One of those clear, robin's-egg blue skies that made a man feel as if he could take on the world. He paused at the curb before swaggering down the street. More than one woman gave him a second look as he passed, and in spite of his scars, and his long ponytail wig, he knew it was not in disgust. There was a bad-boy air of danger about him that never failed to attract the women. Granted, they were always the wrong kind of women, not like his beloved Martha, but they were always there just the same.

He stopped at a crosswalk, waiting for the red light to change, and thought of what he had lost. His identity was unimportant. He'd lived so long in the shadows that another assumed name would be a small price to pay for peace of mind. After his confrontation with David was over, maybe he'd find himself a good woman and settle down again. Despite the fact that his sixtieth birthday had come and gone, he had the body and constitution of a much younger man, and he knew it. It wasn't too late to make a new life for himself. He would have the time, and he already had the money.

The light changed, and he started across the street, losing himself in the crowd of pedestrians. By the time he got back to his hotel, he'd made up his mind to head south after he rid himself of David. Maybe the Florida Keys. He liked the sun. It was why he'd settled in Australia, but he'd had enough of the outback. This time, he wanted to be where there was water. A whole lot of water.

Inside his room, he tossed the bags with his purchases onto the bed and began to go through them, searching for certain items. A few minutes later, he had changed into khaki-colored cotton shorts and a navy blue T-shirt. He put on a baseball cap with the Denver Broncos logo and then transferred a number of items into a medium-size fanny pack, patted his pockets to make sure he had his wallet and room key, as well as some other identification, and headed out the door. He had an appointment he didn't want to miss.

A half hour later, a cab dropped him off at a public firing range. He sauntered inside as if he owned the place.

The clerk at the front desk looked up. "Can I help you?" he asked.

Frank nodded, flashing a badge. "Detective Ferraro out of New York City. I'm here on vacation. Thought I'd get in some target practice while the little woman spends all my money."

The clerk grinned. "Yeah, I can identify with that, buddy," he said. "Sign in here. I'll get an escort to take you into the range. He'll get you all set up."

"Great," Frank said, signing his fake name with a flourish.

A few minutes later, he stood within his cubicle, safety glasses and headphones on, his 9mm Glock loaded and waiting for the first target to appear. Someone tapped him on the shoulder. He turned.

"Are you ready, sir?"

Frank nodded, took aim and waited. About fifty feet in front of him, a paper target appeared. He squeezed off a couple of rounds, taking satisfaction in the weapon's kick against the palms of his hands. The muffled sounds of gunfire, the smell of burning gunpowder, the surge of adrenaline—everything combined within his senses and sent his memory into overdrive. David's face suddenly appeared on the target, taunting him like the ghost that he'd become, and when it did, Frank snapped, emptying his gun into the target. Moving in robotlike motions, he ejected the empty clip and slipped a full one in place before pressing the button on the wall beside him to bring the paper target up close.

Yanking it from the wire, he grunted in satisfaction. Every shot he'd fired had hit within a three-inch radius of where a man's heart would be. He dropped it onto the floor beside him, hit the switch, then adjusted his safety glasses as he waited for a new target to appear. He'd done fine, just fine. But he could do better.

He set the distance on the new target at fifty feet farther back than before and took aim. Again, David's face appeared before him. He squeezed the trigger in rapid succession again, this time peppering the head until there was nothing left of the target above the shoulders and no bullets left in the clip.

Muscles in his healing shoulder protested, but he ignored the painful twinges as he took off the headphones and goggles, then mopped the sweat from his face with his handkerchief.

A passing attendant glanced into Frank's cubicle and whistled softly.

"Good job, sir. Whoever he is, he's definitely dead."

Frank turned abruptly, still holding his weapon and making sure that he'd never seen him before. Luckily for the attendant, he was a stranger to Frank, or he might never have lived to see another sunrise. Then Frank smiled, pulling the scarred side of his mouth into a grimace.

"Yeah...he's that, all right," Frank said, and headed for the exit.

Morning dawned on a gray, overcast day. It looked like rain. David stood at the living room windows staring out into the yard, but he wasn't looking at the view. His thoughts had gone inward, mentally plotting out a course of action. The scent of coffee still permeated the air from their breakfast. Cara had scooted David out of the kitchen, claiming she was making him a surprise. Then she'd argued he should be resting in bed and he'd retaliated by ignoring her.

Now, although they were but a room away from each

other, the distance between them couldn't have been further. He wasn't thinking like David. He'd become Jonah again—planning the best way to trap and dispose of a killer.

Happy with the pie she was baking, Cara never knew when David went out the front door and checked the contents of his trunk. He needed to check in with his agents and the powers that be again. If God had been listening to his prayers, maybe they'd already fished Frank's body out of the East River, but he wasn't betting his future on that. At least not yet.

He looked at the house. He wasn't in the mood to go to the lake, but no way was he ever going to destroy the sanctity of that home by bringing any part of his old life into it. Anxious to get things in motion, he set the bag in the front seat of the car and ran into the house.

Cara heard the front door slam, then the sound of running footsteps. She turned just as David entered the kitchen.

"What's the hurry?"

He hesitated. "Something smells good."

She frowned. "David. I raised three children and I've heard just about every excuse in the book. That's not what you came here to tell me."

He grinned. "Damn, you're good."

"Yes, and don't you forget it," she muttered. "So, what's up?"

"I'm going to take another little drive. I won't be gone long, okay?"

Her fingers tightened around the handle of the knife she was holding. It was the only outward sign of her unease.

"Okay. If you get as far as Chiltingham, would you mind bringing back a gallon of milk?"

His eyes widened, then a genuine smile spread across

his face. He hadn't done anything that ordinary since before he'd left for Vietnam.

"No, I don't mind. I don't mind at all," he said, and then suddenly swooped, swinging her up in his arms and dancing her across the kitchen with her feet dangling above the floor.

"Be careful of your stitches," she cried.

"To hell with the stitches. I'm going to kiss you."

Cara laughed from the joy in his eyes and from the silliness of it all. By the time he stopped moving, she was dizzy from all the spinning.

"You're a crazy man," she said, and planted a hard kiss in the center of his mouth.

"That kind of behavior will make a man crazy," he muttered, and kissed her back. Then he turned her loose with a reluctant groan. "I won't be long," he said.

She eyed him cautiously, afraid to say what was in her heart, but David read the expression on her face.

"I swear I'll be back," he said softly.

"I knew that," Cara said. "Now get. This pie won't be ready in time for supper if I don't get it in the oven."

But David didn't move and he wouldn't turn her loose.

"Cara..."

"Yes?"

"I love you very much."

Quick tears blurred his face. It had been forty years since she'd heard him say those words and yet her heart still skipped a beat. She cupped his face with her hands, fingering the silver strands of hair above his ears and then smiling.

"Thank you, my darling. I love you, too."

He laughed and then hugged her fiercely before bolting out of the house. Only after Cara could no longer hear the sound of the car's engine did she sit down and cry.

Still riding on an emotional high, David drove with focus, searching for the same road that he'd taken before. The radio was on, but turned down low, little more than background noise for bigger plans. But when he heard the disc jockey giving a brief update on a breaking story, he turned it up, then began to frown. Another business had been robbed, presumably by the same three thieves who'd been terrorizing the area.

"They'll make a mistake," he muttered. "They're getting too cocky."

A few miles down the road, he saw the cutoff he was looking for and swerved. The car bumped and bounced along the graveled road before he had a chance to slow down. Just like before, no one was anywhere in sight, not even on the water.

A few minutes later, he was set up and running. As he dialed the first number, he felt himself slipping back into the Jonah mind-set, and as he did, realized that it felt uncomfortable. Just these few days with Cara were easing forty years of scars from his military service. Seconds later, his call was answered. He gave a one-word code, which instantly connected him to another line, then another. Finally, his call reached its final destination.

"Hello, Jonah, this is the President. How have you been?"

"Better, sir," David said briefly. "Has there been any word on our quarry?"

"No, I'm sorry to say there has not. It looks like your assumptions were correct after all."

David slumped in disappointment and was glad the President couldn't see his face.

"Yes, sir. I'm sorry, too, sir."

"Is there anything you need?"

"Not at the moment, sir. I'll let you know when it's over."

"Thank you, Jonah. I appreciate that."

"Oh...sir?"

"Yes?"

"About looking for my replacement."

"Yes?"

"I suggest you start the process."

"It's your call," the President said, and then added, "I hope you know how much I regret it had to come to this."

"Yes, sir. Thank you, sir, but it was inevitable. We don't last forever in this job."

The President's chuckle rumbled in David's ear. "Longer than I do in mine, I can assure you."

David grinned. "Yes, sir." Then he added quickly, "I'll be in touch."

The line went dead in his ear. Satisfied that was done, he dialed another number. Seconds later, a woman's voice answered.

"MailBin, Birmingham branch, Jennifer speaking."

"Hello, Jennifer, this is David Wilson."

"Oh, hi, Mr. Wilson. Long time, no talkie," she said, and then giggled at the joke she'd just made.

"Yes, it has been a while," David said. "I need you to do something for me."

"Are we forwarding your stuff again?" she asked.

"Yes."

"Okeydoke. Even though I recognize your voice, I need your password."

"Fourth of July," he said.

"All righty, then. Where do you want your stuff sent this time?"

"I'll be in Washington D.C. by Monday. Please send the contents of the box to the Wardman Park Hotel. Here's the address."

A couple of minutes later, he hung up again, satisfied that whatever mail had been accumulating for him would be awaiting his arrival at the hotel. Then he dialed another number, checked upon the situation at the Texas/Mexico border and deployed another agent to help the one already on-site, then sent another agent to assist the two in Illinois who were investigating the death threats on the President.

Once he'd finished with the business of SPEAR, he dialed one more number, this time his last.

"Marriott Wardman Park, how can I direct your call?"

"Reservations, please," David said.

"One moment, sir."

A couple of rings later, David was connected.

"Reservations, how may I help you?"

"This is David L. Wilson. Number fifty-one. I will be arriving Sunday afternoon."

The moment the name was typed into the hotel computer, it automatically opened into a security file with a predestined room ready at his disposal.

"Yes, Mr. Wilson, I have entered you into the system. Will you be needing a driver at the airport?"

"Not this trip," David said. "I'll catch a cab. Oh…there will be a package arriving for me within a couple of days. That is to be held for me to pick up upon my arrival."

"Yes, sir. Have a safe flight."

David hung up, set the laptop aside and crossed his arms upon the steering wheel then leaned forward. The sun was close to setting, giving the glassy surface of the lake a mirrorlike appearance. It seemed almost impossible to believe that only the day before yesterday they'd been here, fishing and laughing and pretending that they were normal people with normal lives.

Although he sat without moving, his thoughts were in constant motion. He'd done all there was to do from this end. There was nothing left to do but get to D.C. and wait for Frank to contact him. And he was in no doubt that it would happen. His brother had obviously invested a lifetime in tracking him down with full intentions of destroying him. All David had to do was make sure it didn't happen.

A simple thing, actually. Just stay alive. It was an instinctive act that shouldn't pose a real problem. The only thing was, Frank was most likely set on the very same thing.

David said a brief but fervent prayer. It wouldn't be the first time brother had fought brother on American soil. He just hoped to God the outcome of their meeting would lie in his favor.

When he looked up, the sun was slipping behind the treetops. He packed up his equipment and then started the car. He had a gallon of milk to buy and a woman to come home to.

By the time he got into Chiltingham, the streetlights were on. The charm of the little town was amazing to him. Everywhere he looked was a picture postcard scene. Perfect little houses with perfect little lawns and perfect little flower beds to accentuate their beauty. He pulled into the parking lot to the supermarket and caught himself whistling as he walked toward the door.

Lord, when had he last done something so innocuous as whistle? Then he grinned. Too damned long, that's what.

As he strolled inside, he grabbed a shopping cart and began to wheel it down the aisles.

What was it Cara wanted me to buy? Oh, yeah...milk.

He headed toward the back of the store, knowing that was where most of the cold storage items were kept, but got sidetracked by the cookie aisle and then sideswiped by a woman he knew he'd seen before. It wasn't until she started to speak that he remembered her name. Macie. The woman with whom Ray had his affair.

"Why...if it isn't Cara's sweetheart," she said, and slid her hand up his arm. "Isn't this cute? I just love to see a big, strong man doing these thoughtful little chores."

David reached for a package of cookies, well aware that as he did, she had to step back.

"I'm sorry, but I've forgotten your name," David said, knowing that wasn't something she would appreciate. From the frown that appeared on her forehead, he was right.

"Macie. My name is Macie."

He nodded. "Now I remember. Sorry. Nice seeing you again," he said, and pushed the cart a little farther down the aisle. Unfortunately, she followed.

"I see you have a sweet tooth," Macie purred, and then lowered her eyelashes to half mast.

David assumed she thought it was sexy, but he could see they were false and wondered if she knew one was coming unglued.

"You know what they say about men who love their food," she whispered.

David grinned. "Yeah, they get fat. Listen, it's been nice talking to you, and I'll be sure and tell Cara you said hello."

Macie looked irritated. "Yes, well…you do that," she muttered, and then walked away.

David didn't bother to watch. He'd spied a box of cereal that he might want to try and tossed it into the cart.

"Milk. Milk. Remember to get milk," he muttered, and kept on going.

By the time he got to the checkout stand, he'd covered the entire store. He now knew where the toilet paper was shelved and where he could find aspirin and cinnamon, as well.

The checker, who couldn't have been more than nineteen or twenty, rang up his purchases, eyeing him curiously as she did. When he handed over a ten and a twenty to pay for his purchases, he caught her staring at him and he winked.

She blushed all the way to the roots of her hair and dropped a dime of his change.

"I'm sorry," she mumbled, as she dug another out of the drawer and handed it to him. "Thank you, and come back again."

"Yes, thanks, I will," he said.

"Do you need any help carrying those out?" she asked.

"Are you offering?"

She blushed even harder. "Why, no, sir, but I could call a—"

David grinned. "No, thanks. I don't need any help. I was just teasing you."

She grinned then, a little more sure of herself.

"Well, I *was* staring. I suppose I had it coming." Then she added, "Are you new here, or just passing through?"

He hesitated and then smiled. "New."

"Then welcome to Chiltingham," she said.

The innocence of her remark took him aback and then touched him greatly.

"Thank you. The longer I'm here, the more certain I am that it's just where I belong."

As he left the store, he had the feeling that he'd just made another friend. Dr. Marvin Edwards had welcomed him home from Vietnam and now this girl, barely past her childhood, had welcomed him to the town. Damned if he wasn't taking a real liking to normal living.

He put his purchases in the trunk and then drove out of town, anxious to get back home. He thought of the pie that Cara had been baking when he left and wondered what other surprises she had in store for him. Whatever they were, they were bound to be good.

Chapter 7

David pulled into the driveway of Cara's house and parked. Before he could get out of the car, she came out the door to meet him. He waved as she circled the car and gave him a welcome-home kiss.

"I got the milk," he said, as he popped the trunk of the car.

Cara peeked over his shoulder and stifled a grin.

"It's sort of difficult to see it among all the other stuff you bought, so I'll just have to take your word for it."

"Do not chide the hunter who brings home sustenance," David said.

This time she let her grin show.

He handed her one grocery sack and then took the other two himself, closed the trunk lid with his elbow and shifted the sacks to a safer position within his grasp.

"Lead the way," he said. "I'm right behind you."

All sorts of wonderful scents assailed David as they entered the house. He could definitely smell that apple pie she'd been baking when he left.

"Smells good in here," he said, as he sat the grocery sacks on the counter.

"I haven't had this much fun cooking in I don't know when," Cara said.

David took the grocery sack from her and then took her in his arms.

"Yeah, and I don't know when I've had this much fun, period."

She smiled and combed her fingers through his hair.

"You're too easy to please," she said softly.

"It's not that. It's the woman who's doing it."

She gave him a quick kiss. "Save that for later. I want to see what the *hunter* has bagged."

"Just stuff," he said, and dug the milk from a sack and put it into the refrigerator.

"Is there anything else in these that needs refrigerating?" Cara asked.

"A couple of things, I guess."

"Like what?" she asked, as she started digging through the sacks.

"Well...like this...and for sure this, and I think this would spoil, too."

Her eyes widened, then she started to smile as she watched him pull out a half gallon of Rocky Road ice cream, a package of hot Polish sausage and a carton of dip to go with the enormous bag of chips in the other sack.

"This looks like the groceries Tyler used to bring home."

"He's the youngest, isn't he?"

Cara nodded. "And my only son. He'll be thirty on his next birthday. You'll like him."

David stilled, watching as Cara began putting the items away that he'd purchased.

"Saw Ms. Macie at the supermarket. She said to say hello."

Cara turned. "And you would be lying to me now."

He nodded. "Well…she definitely said hello to me."

"She's a snake," Cara muttered.

"More like a barracuda," David offered.

The simile made Cara smile.

He handed her a couple more items from the grocery sacks, which she put on the refrigerator shelves, then moved to the pantry to store the rest.

As she worked, she realized David had gotten very quiet. She turned and looked at him, trying to judge what he was thinking against the expression on his face. As usual, it was impossible to tell.

"Well," she said. "Are you going to tell me, or is this going to be another game of twenty questions?"

"This life is so simple—so ordinary. I keep worrying if I'll ever fit in. And your children… I'm trying to put myself in their places when confronted with someone like me. I'm not so sure this is going to be good. If I was them, I don't think I would like me."

"Well…I like you, which is all that matters. Besides, you don't know them or you wouldn't be worrying," she said, and handed him the ice cream. "Put this in the freezer, please."

He did as she asked.

"Now go wash up, super shopper. Supper is ready."

David sighed and then headed for the bathroom. For a man used to being the one giving orders, this was a definite change in his routine, but one he could get used to.

He paused at the doorway and looked back. Cara was already at the stove, dishing up the food.

So beautiful. Then he shook his head and then hurried down the hall, anxious not to waste another moment of his time with her.

By the time he returned, she was carrying the last of the dishes into the dining room. He followed, his eyes widening with appreciation as he entered. The cherry wood table was set with china instead of the stoneware she used every day. There was a bouquet of her own flowers in the center of the table and lit candles on the mantel as well as on either side of the flowers. He thought of all the lonely days and nights of the last forty years and words failed him. When Cara turned, she saw him standing in the doorway and held out her hand. He took it, kissing it twice— once on the back, then again in the center of her palm.

"For you," Cara said softly. "For all the meals you ate alone."

He took her in his arms, too overwhelmed to speak. Cara was the first to move.

"Let's eat before it gets cold."

He seated Cara and then himself, missing nothing of the elegance. Everywhere he looked he saw beauty, and all for him—all in the name of love. Cara handed him the carving knife, indicating that he carve the roast she had cooked.

He looked at the long, thin-bladed knife, trying to relate it to serving food, but the images it evoked were deadly and ugly. Almost immediately, he laid it down.

"There's something I need to do first," David said, and took her by the hand. His thoughts flashed to Frank, lying in his own blood, and he shook his head as if clearing away the ghosts.

Cara waited.

David bowed his head, uncertain how to proceed, but the need to acknowledge a greater power was, at that moment, overwhelming.

There, in a deep, quiet voice, David Wilson asked a blessing for the food and the woman who had cooked it, ending his awkward plea with a soft amen.

Cara squeezed his hand. "Thank you, my darling, that was wonderful. Would you carve?"

This time when David picked up the carving knife, it didn't feel lethal in his hands.

"I would be honored."

After that, time passed in a series of moments that would forever be in his heart.

The flickering candlelight softening the passage of time on their faces.

The dark, blood-red wine as he filled their crystal goblets.

The purity of the *clink* as they toasted their future.

The look of joy in Cara's eyes when he took his first bite of roast.

The sensation of crisp, sugary crust, warm, cinnamon apples and the cold, silken sensation of vanilla ice cream as they ate the dessert, apple pie à la mode.

Finally, David pushed back his dessert plate with a groan.

"I have never had such wonderful food in my entire life."

Cara beamed, then held out her hand. "Come with me. The evening isn't over yet."

He groaned again. "Whatever it is, I better not have to eat it."

She laughed. "Come on. You won't be disappointed. I promise."

They got as far as the living room when Cara ordered him to take a seat.

"Just remember to save room for me," she said, and headed for the television across the room.

While David watched, she slipped a video from a case and put it into the VCR, then took a seat beside David on the sofa and punched the remote.

He grinned. "What's playing?"

"Your daughter's life."

The grin slid sideways. "They're videos of Bethany?"

She nodded. "And later Valerie and Tyler will be in them, too."

He looked at the screen, his expression fixed. When the first images appeared, she heard him grunt as if someone had just kicked him in the belly. It was easy to see why. Ray had taken it the day of her release after giving birth to Bethany. A nurse was wheeling her out of the hospital with the baby in her arms.

"Oh, Lord, I always forget how long my hair was then," Cara said, but words were beyond David.

He saw the sadness of her smile and knew it was because of him. Then the camera panned to the baby she was holding. The focus was bad and the picture kept bouncing, as if the photographer was walking as he filmed, but there was no denying the tiny little face peering out from the blankets, nor the dark wisps of hair framing her features.

"Even then, she looked like you," Cara said. "It was at once a blessing and a pain. She was a constant reminder of how much I loved you and how much I'd lost."

"Lord," David muttered.

Cara rubbed her hand across his shoulder in a comforting motion.

"It's okay, honey. Just watch. If you have questions, ask. Otherwise, most of the stuff is self-explanatory."

He leaned forward, his elbows resting on his knees. For the next two hours, he was virtually mute. When that video was over, he looked up with a start, like a man who had been rudely awakened.

"That's not all, is it?"

He'd only seen the first year of her life. She had just been learning to walk.

Cara was already up and changing the tape.

"Oh, no. There are far more than you could possibly watch in one night. You haven't even gotten to the part where she finally gets a whole spoonful of cereal into her mouth without spilling it.''

"You have that on tape?"

"Yes, thanks to Ray."

He swallowed around the lump in his throat. "It seems I have a lot to thank Ray Justice for."

"Don't be sad, David. I couldn't bear it if this hurt you. I only wanted you to see the little milestones in her life. They weren't all caught on tape, but enough were so that you will see part of her growing up."

"Not sad. Just so damned sorry."

She hesitated before putting the next tape in the VCR.

"No regrets, remember?"

He sighed. "I remember."

"Okay. Then here goes."

And so David sat, reliving his daughter's life in silence, from birthday parties and swimming lessons, to learning to ride a bike. When the camera caught her taking a spill, David flinched. He watched her get up crying—saw a tiny trickle of blood on her knee and the pain in his chest was so great he thought he would die. She'd hurt and someone else had wiped away her tears.

He saw her hit a home run at a softball game and the joy on her face as she rounded third base to home made him laugh aloud.

Cara hugged him, her cheek against his shoulder, but she remained silent, answering questions only when he asked, letting him see and accept this in his own way—in his own time.

Bethany's life unfolded beneath his gaze, from the gap in her smile when she lost her first tooth to her first date. He saw it all, unaware that Cara had fallen asleep beside him. When the tape in the VCR ran out, he glanced at his watch, then at Cara. She was asleep on the sofa beside him, and no wonder. It was ten minutes to three in the morning.

He switched off the TV then picked her up and carried her to their bed. As he laid her down, she roused briefly.

"Ssh, just sleep," he said softly, as he took off her shoes.

She rolled over with a sigh. He pulled a sheet over her shoulders, not bothering to help her undress. He'd slept many nights in his clothes and it hadn't changed the gravity of the earth. She could surely do the same. But when he started to undress and get into bed beside her, he hesitated, then stopped. Knowing himself too well, he knew there was no way he would be able to sleep. Not after the evening he'd just had.

Instead, he moved quietly through the house and began to clear the dinner dishes from the table. There in the quiet of the house with the memories of his baby girl's face in his heart, he washed the dishes from the meal that Cara had prepared. The hot soapy water felt good on his skin, cleaning the ugliness of his past just as he cleaned the china. Uncertain where to put the things he had washed, he left the china in neat stacks on the kitchen counter instead, then hung up the dish towel and turned out the light.

As he exited, he stopped in the doorway and turned, looking back at the room to make sure he'd left nothing undone. The table was clean. The dishes were shadowy stacks against a darkened counter—the curtained windows like judgmental eyes looking back at him. He shuddered, and as he did, sensed he wasn't alone in his inability to sleep. Somewhere, his brother was also awake—and thinking of ways to kill him.

Frank Wilson was a haunted man. The past year had been one disappointment after another, and with each failure to get to David, his frustration had risen, multiplying into a dozen different symptoms.

Spicy food made him nauseous and he couldn't remember when he hadn't had a headache. He had intermittent bouts of insomnia that would often last for days and when his body finally gave out and he could sleep, it wasn't rest. Instead, he seemed destined to relive the failures of his past.

Inevitably, the dreams always spiraled into one horrible, recurring nightmare—of fire and burning flesh, of the mind-bending pain that came afterward. His brother's traitorous face was etched in his brain and he would know no peace until David was dead.

Tonight wasn't any different. The silhouette of the Colorado Rockies were visible from his hotel room. They rose above the landscape like jagged rips in the horizon. But the grandeur of the presence completely missed him. He rubbed a weary hand across his face and wished for peace.

At night, without his wig and mustache, he couldn't hide from himself. The face looking back at him in the mirror was the same man who was on the run, not the cocky New York cop he was pretending to be. He hated that face. He hated the man behind it.

He paced before the windows, ignoring the traffic on the street below for the blanket of star-littered sky. It was nights like this that he missed Australia. It seemed that the sky there was larger and the stars closer. Martha had loved to camp out with him, lying on their bedrolls beneath the wide open spaces and sleeping beneath the stars.

His chin jutted angrily as he slammed a fist against the windowsill.

Get over it, sucker. Those times are gone forever.

"Damn it," he muttered, and sank onto the side of the bed, then covered his face with his hands, unconsciously tracing the road map of burn scars with his fingertips.

A car horn sounded on the street below, and in the distance, he could hear approaching sirens.

God, but he missed the quiet of the outback. Maybe retiring to Florida wasn't such a good idea after all. Quiet would be the last thing he'd find in such a place.

Swamps and alligators—oranges and hurricanes.

Hundreds of thousands of people whose first language was not English.

Old people who'd moved there to live out what was left of their lives.

He sighed. Damn it all to hell, wasn't there a place left on earth to which he could belong?

He laid back on the bed and closed his eyes, and while he was feeling sorry for himself, exhaustion came and wrapped him in a blanket of deep, dreamless sleep.

The unexpected night of rest had given Frank a whole new outlook on life. He awoke with the feeling that he could conquer the world. For the first time in months, he was confident of what he was doing. As he dressed, he began to lay out his plans for the day. Maybe another round of practice at the firing range, a good meal around mid-afternoon; after that, find a good travel agent. Another night or so here in Denver and it would be time to move on.

This hotel suite was a far cry from the roach motel he'd been at in L.A., but then, he'd had few options. It had been easier to disappear into the seedy life of a city than to explain away the bandages he'd been wearing at the time. Now that they were gone, his lifestyle had taken a big change for the better.

He sat down on the sofa, opened his laptop, plugged in the modem and logged on to the Internet. His hands were steady as he opened his e-mail, but his heart was pounding. He'd been sending the same message to the same mailbox each day, certain that he would eventually get the answer he wanted. It began to download, zapping one message after the other through a medium he still found amazing. He'd seen a lot of things in his lifetime, but in his opinion, the public availability of the Internet was the most life-altering one of them all.

The little You've Got Mail logo centered on the screen. He scanned the contents rapidly, deleting any and everything that didn't have David Wilson's name on it. Thirty-nine messages later he leaned back with a frustrated sigh. Still no answer.

He shrugged. It didn't matter. It wasn't like he was on a time schedule. Hell. Time was all he had. He could wait.

He typed in the same message that he'd been sending regularly each day and then pressed send. When the process was finished, he shut down the computer and set it aside. His stomach was growling and he had a need to feel the sun on his face and the wind in his hair.

A few minutes later, he exited the hotel and strode to the curb to hail a cab. As he did, he heard the shrill and strident voice of an insistent child. He looked out of curiosity and suddenly found himself on the receiving end of a little girl's delight.

"Ganpa! Ganpa!"

He froze. The little girl, who couldn't have been more than two or three, had wrapped herself around his leg.

"Up!" she shrieked. "Want up!"

Before he could react, a young woman emerged from a doorway, her expression frantic.

"Martie! Martie! Where are you?" she shouted.

Frank turned again, this time waving to get the woman's attention.

"Lady…is this your kid?"

"Oh, my God!" the woman cried, and then bolted toward them. Seconds later she was on her knees, unwinding the child from Frank's leg. Then she stood and picked her up in her arms. "Bad girl! You ran away from Mommy."

The baby's lower lip slipped forward in an instinctive pout.

"Ganpa!" she muttered.

For the first time, the woman got a good look at Frank's face, and as she did, a smile of recognition replaced her frown.

"Oh, my goodness," she said. "No wonder Martie ran to you."

"I'm sorry?" Frank said, certain that he'd never seen them before in his life.

"No, I'm the one who should be apologizing," the woman said, and then held out her hand. "My name is Beth Stalling. This is my daughter, Martha. We call her Martie, for short. You look enough like my father-in-law to be his twin." Then she hugged her daughter to her. "And Martie loves her grandpa Jules. She must have thought you were him."

Frank shook her hand, but he had quit listening to what she was saying after hearing the little girl's name. Martha. Martha of the blue eyes and platinum blond hair. And this little girl had blue eyes and almost cotton-white hair, just like *his* Martha.

"...so I hope you understand," the woman finished.

Frank blinked, suddenly realizing that she'd still been talking.

"Of course. No harm done," he said briefly, and then something—maybe the last good part of his soul—prompted an action quite out of character. He reached for the little girl's hair and lightly fingered the soft, cottony whorls.

"I'm thinking Grandpa Jules is a very fortunate man."

The woman beamed. "Why, thank you."

Suddenly uncomfortable with the whole incident, he

muttered something about being late for a meeting and
headed for the curb. Saved from having to make further
conversation by the immediate arrival of a cab, he slid into
the back seat and actually breathed a sigh of relief as the
door slammed behind him.

Unwilling to be reminded of a life he'd chosen to forgo,
he wouldn't look back. Yet the farther they drove, the
heavier his heart became. He even toyed with the notion
of walking away now. Just quitting on the idea of revenge
and losing himself in America. He could do it. He'd done
it before. Everyone knew that you could buy anything in
America for the right amount of money. It would be cheap
to buy a new identity and live out the rest of his life in
relative comfort. But as he glanced at the window, he
caught a glimpse of his reflection and realized it was not
his own. With his mask in place, the man beneath did not
exist. But night always came and the mask always came
off.

The notion of forgive and forget quickly disappeared.
David had wronged him. He had to pay.

"Let me out here," he told the cabby, tossed him a
handful of dollars and all but bolted from the cab.

His steps were hasty as he started down the street, as if
he was trying to outrun a new enemy. But the farther he
went, the more he realized that there was no escape for
him as long as David still lived.

Once the thought was firmly in his mind, he began to
relax. His steps slowed, his thinking cleared. He spied a
travel agent on the opposite corner of the street. Now was
as good a time as any to make his plans. But as he stood
at the corner, waiting for the light to change, he knew it
would be a long, long time before he forgot the silken
texture of baby hair against the palm of his hand.

By the time night came to Denver, Frank Wilson was
long gone. As his plane landed in Chicago, he had security

of knowing that the next four days were securely mapped
out in his mind. This time when he got to a hotel, he was
digging in until he heard from David.

Cara came out of the kitchen with a vase of flowers in
her hand, heading toward the dining room table. Every
wood surface in the house gleamed from the polishing
she'd given it, and wonderful scents were coming from the
kitchen. In spite of the enticing aromas, David knew they
were not for him.

Last night, just as Cara had come out of the shower,
she'd glanced at the calendar and gasped. The planning
committee for the annual fall church bazaar was being held
at her house. And the meeting was going to be tomorrow!
She'd known about it for weeks. But with all the excitement of David's arrival, she'd completely forgotten the
date and that she was expected to serve lunch in the process.

He'd laughed and told her not to worry, that he'd help
her straighten up the house, but that was before he had
completely understood.

Twelve women were coming to her home. Twelve
women who had husbands and children and homes of their
own. Twelve women who would be judging Cara's worth
on this earth by how clean she kept her house and how
tasty and unique her menu would be.

She had set the alarm for six-thirty and was up before
it went off. And she hadn't just straightened the house. In
David's opinion, she'd done everything short of rebuild it.
Wisely, he'd chosen a simple bowl of cereal for breakfast
and then when he was finished, washed and dried the dish
and put it back where it belonged.

By the time she had moved into the kitchen to begin
preparing the food she would serve, he'd made another
wise decision and dragged the lawn mower out of the shed

and begun mowing the front yard. Her pleasure at his choice of occupation was obvious when, an hour later, she brought him a cold drink and gave him a kiss that rocked him back on his heels.

"The yard is looking wonderful," she said. "I've got to run. The oven timer is about to go off."

"I may not get through in the back before they come. Is that all right?"

"Oh, sure. It won't matter if you're still mowing."

He sighed with relief. If he was still working in the back, he would have a very good excuse to absent himself from their presence.

By the time he had finished in the front and come in the back door for another drink, the food in different stages of preparation looked like something from a five-star restaurant. The elegance of the presentation was surpassed only by the aroma.

"Wow, Cara. I didn't know you could do stuff like this."

She gave him a harried smile and shrugged.

"You'd be surprised what a female can do in an emergency."

He shook his head without comment. This church bazaar had taken on the undertones of a life-and-death situation. Her emergencies were certainly different from the ones that he'd faced, but something told him that it would be easier to deal with an international terrorist than to face these twelve women.

"I made you some food," Cara said. "Although you are certainly welcome to sit and eat with us at noon."

"No," David said, and then countered the abruptness of his answer with a smile. "But thank you for inviting me."

She sighed. "I wouldn't want to eat with us, either. I can't believe I'd forgotten this."

David shoved aside her hair and kissed the back of her neck.

"I'll eat later, after I've finished mowing the back yard, okay?" Then he added, "And, if you're not finished with your meeting by that time, I'll be eating in the kitchen."

She laughed and tweaked his nose.

"Coward."

"Devout and proud of it," he said, and then turned at the sound of a car coming up the drive. "Looks like your first guest is already arriving."

Cara turned to the window and peered out.

"Oh, Lord! It would be Hillary. She's the most critical of the lot."

He put his finger under the edge of her chin and lightly pushed up.

"Chin up, baby. Just remember that all the time they're looking at you and the house, you've got a man in your yard who likes to jump your bones."

Having said that, he gave her a devilish grin and winked, then walked out the back door just as the front doorbell began to ring.

David's words were still in her head as she rushed to the front door. Thankful that thoughts were not visible, she smoothed her hair and then straightened her blouse before opening the door.

"Hillary! You look gorgeous as always. Come in."

Hillary Redford sauntered into the house. Cara knew that Hillary was well aware her friends dreaded her arrival and she liked it that way. It gave her a sense of importance to think they valued her approval enough to be worried.

"How nice everything looks," she said, raking the gleaming wood and fresh flowers with quiet approval.

Cara resisted the urge to snort beneath her breath. Nice? It looked great and she knew it.

"Have a seat, will you? I need to take one more thing out of the oven and then I'll be right back."

Hillary sat, tentatively testing the cushions of the sofa and finding the one that suited her best. Within moments, Cara was back, and one by one, the other eleven women began to arrive. The noise level rose with each arrival until the front part of Cara's house was as noisy as a Saturday night at the local bar.

Cara flitted among them, serving dainty little appetizers and flutes of white wine, knowing that each time she left the room, they resumed their conversation, which was all about her.

As they nibbled and talked, Cara finished carrying the last of the food to the dining room where she'd set up a buffet on the sideboard. With one last glance to make sure she'd forgotten nothing important, she went to the living room to call them to eat.

"Ladies, the food is ready. Let's adjourn to the dining room where you can continue your discussion about my life and if somewhere in the midst of it someone should happen to remember we are planning a bazaar, then that would be wonderful."

There was a moment of embarrassed silence and then everyone laughed while Hillary felt the need to explain.

"Oh, Cara, you funny thing. We weren't really talking *about* you, just curious about the new man in your life. After all, you can't really blame us for that."

Cara smiled and then led the way into the dining room, comfortable with the fact that she'd taken the wind out of their sails by acknowledging the gossip and then ignoring it.

"Mm, everything smells wonderful," one of them said, while Hillary Redford silently applauded the elegance of the dishes she'd fixed.

"Thank you," Cara said. "Although they're really simple, they are some of my favorite recipes."

As they began to round the buffet and fill their plates, their chatter lessened. And for the first time, the sound of David mowing in the back yard could be heard. Hillary was the first to comment.

"I noticed your yard was freshly mowed when I came to the door," she said.

"Yes, but David's not quite through in the back."

"Who is David?" Hillary asked.

"Bethany's father," Cara said simply.

Twelve pairs of eyes turned instantly toward her. Twelve mouths dropped to an equal degree of shock.

"Oh, I've just got to have a look," Hillary said, and set her plate on the table without filling it and headed for the kitchen.

Eleven other women followed suit without waiting to see if Cara minded that they were trooping through the kitchen where she'd been preparing the food. She smiled to herself and followed, thankful that almost everything she'd been cooking with had been cleaned up and put away or was in the dishwasher waiting to be washed.

But when she got to the kitchen, she couldn't see outside. Every window in the room was lined with women who seemed too dumbstruck to move.

"That's him?" Hillary asked, and did something quite unlike herself and smeared the glass when she put her finger against the window to point.

Cara peeked over Hillary's shoulder.

"Yep, that's him."

"Have mercy," someone whispered. "He looks like that actor...oh, what's his name? He was in that movie *Sniper* and a whole bunch of others."

Someone offered the name Berenger.

"Yes! That's it! Berenger! He looks like Tom Berenger."

Then they all turned and stared at Cara as if they'd never seen her before—then turned again, their faces glued to the sight.

Cara crossed her arms as she watched them, resisting the urge to laugh. In spite of all her cleaning and cooking, a bare-chested man had been the hit of the day. And she couldn't blame them for gawking.

"Um, Cara?"

It was Susan Hanover, the banker's wife, who was standing near the door and waving her hand to be seen in all the shuffle.

"Yes?"

"Is he that, uh, *fit* all over?"

The eleven other women turned, all but salivating as they awaited the answer.

Cara smiled politely, as if they'd just asked for the recipe for her cake, although she knew her cooking was no match for David, naked or dressed. And the fact that he wasn't wearing a shirt and that his shorts were riding low on his hips didn't hurt. That hard, flat belly and that beautiful face were hard to ignore.

"Yes."

"Oh…my…God," Susan moaned, and leaned against the wall as if pretending to faint.

The question broke the ice of curiosity. The questions began coming at her from right and left.

"What does he do? Where has he been? Is he going to stay? Are you going to marry him? Is he going to come inside?"

Cara just waved away the questions.

"Food's getting cold," she said, and went into the dining room.

One by one, courtesy demanded that they follow, but

when they finally all sat down to eat, they were looking at Cara with new respect. And as they chewed their first bites, they were thinking of their respective husbands, most of them soft, overweight and going bald.

After a few minutes, they seemed to settle down and as they talked and ate, they actually settled on most of the planning committees that they'd come to put in place. It wasn't until Cara was serving cake that she heard the back door slam. David was obviously through mowing the yard.

Again, twelve women froze; in the act of putting cake in their mouths, they seemed to hold their breaths, hoping against all hope they would get a closer glimpse. David gave them way more than they bargained for.

Still bare-chested and carrying his T-shirt in his hands, he stuck his head into the room. Everywhere he was bare was glistening with sweat, and his thick, dark hair was spiky and damp.

"Cara, I'm through with the back yard. I'm going to shower before I eat." Then he gave the woman an all-encompassing smile. "I sure hope you pretty ladies saved something for me."

Having dropped the verbal bomb in their midst, he sauntered off, giving them an all-too-generous view of his tight buns and long legs.

Susan, the banker's wife, laid her fork on her cake plate and covered her face with her hands.

"Lord forgive me for my thoughts," she muttered.

They all burst into laughter, glad that she was the one who'd said what they'd all been thinking.

They lingered through coffee. Some even ate a second piece of cake just to prolong their presence in the house. When David finally emerged from the bedroom, he was dressed in slacks and loafers and a blue knit shirt.

"He looks good in clothes, too," Susan muttered, as he passed them by on his way to the kitchen.

David heard her and grinned. Well aware of the fuss that he'd caused, he didn't know whether to make himself scarce or go say hello.

Cara saved him the trouble of deciding by following him into the kitchen.

"We saved you a piece of cake," she said.

"Sure you want me in there?" he asked.

She sighed and then shrugged. "You'd have to be blind, deaf and dumb not to know that they're quite taken with you."

"Oh?"

"Yes. It started when they saw you naked."

"Naked?"

"Honey, when a man has nothing on but a pair of shorts and wears them as well as you do, women can figure out the rest."

He grinned.

"So you may as well come in and finish them off."

His grin widened as he followed her into the other room.

"So, you did save me some cake after all," David said.

"Here! Sit here!" one of them said, and jumped up from her chair and gave him her seat.

"Oh, no, but thank you," he said. "A gentleman never sits in a room full of ladies. You sit yourself right back down. I'll eat my cake standing up. That way I can eat more."

Just the knowledge that the cake they'd been eating was now going into his stomach was all it took for twelve pairs of eyes to stare at his shirt, remembering the hard, washboard surface of his belly underneath.

"Have you finished?" David asked.

Twelve startled women looked at his face and then at their plates.

"With your meeting, I mean," David said.

Cara laughed. He was playing them like a fiddle.

"David Wilson, you are awful," she said. "Stop teasing them this minute, do you hear?"

He grinned and then leaned over and kissed her square on the mouth before taking another bite of the cake.

Twelve sighs of appreciation rose in accompaniment.

Cara smiled to herself.

Her luncheon had been a success.

Chapter 8

David woke up before sunrise, savoring the quiet of the room and the warmth of the woman snuggled against him. It was Friday and his time with Cara was already almost gone. Bethany and her family would be home the day after tomorrow and he would be in D.C., and he still hadn't told Cara he was leaving. Truth was, he was scared to tell her. They'd fought horribly the last time he'd announced his exit from her life. He didn't want it to happen again.

His thoughts scattered as Cara sighed and rolled onto her back. He watched her eyelids fluttering slightly and knew she was waking. Unable to wait, he leaned over and kissed her the rest of the way awake.

Cara stretched, then wrapped her arms around his neck.

"What a wonderful way to wake up," she said.

"Are you good and awake?"

She smiled. "I think so, why?"

"I don't want it to be said that I took advantage of an unconscious woman."

She laughed as he pulled her nightgown over her head and tossed it aside, then rolled over on top of her, pinning her to the mattress with the weight of his body.

"Are you paying attention?" he growled.

Another laugh bubbled up her throat.

"Woman...I'm trying to be serious here."

Suddenly, the laughter was over. Cara had her legs locked around his waist and her arms around his neck.

"How serious?" she whispered.

"Oh, baby, let me show you the ways."

Without foreplay.

Without sweet-nothing whispers.

Without warning.

Between one breath and the next, he was inside her.

Cara would look back on it later and realize that there was as much desperation in the act as there was love. But for now, she had no focus save the man above her and the hard, rhythmic pounding of his flesh against hers.

One minute spilled into the next and then the next and just when Cara thought she would die from the intensity, it shattered within her, splintering the power and flooding her body with a bone-melting ecstasy. She lay within his arms, her eyes closed, her heartbeat little more than a ricochet of its normal rhythm, while savoring the sensations from the act of perfect love.

She didn't know it wasn't over.

David paused, raising himself above her on tightly tensed arms, as if judging her expression. She groaned then sighed.

At that point, he seemed to shift gears.

She opened her eyes and looked up.

One slow, sensuous stroke after another, David started again, and all the while, he was watching her face. In her entire life, Cara had never felt so vulnerable or so loved.

A long minute passed, and then another, and time

seemed to stop. There was nothing in their world but the sensual body-to-body hammer, seeking that fleeting and volatile burst of sweet pleasure. Sweat beaded across David's forehead and dropped into the valley between her breasts as, again, they danced the dance of love.

One moment Cara was aware of David above her, and then her mind suddenly blanked. Clutching his forearms, she arched beneath him, her eyes wide, unseeing. Shattered by the force of her climax, her moan became a scream.

It was the sound as much as the spasms of her body that sent David over the edge, spilling forty years of loneliness and denial into the woman beneath him.

Moments later, he collapsed with a gut-wrenching groan and then rolled, taking her with him so that she would not be burdened any longer with his weight. What had just happened was so perfect, he didn't even feel twinges from the stitches on his shoulder. So they lay locked within each other's arms, awaiting the end of the world or a steadying heartbeat, whichever came first.

Sometime later, she groaned and raised her head.

"David...I..."

He arched an eyebrow. "You're welcome."

She snorted lightly beneath her breath and teasingly pulled at his hair.

"Are you going to brag?"

He grinned. "Honey, after that, if I could walk, I'd be strutting."

She laughed. It was the most perfect sunrise of her life.

"Authorities are still searching for the perpetrators of the ongoing tri-county crime spree. The trio struck again around midnight last night, robbing the clerk at an all-night quick stop and beating him unconscious. The clerk, a thirty-two-year-old father of two, is in the intensive care unit of Burney Hospital. He is in critical condition."

Cara paused in the act of putting on her makeup and stepped out of the bathroom into the bedroom where David was watching the news on the wall-mounted television opposite her bed.

"That poor man...and his family," she added. "I can't believe they haven't caught those awful people yet."

David nodded without answering, his thoughts in a whirl. This wasn't something that SPEAR got mixed up in, yet his sense of justice was being sorely tried. Unless he'd missed a report, this was the third incident in the area since he'd arrived at Cara's house and the sixth in less than two weeks. That was close to one robbery a day. He knew how criminals like that thought. They were cocky now, confident of their ability to get away with anything, even murder. Besides the countless assaults, there were two deaths attributed to the criminals. If this young man died, it would make three. Unconsciously, his fingers curled into fists and his expression darkened.

Cara leaned over his shoulder and pressed a kiss on his cheek.

"You can't fix everything, darling," she said softly.

The gentleness in her voice touched him. He turned, pulling her into his lap and nuzzling the side of her neck before giving her a long, silent hug.

Cara sensed something was bothering him and suspected it wasn't all connected to the broadcast they'd just heard.

"Is there anything you want to talk about?" she asked.

He froze. Damn, she *was* good. There was plenty he needed to say, but now was not the time.

"No, honey...at least not now." He lifted his head and made himself smile. "You look good enough to eat, but I'd settle for a hamburger instead."

"Okay, David, I'll play your game. I'll be the silly, airheaded blonde who's blindly unaware of underlying currents, and you be the big, strong hero who needs to protect the little woman from herself.''

A startled look crossed his face before he could hide it. She'd read him right down to the bone, and it shamed him that he couldn't deny it.

In a moment of blinding pain, understanding came to Cara.

Ah, God, he's going to leave me. But instead of crying, she slid off his lap and straightened her slacks and shirt. ''Just remember that games eventually come to an end. At that time, I expect the truth. Deal?''

She fixed him with a steely gaze and held out her hand.

He sighed and then stood.

''Deal,'' he said, enclosing her fingers in his grasp.

Fear shifted within her, but she wouldn't give in. Not now. Not when they had precious little time left.

''Are you ready to go into Chiltingham?'' David asked.

She nodded. ''I just need to get my grocery list from the kitchen.''

''I'll meet you out front,'' he said.

''Want to take my car?'' she asked.

He hesitated, then shook his head. ''No, let's take mine. I need to get gas, anyway.''

Cara couldn't look at him yet. More proof he was getting ready to leave. Again, her heart twisted, but she refused to comment.

''Be right there,'' she said, and walked out of the bedroom before she made a fool of herself.

All the way to the kitchen she was blinking back tears, but by the time she walked out of the house, her emotions were under control. David was standing at the passenger side of his car, the door ajar, waiting for her to enter.

''Why, thank you, sir,'' she said, as she slid into the seat.

''My pleasure,'' he countered, as he closed the door and

then circled the car to get in. He started the engine and then drove out of her drive onto the blacktop road. "Where to first, ma'am?"

"I'd say Hawaii, but I don't think you have enough gas."

He heard the desolation in her voice and reached over and squeezed her hand.

"Not this time around, I don't, baby. But maybe soon. Have you ever been to Hawaii?"

She sighed. "No, but I've always wanted to see if the water is as blue as they say."

"It is."

She smiled sadly. "I should have known you'd already been there."

He thought of the drug runner he'd chased for six weeks before cornering him in an inlet off the eastern coast of Oahu.

"It wasn't a vacation," he said softly.

"Oh."

"When do you want to go?" he asked. "This fall? Next spring? You name the time and we're there."

Her eyes widened. "Are you serious?"

He pulled over to the side of the road and put the car in park, then took her in his arms.

"Yes, I'm serious. I'm committed. I'm in love. And I was going to wait until tonight to ask, but something tells me the time is now."

"Ask what?" she said.

"If I'm able to come back...and I will do everything in my power to come back...will you marry me?"

It was the last but best thing she would have expected him to say. Good sense demanded more time with the man before committing the rest of her life to him, but the good sense she'd used before had cost her forty years without him. She wasn't going to do it again.

"Yes."

David was all ready to plead his case. Her positive, one-word answer took him aback.

"You will?"

She nodded.

"Just like that? Without knowing if—"

She put her hand over his mouth, silencing the rest of what he'd started to say.

"Don't say it aloud. Don't give the words power, David. Just do what you have to do and come back to me when it's over."

"Ah, God," he groaned, and took her in his arms. "You won't be sorry, I swear."

"I told you no the first time and have regretted it for forty years. I'm not about to make the same mistake twice."

"Hallelujah," he muttered, and kissed her hard on the mouth.

A speeding car passed them by as they embraced, the driver blaring his horn as a taunt to the lovers.

Cara jumped at the sound, and David groaned and pulled back.

"Who was that?" David asked, as he stared at the disappearing taillights of the car.

Cara sighed. "Um, I'm not sure, but it looked a bit like Harold Belton's car."

David grinned. "Hasty Harold?"

"The same. And wipe that satisfied smirk off your face."

David put the car into gear and then pulled onto the highway.

"I wasn't smirking."

"You were smirking."

"It was more of a—"

"You were smirking, David. Have the grace to admit it."

He glanced at her, his eyes glittering darkly, a wide grin on his face. At that moment, Cara saw the young boy that he'd been. She couldn't help but smile back.

"Okay, I was smirking," David said.

"I know. Thank you for being honest."

"I was smirking because I got the girl and he didn't."

"True," Cara said. "But you had an unfair advantage coming in."

"What? You mean Bethany?"

"No. A flat belly and a dynamite kiss."

His smile widened.

"You're smirking again," Cara warned.

"You just keep on talking like that and by the time we get to town, I'll be ready to do that strut I promised you earlier."

She threw back her head and laughed. God, but she loved this man.

A short while later, he pulled up in front of the supermarket, but he didn't kill the engine.

"Aren't you coming in?" Cara asked.

"Not right away. I need to run a quick errand. It won't take me long. I'll be back before you finish, okay?"

"Sure. Just look for me in the aisles. I'll probably still be shopping. I want to get some food to make a special meal for Bethany and her family on Sunday." Her face lit up. "Oh, David, she's going to be ecstatic about you…and about us."

Sunday. He wasn't going to be here on Sunday. Damn. He had to tell her, but not now.

"I'll find you," David said. "Count on it."

She flashed him a smile. "I love you very much, you know."

"I love you, too, now scoot or I'll be tempted to dash

your reputation even more by kissing you again.'' He pointed to the people going in and out of the store. "And we're not exactly alone this time."

"So what," she said, and gave him a quick kiss before getting out of the car. "If I finish before you get back, I'll wait for you inside where it's cooler, okay?"

"I'll be here before you're through, I promise."

She nodded and then shut the door behind her.

David watched her until she was inside the store, then he backed up and drove to the main street. If memory served, he distinctly remembered a jewelry store a couple of blocks down on the corner. He wasn't leaving Cara again without his ring on her finger.

Ten minutes later, Cara had yet to get down the first aisle. Two women from her church had stopped to ask her if it was true that Ray wasn't Bethany's father. Before she could answer, they'd followed that question with another. Was it also true that the real father was staying at Cara's house?

Cara had answered truthfully without elaborating and told them goodbye, knowing the moment she turned the corner they were going to rake her reputation over the coals. Instead of being bothered about it, she just smiled. She wouldn't trade David's presence in her life for anything, not even a perfect reputation. Besides that, she was more than slightly amused at being thought of as a loose woman. It certainly beat the loneliness and tedium of the last three years of her life.

Glancing over her shoulder, she saw the two women huddled together at the end of the aisle and looking her way. Impishly, she waved. They scurried away like flushed quail.

Still chuckling to herself, she continued with her shopping and was halfway up the next aisle when she heard a commotion at the front of the store. Remembering the large display of canned goods near the door, she assumed someone must have knocked it over and gave it no more thought.

Then she heard a woman scream and another start to cry. Those sounds changed everything. Afraid that someone had surely been hurt, she hurried toward the front of the store, but it wasn't an accident, as she feared. As she rounded the corner, she found herself face to face with an armed trio of men. The store was being robbed!

Instinctively, she pivoted and started to run when someone grabbed her by the arm and dragged her toward the group of shoppers they'd already corralled.

"Get over there and shut up," the man said.

"Ow," Cara cried, as he twisted the flesh on her arm.

"Shut up, woman, or I'll give you something to cry about."

Cara flinched as he shoved her toward the others. She did as she was told. And even though she was standing here, watching three armed men tear through the cash registers for the money, the reality of the situation had yet to sink in. It wasn't until one of the armed men shoved his gun in the manager's face and demanded he open the safe that it hit her who they must be.

Less than an hour earlier, she'd been horrified by the television broadcast of the poor clerk who had been robbed and was in critical condition, and now she had become one of their latest victims.

Anxiously, she glanced out the window, praying for David's return. She knew he would come, and she also suspected that he was, quite possibly, their only hope.

"Move!" one of the robbers suddenly shouted, and as he did, the other two armed men herded the hostages toward the back of the store.

Cara's panic renewed. *Dear God, don't let this be the day I die.*

David slapped a credit card down on the counter, smiling to himself as the jeweler slipped a small velvet box into a sack. It was, without doubt, the most important purchase he'd ever made, and it had taken him less than ten minutes to make up his mind.

"I think your lady is going to be quite pleased with your selection," the jeweler said, as he handed David his credit card.

"So do I," David said, and hurried out of the store.

He got into the car, the smile still on his face. But by the time he was pulling into the supermarket parking lot, a sense of urgency had replaced his glee. It was that same hair-raising, flesh-crawling feeling that he'd had so many times before, and it didn't make sense until he tried to get into the store.

When he realized the front doors were locked, he began to frown. As he cupped his hands against the window and peered inside, he saw the drawers of the cash registers were all ajar. Added to that was the fact that not a shopper or clerk was in sight. It was gut instinct that made him go back to the car for a lock pick and his gun.

A woman drove up just as he was heading to the store.

"Do you have a cell phone?" he asked.

She nodded.

"Then call nine-one-one. The store is being robbed."

She looked askance, staring wildly at the gun he was holding and then at his face.

"Not by me," he said shortly. "The doors are locked and the cash registers are open. I'm going to try and get in, but I need you to help me, understand?"

She nodded, her expression startled.

"After you make the call, drive your car to the street

and keep everyone else away. We don't need any innocent bystanders getting hurt, do we?''

"No! Oh, my! I can't believe…''

"Lady! Just make the call and then get the hell out of the way.''

She bolted for her car.

Satisfied she would do as he'd asked, he headed toward the front doors again. He wouldn't let himself think of what might have already happened. Instead, he palmed the lock pick and with a few deft strokes, opened the door and quietly slipped inside.

He stood against the wall, his gun raised, listening for something that would tell him where everyone had been taken. The silence was more horrifying than any scream would have ever been. When he finally heard angry shouts coming from the back of the store, he closed his eyes momentarily, recalling the layout of the floor plan from his earlier visit, then started to move.

"Damn it, Travis, shut that woman up now or I'm gonna do it for you,'' Darryl Wayne shouted.

Cara flinched as the short man, the one who was shouting, grabbed a can of peas from a shelf and threw it at the hostages. Cara ducked, covering her head as the can sailed past her ear, only to hit one of the grocery clerks on the head. The woman never saw it coming, and when it hit her, it knocked her out cold. She dropped to the floor in a slump.

Cara scrambled over to her side, trying to staunch the flow of blood with the tail of her shirt, and was backhanded for the trouble.

"I told you people not to move and I meant it.''

Pain-filled tears blurred her vision as she grabbed the side of her face. Already it was beginning to throb.

"Please," she begged. "Her head...it's bleeding badly."

Darryl grabbed her by the hair and yanked her to her feet.

"Look at me!"

Cara stared, too frightened to move.

"Can you see my lips?"

She nodded, wincing when he tightened his grip on her hair.

"I'm telling you for the last time, don't move. Can you do that?"

She nodded again.

He shoved her hard. She fell backward over the unconscious woman's feet, then onto the floor. From where she was lying, she could see the third man in the office with the manager, holding a gun to his head as the manager opened the safe. Never in her life had she been so certain she was going to die. The moment that safe came open, they were all expendable.

Oh, God! Oh, David! Where are you?

"Hurry up with that safe!" Darryl shouted. "We ain't got all day."

The third man stepped out of the office. "He says he can't get it open."

"Bull!" Darryl yelled, turned toward the hostages and fired at the nearest one, who happened to be the Methodist pastor's wife. The bullet tore through her shoulder and ricocheted against the concrete wall behind her. She slumped over without a sound. "One down, ten to go," he yelled. "Now see how fast he can open that safe."

The third man grinned and stepped back into the office. A horrified silence permeated the area. No one dared look up for fear they would be next. And because their heads were bent, they didn't see the man who slipped through the open door of the loading area and disappeared behind a stack of wooden pallets.

David's gut was in a knot. He'd been only feet away from the door when he'd heard the shot, and even though he knew there was bound to be other hostages, his heart sank. All he could think was, *Please, God, don't let it be Cara.*

A second later he was peering through the half-open door. He counted eleven hostages, two unconscious, maybe dead. When he saw the top of Cara's head and realized she wasn't one of the bodies on the floor, he said a quick prayer of thanksgiving, then slipped into the room behind a stack of pallets.

Two gunmen had their backs to him, and they were still talking to a third, who he figured must be in an office somewhere nearby. He glanced at his watch, trying to figure out how long it would be before the sound of police sirens alerted the men to their arrival. He'd been inside for more than four minutes, and if the police were on the ball, he didn't have much time.

Suddenly, a third man came into view, holding another at gunpoint. David froze. With less than five feet between them, he could have reached out and touched the back of the gunman's head.

"I got it!" the gunman shouted. "Let's get the hell out of here now."

David held his breath. If they would just leave, it would be the safest move for all concerned. Unfortunately, the short, stocky one who seemed to be in charge had other ideas.

"No witnesses," he said abruptly, and took aim at the people on the floor as calmly as if he was about to squash a bug.

To David's horror, Cara was the closest to the gun. There was no time left to wait.

David coldcocked the man closest to him on the back of the head, then grabbed him before he fell, using him for a shield as he took aim. He fired twice in rapid succession, hitting the short man first and the next man as he was spinning around.

A stunned silence momentarily enveloped the hostages, and then they erupted into a melee of shouts and screams. Several started to run. David stopped them all with one shout.

"Wait."

They froze.

He looked at Cara, who was on her knees, trying to stop the blood pouring from the shoulder of one of the victims.

"Cara!"

She looked up, her eyes filled with tears, but there was a look on her face that told him she was all right. He yanked his T-shirt over his head and tossed it to her.

"Use pressure, honey. Help is on the way."

One of the stock boys followed suit and removed his T-shirt for her, as well. She nodded, quickly folding the shirts and pressing them against the front and back of the wound. The woman who'd been knocked out was coming around. To David's dismay, he realized it was the young cashier he'd teased only the other day. The one who had welcomed him to Chiltingham.

"See about her, too," he ordered, and immediately, a couple of the other hostages began to attend to her.

David motioned to the manager.

"I hear sirens. Go up front and meet the police and the paramedics. Make sure they know everything is under control. We wouldn't want anyone to be mistaken for a bad guy, would we?"

The manager nodded, still wide-eyed and shaking, unable to believe the ordeal was over. He bolted for the front of the store without looking back.

The man David had hit was moaning at his feet. He grabbed some reinforced strapping tape from a nearby shelf and quickly bound his hands and feet, then checked the two that he'd shot. They were dead.

Confident now that danger was past, he moved toward Cara, needing to touch her. When he knelt beside her, she looked up.

"I knew you would come."

He cupped the back of her head and pulled her to him, kissing her quick and hard.

"Let me help," he said quietly, and took over the job of keeping the pastor's wife alive while Cara rocked back on her heels and started to cry.

"It's all right, baby," he said quietly, as he inspected the woman's wound. Satisfied that it was a through shot and high enough that nothing vital had been hit, he kept pressure on the makeshift bandages and waited.

As they waited, the young clerk who'd been knocked out began to sit up. Looking around in stunned confusion, she saw Cara's face and then the blood all over the dress the preacher's wife was wearing and started to cry.

"Hey!" he said quickly. "Look at me!"

She blinked as recognition dawned.

"I know you," she whispered. "You're the new guy who moved to town."

"And it's a good thing he did," one of the hostages said. "They were going to kill us. He saved us all."

"Oh, my," she said, and then clutched her head and closed her eyes.

"Are you feeling sick to your stomach?" David asked. She nodded.

"Put your head between your knees," he said, and then

pointed with his chin toward a couple of the young grocery sackers. "Isn't that an ice machine over there?"

They nodded.

"Get a plastic bag, fill it with ice and put it on her head."

They did as he ordered, thankful to have something to do besides stare at the blood pooling beneath the two dead men.

David looked at Cara and the mark upon her face.

"Bring two of those bags of ice, will you? Give one to Mrs. Justice so she can put it on her face."

Cara tried to whisper a thanks, but she knew if she talked, she would scream. The horror of what had just happened was finally sinking in.

When one of the boys suddenly thrust the cold, wet plastic into her hands, she laid it against her face in mute thanksgiving.

Chapter 9

Moments later, they heard shouts at the front of the building, then the sounds of running feet. Suddenly, the back room of the supermarket was overflowing with uniformed officers as well as medical personnel.

"Here!" David called. "This woman is hurt the worst. She has a clean shot all the way through the shoulder but she's lost a lot of blood." Then he nodded toward the young clerk who was holding a bag of ice against her head. "She was knocked out for a short while. Might have a concussion."

"What about those two?" one of the paramedics asked, looking toward the two men on the floor.

"They're dead, and it's a better fate than they deserved," David muttered, then got to his feet and got out of their way.

A second later, Cara was in his arms, her face pressed against his chest, the melting ice clutched tightly in her hand. David could feel the cold against his bare back, but didn't give a damn for the discomfort. Nothing mattered but Cara's welfare.

"It's all right now, honey," he said softly, holding her tight. "It's over."

"You saved us, David. You saved us all," she muttered.

"Yes, God bless you, mister," someone said, and patted him on the back, their hands warm against his bare flesh.

One after the other, the hostages thanked him, some hugging him, some unable to do anything but touch him as they were led away.

Just when David thought it was over, another set of officers arrived. These were in suits. He sighed. Detectives. Now the questions would really commence. But how to answer? Identifying himself and not giving himself away could be tricky, especially since he'd only left them with one live body to take to trial.

"So where's this Rambo they're all talking about?" one of the men asked.

"It was him, Robert! That's the man who told me to call the police."

David turned around. It was the woman from the parking lot. He looked back at Cara, assessing her condition. Her face was swollen where she'd been hit and she was still shaking. He needed to get her out of the building, but it wasn't going to happen. Not yet.

The detective looked first at David, then at the woman in his arms. Surprise spread over his face.

"Mrs. Justice, is that you?"

Cara looked up. "Oh…Robert, I should have expected you, but this all seems so surreal. I still can't believe it. If it hadn't been for David, we would all be dead." Then she laid her hand on David's arm. "David, darling, this is Robert…oh, excuse me, Robert. I forget all of you boys have grown up. It's Detective Foster, now. He and my son, Tyler, grew up together."

David shook the man's hand.

"Detective," he said, reluctantly acknowledging the man's need to be here.

Robert Foster nodded cordially.

"Care to tell me what happened?" he asked, wondering about David's lack of shirt, and then saw one wadded up on the floor where the paramedics had discarded it. It was stained with blood. "Is that your shirt?" he asked.

But David was more concerned with the trembling in Cara's muscles than his lack of clothing.

"Can we go somewhere and sit down?" he asked. "Cara is going into shock."

"I'll be fine," Cara said, but when she started to walk, her legs went out from under her.

David caught her before she fell. "Are you sure he didn't hurt you?"

She shook her head. "Just a slap across the face. It was nothing compared to Margie being shot." Then she started to cry again. "My God...my God...I thought we were going to die."

David held her close against him and headed for a nearby stack of boxes. He sat, still cradling her in his arms.

"She probably needs to see a doctor," Foster said.

"No," Cara muttered. "I wasn't hurt, just terribly afraid."

"He could give you something to sleep, though," Foster insisted.

"I don't need anything but David."

"Look, could you make this kind of quick?" David asked. "If there are any details you need to fill in later, you can reach me at Cara's. I'll be there another day or so."

"You're leaving town?" Foster asked.

David felt Cara stiffen in his arms, but there was no denying what had to be said.

"Yes, but only for a few days."

"Then could you tell me...briefly of course...exactly how you got involved in this?"

David gave Cara a quick, gentle squeeze as he settled her securely within his embrace.

He went into a brief, but concise account of what had occurred, right down to the moment he made the decision to fire the first shot.

"The short, stocky perp had already shot one hostage and knocked another unconscious. When he said no witnesses and turned his gun on Cara, he lost whatever breaks I might have given him."

"I see," Foster said, then picked up David's gun, turning it over in his hands and casually eyeing the weapon. "You must be a good shot."

"Yes."

"Never saw a gun like this before. Where did you get it?"

David hesitated. "That's because there's not another like it."

Foster noted that David had only answered half his questions.

"Prototype?"

David nodded.

"Interesting. How did you come by it? Did you design it?"

"No, I'm not that skilled."

"I don't suppose you stole it? I wouldn't want to hear something like that, especially since you're going to be the hero of the hour."

David sighed. "It's not stolen. Look, just run the serial numbers through the computer along with my driver's license number. It will explain itself."

Foster nodded. "That sounds simple enough," he said.

"Can we go home now?" Cara asked.

David looked at the detective.

Foster nodded reluctantly. "You say you'll be at Mrs. Justice's house for another day or so?"

"Yes."

"Then I'll just run the numbers on your gun and bring it out to you later this evening, if that's all right?"

"I'll be there," David said.

Cara slid out of his lap. "I can walk," she said.

David pulled her into the shelter of his arms.

"I know, but if you need to, just lean on me, honey."

Cara leaned. Not because she particularly needed to, but because she still could. She'd heard it from his own lips, even though it hadn't been said to her. Within a couple of days, he would be gone, maybe walking into something far worse than what she'd just witnessed, but she swallowed her fears and kept on walking.

The parking lot was a mess. Ambulances were coming and going and from the appearances of the police on the scene, they'd had to call in their reserves. Some weren't even in uniform, but were doing their best to keep curiosity seekers at bay.

When David and Cara emerged from the store, a smattering of applause sounded from some of the bystanders. Obviously, word had already spread that he was the hero of the day. When he saw a television crew pulling into the parking lot, he kept his head down, tightened his hold on her hand and kept on walking.

"Hurry, Cara, I can't have my face splashed all over the news."

Cara looked startled, only then realizing the consequences of what he had done. By saving them, he'd blown whatever cover he'd had left. No one in the world would recognize him as Jonah, but Frank would damn sure recognize him as the man he sought.

With the help of a couple of the officers, the police

cruiser blocking David's car was quickly moved. As soon as the car was free, he sped away. Only when they were on their way out of town did he breathe a sigh of relief.

"Thank God, that's over," Cara muttered, as she leaned back against the seat and closed her eyes.

David glanced at her, but didn't comment. If she only knew, it was probably just beginning. The moment Detective Foster ran the serial numbers of that gun through NCIC, it was going to set off so many bells in Washington that they'd probably hear them in heaven. And then there was Frank. David couldn't depend on anonymity any longer. He needed to start laying a trail for his brother to follow that would lead him as far away from Cara as possible.

A short while later, they arrived at Cara's home. She staggered as he helped her out of the car, then weakly apologized. He glared at her for apologizing again, then scooped her up in his arms. This time, she didn't argue. By the time he got her into the house, she was sobbing. The tenderness in his voice was even more of her undoing.

"That's all right, baby. Go ahead and cry. Lord knows you've earned a few tears after the morning you've had." He set her on the side of her bed and began helping her take off her bloodstained clothes. "There was a time or two when I felt like crying, myself."

She hiccuped on a sob and tossed her bloodstained bra onto the floor. Gently, he cupped the side of her face, wincing at the bruising already taking effect.

"The son of a bitch," he muttered, and then kissed her there. "If I could, I would have killed him twice."

She sighed and leaned forward until their foreheads were touching.

"Oh, David, if you hadn't come back for me when you did, today would have been the day I died."

He shuddered. "Don't! Don't play that if game. It'll make you crazy. I know."

She wrapped her arms around his neck and hugged him fiercely.

"Before today, I hated what the government had done to you, but now..."

A sad smile came and went. He knew what she meant. He and Cara had been cheated out of a normal life, but because he knew how to kill, he'd saved her—saved them all—to live another day.

"Let's get the rest of these bloody clothes off of you," he said. "Can you stand on your own in the shower, or do you want to take a bath?"

"Shower, please, and yes, I can stand."

When she dropped the last article of her clothing in the pile on the floor, she kicked it aside with her toe.

"Throw them away."

"All of them?" he asked.

She nodded. "I don't ever want to wear them again."

He gathered them up in his arms and started for the door, then hesitated.

"Cara?"

"What?"

"The clothes will wash."

"But I—"

The despair on his face confused her, then suddenly she understood. David not only had blood on his clothes, but blood on his hands. And if she was so disgusted by something as inconsequential as bloody clothes, then what must she think of a man who had shed blood?

She made herself smile. "You're right. I just overreacted. Besides, those are my favorite slacks. Maybe if you just tossed them in the washing machine in cold water and let them soak for a while?"

A rare smile of approval appeared on his face, before he turned and walked away.

A couple of hours later, they were in the kitchen eating some sandwiches David had made for them when the phone began to ring.

Cara looked at David.

"Want me to answer?" he asked.

She sighed. No use running from something she would inevitably have to face.

"No, I'll get it, but thanks anyway."

She picked up the portable, eyeing the caller ID screen, then rolled her eyes.

"Hello."

"Oh, my God, Cara, we just heard."

"Hello, Debra. Looks like news travels fast."

"Are you serious? It isn't gossip, honey! The whole thing is on the news."

"Now?" Cara asked.

"Yes, now."

"The television," Cara whispered, pointing to the living room. "Debra says the incident is on TV."

David bolted for the living room. Cara followed, still talking to her friend. To her dismay, she realized it wasn't a local news show, but a national network broadcasting live from the scene, where police were still working the area. She quickly disconnected and then slipped into the seat beside David.

"This isn't good, is it?" she asked.

"They don't have any tape of us. It should be all right."

At that moment, someone blurted out his name.

"Oh, no," Cara moaned.

David's expression darkened perceptibly. She was right. It wasn't good. Even though there were probably thousands of David Wilsons in the United States, there wouldn't be many who could have pulled off the rescue of eleven hostages single-handed. Hooray for the training he'd received at SPEAR and to hell with any anonymity he might have hoped to retain. When she clutched his hand, he slipped an arm around her and pulled her close, shoving all thoughts of Simon from his mind.

Less than ten minutes later, the phone rang again. This time, Cara handed the phone to David with a pleading expression.

David took it unwillingly.

"You could unplug the phone," he said.

"Please?"

He smiled, then answered.

"Justice residence."

"Is this David?"

He flinched. He'd only heard her voice once, but it was as firmly etched in his mind now as was Cara's face.

"Bethany?"

"Yes! We just saw the news about the supermarket in Chiltingham being robbed."

"Yes, so did we," David said. "Here's your mother."

"Thanks. Oh, David..."

"Yes?"

"Nice talking to you."

He found himself smiling. "Nice talking to you, too, honey."

He handed the phone to Cara and then started to get up and give her some privacy, but she grabbed his hand and pulled him back down beside her.

"Hello?" Cara said. "Bethany, darling, how are you?"

"We're all fine," she said. "I just had to call, though. It was so weird, seeing our little hometown on the evening news. Isn't it awful? They said someone was shot. Do you know who?"

"Yes, it was Margie Weller, the Methodist pastor's wife."

Bethany gasped. "How horrible! Was it serious? Is she going to be all right?"

"Yes, it was terribly frightening, but last word we had, she was in surgery and her prognosis was good."

"Thank goodness," Bethany said. "I guess you never know about things like this, but who would have thought it could happen at home, right?"

"Right," Cara said.

"They said there were eleven hostages and some guy named Wilson saved them all."

"Yes, he did," Cara said, wanting so badly to tell Bethany that it was her own father who'd been the hero that day. But telling her something like that over a phone was unconscionable.

"Is he new to the force?" Bethany asked.

"He isn't a member of the police force."

There was a moment of silence and then suddenly Bethany's questions took on the feel of an inquisition.

"Mother, is there something you aren't telling me?"

Cara sighed. "Everything is fine. We'll talk about it when you get home."

"Mother! Please God, don't tell me you were there?"

Cara's hesitation was enough to send Bethany into hysterics. She could hear her daughter screaming at her husband on the other end of the line. She looked at David and rolled her eyes.

David patted her leg. "It's to be expected, honey. It would be enough to scare the hell out of anyone, never mind that it's your mother."

"I guess," Cara said, then put the phone back to her ear. Bethany was shouting her name. "Yes, darling, I'm still here. Are you through screaming?"

Bethany was crying now. "Mother, my God…are you all right?"

"I'm fine."

Bethany moaned. "I can't believe this."

Cara tried to laugh, but it sounded awkward, even to her. "I know how you feel. It's a bit hard for us to believe and we were there."

There was a long moment of silence on the other end of the line and then Bethany spoke.

"He was there, too?"

"By he, I suppose you mean David? Oh, yes. Actually, he's the man of the hour in Chiltingham. I wouldn't be surprised if they name a street after him."

Now David was the one rolling his eyes.

"Is he the one they're talking about...the man who saved all of you?"

"Yes."

"I want to speak to him," Bethany said.

"Just a minute," Cara said, then covered the mouthpiece with her hand and looked at David. "She wants to talk to you."

David nodded, gearing himself for the sweet sound of her voice.

"Bethany, I promise your mother is fine."

At first she didn't answer and he thought he could hear her crying.

"Honey...are you there?"

"David, whoever you are, I just want to tell you that I'm so sorry for everything I first thought about you, and I will never be able to thank you enough for saving Mother's life."

"You're welcome," he said softly, and heard her sigh.

"I want to apologize to you," she said.

He smiled. "For what?"

"For thinking you were some kind of con man who was after my mother's money. It's not like she's rich or anything, but she has her home and Dad's retirement and...well...you know what I mean."

It hurt to hear the word *Dad* come out of her mouth and know she was referring to Ray Justice, but it was a title Ray had earned.

"I understand, and I don't care that your mother doesn't have a lot of money, because I do, okay?"

Cara's mouth dropped. "What on earth is she saying to you?" she whispered.

"She thought I was a con man after your money," David said.

"Oh, my word," Cara muttered. "Give me that phone." She took it out of David's hand with a yank. "Bethany Gail, you might be an adult, but you will never get old enough to question my behavior, is that understood?"

"Yes, ma'am."

"All right then," Cara muttered. "As long as we understand each other on that count."

"We're coming home a day early," Bethany said. "We'll see you tomorrow sometime after noon. Our plane is due in at Canandaigua around ten in the morning."

Cara hesitated. "Well, I'll be glad when you get home, but please don't shorten your vacation on my account."

"Mother, after this, do you think any of us could find a way to forget what happened to you and have fun? We want to come home…all of us."

"Then come," Cara said. "And have a safe trip."

"We will," she said, then added, "tell David goodbye for me."

"Tell him yourself," Cara said. She handed the phone back to David.

"Hello?"

"David, thanks again."

He smiled. "You're welcome."
Then she added, "David?"

"Yes?"

"I'm looking forward to meeting you."

He sighed and closed his eyes. "I'm looking forward to meeting you, too."

"Well...goodbye then."

"Yes, honey. Goodbye."

The line went dead in his ear. He handed the phone to Cara and then took her in his arms.

"My God, I don't think I've ever been this scared in my life, except maybe when that bastard put his gun in your face. Not even in Nam. She has every right to hate me."

"She doesn't have a right to hate anyone," Cara said. "She didn't do without a single thing in her entire life. She was loved from the moment of her birth, by both Ray and me. She had loving grandparents on both sides, and siblings, as well. She has known all her life that Ray Justice was her adoptive father. Knowing that you're still alive will be just as big a joy for her as it was for me."

"Swear?" David asked.

"I swear."

He smiled, and then leaned back on the sofa, eyeing the woman who'd given him something he thought he'd never have again—hope.

"You remember this morning...before we got to town?"

She grinned. "You mean when you proposed? Yes, I remember it, so don't think you can change your mind now."

"I don't want to change my mind. I want to make sure you don't change yours," he said, and then pulled the little velvet box out of his pocket and got down on one knee.

Suddenly, Cara was looking at him through a blur of tears.

"Oh, David."

"This is where I went when I let you off at the store. You know I have to leave again, but I pray it won't be for long. I love you so much, and I owe you so much. A war cheated us out of a lot and I want to give you everything, all at once. I can't make any guarantees about the future, so you'll have to settle for just this, right now.''

Her hand was shaking when he slid the ring on her finger.

"It fits,'' she said, more than a little surprised.

"Yeah, I'm a pretty good judge of things like that.''

She shook her head and then threw her arms around his neck. "You're good at a lot more than that,'' she said. "I can't wait for the day when we can start living our life...for us.''

"Me, too. Do you want to—''

Before he could finish, the doorbell rang. Cara jumped at the noise and then glanced at the clock. It was after nine. Surely it wasn't well-wishing friends coming this late?

"I'll get it,'' David said, and then strode to the door.

It was Detective Foster. Then he looked past Foster to the two dark-suited men behind him and sighed.

"Gentlemen, come in. I've been expecting you.''

Chapter 10

Robert Foster glared at David as he stepped inside. He was still sweating from the unexpected confrontation he'd just had with these two federal agents.

All he'd done was what he'd been hired to do, which was investigate crimes. He'd entered the serial numbers from David's gun into the computer, and then proceeded to finish his report while he'd waited for the program to run.

Half an hour later, two strangers in suits had walked into the room as if they owned the place. Flashing their badges, they tossed him a hard copy of the file he'd sent through NCIC and demanded he bring them to the man who owned the gun.

Now, here he was, still reeling from being treated like an underling. No courtesy from one officer to another. No nothing. He didn't like it. He didn't like it one damned bit.

He turned back to the agents, still pissed and glaring. "Happy now?"

They looked at David, comparing this man's physical description against the one they'd been given. They didn't know who the hell he was, but when they got orders direct from the President, they knew enough to respond without question. Convinced that they had their man, one of them stepped forward and handed David his gun while Detective Foster continued to fume.

"You knew this would happen, didn't you?" he said, giving David a share of his anger.

"Knew what?" David asked, eyeing the two men who followed Foster inside.

The detective turned, waving his hand toward his uninvited escorts.

"That Tweedledee and Tweedledum would show up and try to eat me for dinner."

David stifled a grin. The man's description of the two men who were with him was funny, but it wasn't in his best interests to laugh.

"They don't bite," David said, and then added, "Unless maybe if I asked them to."

The federal agents looked surprised as their curiosity grew, but they knew better than to voice it.

Foster was over his head and he knew it. He threw up his hands in defeat.

"Look, I don't know what's going on here, and I'm thinking it would be in my best interests not to ask."

"Cara said you were bright," David said.

Foster shifted nervously. "You're someone special, aren't you?" Then he shrugged. "Hell...I already knew that when you walked into the supermarket and took down three armed men. What I'm trying to say is...you have that damned gun back, and whoever you are, it's been a pleasure meeting you."

David shook the young detective's hand. "Likewise."

"David, is everything all right?"

All of them turned, acknowledging Cara's arrival into their midst.

"Mrs. Justice, I trust you're feeling better?" Foster asked.

"Much." Then she looked at the two men accompanying the detective. "Detective Foster, are you going to introduce your friends?"

"If I knew their names, I might," he muttered.

"They're here for me," David said.

It was the quiet, resolute tone in his voice that made her heart sink. She turned to David, silently begging him to deny what she feared. To her dismay, he shook his head.

"It will be okay," he said. At that moment, the two agents stepped forward, one of them handing David a phone.

"Sir, I'm Federal Agent Thomas Ryan, and this is Agent Patrick O'Casey. In less than a minute, the President will be calling you. We have instructions to await your orders."

Cara gasped and Detective Foster muttered, "Lord have mercy," beneath his breath.

Seconds later, the phone David was holding rang. He answered abruptly.

"Sir?"

"I must say, when you take a leave of absence, you don't do it quietly, do you, son?"

David almost relaxed. He'd expected a dressing down for getting mixed up in public matters.

"It was a choice I made. I would do the same thing again," he said.

"And I would expect you to," the President replied. "Now to more important matters. Our people have been monitoring your old contact station. You are receiving e-mail from the quarry."

One moment David's face was animated and the next expressionless. Cara shivered. It was like looking at a stranger. She took a step backward, unconsciously distancing herself from the fear that came with it.

"Sir, I'm assuming this line is secure."

A soft chuckle rippled in David's ear. "Yes. Feel free to speak your piece."

"The messages, what do they say?"

"He wants a meeting."

David pivoted sharply and walked into the other room alone.

"Can you see that he gets an answer?" David asked.

"Just a minute, son, I'm putting someone else on. Tell him what you want sent. It will get done."

"Yes, sir, thank you, sir."

Seconds later, another voice was on the line. It didn't matter to David who it was. If the President had him standing by, then he was okay.

"Ready to transmit," the voice said.

"Just tell him…Washington D.C."

"Got it. Anything else?"

"No."

Moments later, the President was back on the phone.

"Is there anything we can do for you?"

David thought of the hundreds of agents who could be instantly at his disposal and knew that their presence would do nothing but drive his brother further underground. It was time for all of this hate to end.

"No. I'll let you know when it's over."

There was a hesitation on the other end, and then a softening in the tone of the President's voice.

"Just make damn sure the call I get is from you, personally, do you understand me, son?"

David almost smiled. It was as close as the President would come to saying "be careful" without actually voicing the words.

"Yes, sir, I understand."

"All right then. Those men I sent are there to help you in any way that they can. Use them or send them home. It's up to you."

"Yes, sir, and once again, sorry about the fuss."

"There was a need. You made the right decision. Now go do your thing."

David disconnected, walked into the other room and handed the phone back to Agent Ryan.

"Thanks for escorting Detective Foster out to see me. You men have a safe journey home."

For the first time, the agent's composure was rattled.

"But sir, don't you—"

"No." Then he softened the answer by adding, "But thanks."

They nodded, ignored Foster's presence and smiled courteously at Cara. "Ma'am," they said, and then stepped aside, waiting for Foster to make his excuses.

He quickly took his cue. "Mrs. Justice, if you need anything, you know where to call." Then he looked at David. "Why do I feel the urge to tell you good luck?"

A wry smile tilted the corner of David's mouth. "Probably because I'm going to need it."

Moments later, they were gone, leaving David and Cara alone in the hall. She bit her lower lip to keep from crying, but he saw the gesture and opened his arms.

"Come here to me," he said gently.

She walked into his arms.

"I'm not going to cry and I'm not going to beg, but so help me God, if you get yourself killed, I will never forgive you," she muttered.

"I'm not going to die on you, baby. I spent too much money on that ring to let it go to waste."

"That isn't funny," she muttered.

"Oh, I don't know about that. I'm smiling."

She looked up. "You're crazy, you know that?"

"Oh, yeah, crazy in love. What do you say we call it a night?" He touched the side of her face where the bruising was starting to show. "I have this sudden need to just lie down beside you and listen to you sleep."

Cara knew he was trying to reassure her that there would be no lovemaking this night because of the trauma she'd suffered.

"We can do more than sleep, if you want," she said.

He shook his head. "Maybe you could, but I don't think I can. I'm still trying to get past the sight of that son of a bitch holding a gun in your face." He hugged her again, this time almost desperately. "When I think how close I came to—"

"But you didn't, and I'm still here. Let's go to bed."

Together, they locked the doors and turned out the lights before walking hand in hand up the stairs toward the bedroom.

A small lamp she'd turned on earlier lit the way as they went. It was a moment in time that was neither remarkable nor different, and yet Cara knew it would be in her heart forever. Small things she might never have noticed became things to remember.

Like the warmth of his hand as it enfolded hers.

The steady clip of his footsteps beside her.

The scent of his aftershave and the tick of the grandfather clock standing in the entryway.

The rush of cool air against her skin as she undressed.

The crisp, clean sheets on the bed as they slipped between the covers.

The way he pulled her into the curve of his body and then promptly fell asleep, as if girding himself for the trauma to come.

Unwilling to waste her last hours with him by sleeping them away, she lay without moving, savoring the rise and fall of his chest behind her.

Sometime after midnight, exhaustion claimed her. When she woke the next morning, there was a rose on her pillow with a note beneath.

Don't be mad at me for not saying goodbye. I did it once and look how things worked out. This time, I'm saying I love you, and please wait for me.

David.

Cara covered her face. To her surprise, her cheeks were already wet. She'd been so certain that the pain she was feeling was too terrible for tears. It would seem that she'd been wrong.

In another part of the country and at the same time they were going to bed, Frank Wilson was lying on top of his covers, smoking his last cigarette of the day and watching TV. But his mind wasn't on the programming. He was going through scenario after scenario, plotting all the different ways he could enact his revenge. A few minutes later, he stubbed out his cigarette and turned off the TV and lights and closed his eyes. Within seconds, he was asleep.

It was the first football game of the season and Frankie was almost ready to go. At sixteen, his voice had deepened to what would be his normal pitch and he'd finally grown into his feet. And he had a girlfriend. At least, in his mind, he did. The fact that Ellen Mayhew had yet to acknowledge he even existed was beside the point. He liked her, therefore he must be in as close a vicinity to her as possible without giving himself away.

He started out the door, his hair combed into a perfect ducktail, his sideburns just brushing the lobes of his ears. He thought he looked a little like Elvis.

"Frankie, you get your little brother back here by ten. School tomorrow," his mother said.

He froze, his hand on the doorknob, and then turned abruptly.

"Why do I always have to have that brat tagging along? How am I ever going to have any friends if I'm always baby-sitting with him?"

Davie leaned against the sofa, his gaze beseeching his brother to relent, yet a little afraid that if he did get to go to the ball game with Frankie, he'd pay for it later.

"Friends are fine," his mother said. "But brothers are family. Brothers are forever."

Frankie glared at the little brat, ignoring the fact that Davie wasn't so little anymore and that the kid's body was probably going to be more muscular than his own when he reached full growth.

"If you go, you're not sitting with me and my friends, you hear?"

Davie nodded. "I won't, Frankie, I promise."

"And I don't want to have to go looking for you when the game is over. You be waiting for me by the ticket gate, you hear?"

Davie nodded again. "I hear. I'll be there."

Their mother hugged them both. "That's fine then. You two go and have a good time, but remember, home as soon as the game is over, and Frankie, Davie's care is in your hands."

"Damn," Frankie muttered, and shoved his kid brother out the door ahead of him.

"I'm sorry, Frankie," Davie said. "I won't be any trouble, I promise."

Frankie muttered a curse word and hoped to God that Ellen Mayhew didn't see him walking into the grandstands with Davie in tow.

Two hours later the game was over. Davie Wilson stood by the ticket gate, watching anxiously for a sign of his big brother's face. Families filed past him, laughing and talk-

ing about the big win that they'd had tonight, and with each group that passed, Davie was certain that Frankie would be in the next group to come along.

But he wasn't.

When the gatekeeper and a couple of teachers came by, he slipped into the shadows, unwilling to be questioned as to why he was still at the field.

The lights went out. The last car drove out of the parking lot. Davie was alone.

He could have walked home by himself and would have, except then Frankie would have been in real trouble for abandoning him. So he waited, knowing they would be in trouble for being late, but at least they would be in trouble together.

A half hour passed, and then another. It started to rain.

He pulled the collar of his jacket up around his neck and hunched his shoulders against the downpour. Everything that had been so familiar under the lights on the playing field now took on ominous tones. Familiar buildings became sinister shapes, waiting to morph into swamp monsters and ghouls. The only benefit to the downpour was that it hid the continuous stream of tears running down his face.

"Hey, kid."

He spun, his heart in his mouth. Frankie was standing before him with a sheepish expression on his face.

"I waited, Frankie, just like you said."

It was one of the few times in his life that Frankie Wilson was truly ashamed. Gently, he cuffed his little brother on the side of the head and then gave him a brief, bearlike hug.

"Yeah, kid, you sure did. I'm sorry, okay?"

Davie smiled. It was going to be okay. Yeah, they were going to catch hell from their folks, but it didn't really matter. Whatever happened, they were in it together.

"What are you gonna tell Mama?" Frankie asked, as
they walked through the rain toward home.

"Nothing," Davie said.

Frankie felt even worse. *"She's gonna be real mad at
us."*

"Yeah, I know."

Frankie paused beneath a streetlight, staring at the rain
running out of Davie's hair and down his face.

"You aren't gonna snitch?"

Davie frowned and shook his head.

"Why?" Frankie asked. *"I probably would."*

Davie shrugged. *"You're my brother."*

An ambulance sped by the Chicago hotel with sirens
blaring. Disoriented, Frank bolted from bed, his heart racing with the image of his brother's face in his head. Just
for a moment, the magnitude of what he'd been planning
to do overwhelmed him and he let out a cry and covered
his face. The sound shattered within him, bringing him to
his knees. He could hear his mother's voice as clearly as
if she was standing by his bed.

You are your brother's keeper.

Thou shalt not kill.

Blood is thicker than water.

He moaned. Could he really do this? The first time had
been in the heat of the moment, wrapped up in the day-
to-day combat and the anger that had dragged him into a
war he didn't understand. And he'd fueled that anger all
these years with the need for revenge. He wanted to destroy him, that was certain. He wanted him defiled as he'd
been—his reputation in shreds as his had been. But could
he rip the heart from a man who was his blood?

Then he fingered his scars, remembering why they were
there, and that his little brother had set him on fire. It didn't
matter to Frank that David had thought him dead—that he

had been trying to hide the evidence that would mark his brother a traitor.

He stood abruptly and strode to the wet bar, pouring himself a very stiff drink. He tossed it back without hesitation then poured himself another. By the time the liquor hit his stomach, his brief moment of uncertainty had passed. He moved to the window overlooking the city and to his surprise realized it was raining. Too restless to sleep, he turned on the television and then lowered the volume as he surfed through the few available stations. With nothing but CNN and some pay-per-view movies for company, he retrieved his laptop and decided to check his messages.

Using the bed for a desk, he crawled onto the mattress and centered the laptop between his legs. The television was on mute on the other side of the room, and only now and then did he even bother to look up to see what newsworthy event CNN was covering. When the You've Got Mail sign flashed across the computer screen, he refused to anticipate the contents of the box. With a click of the mouse, e-mail began to download. As it did, he glanced at the television screen across the room and then hit the mute button to reinstate the sound.

A spokesperson for some local police department was making a statement regarding the deaths and capture of suspects involved in a week-long crime spree somewhere in the state of New York. He was reiterating the well-being of one of the victims when the laptop signaled the end of the download.

Immediately, Frank hit mute again and looked at the screen. As he did, he missed hearing the location of the incident and the name of the man who was credited with the rescues. He didn't know it yet, but fate was already dealing him a handful of bad cards.

He scanned the list of messages, and as he did, his heart skipped a beat. Quickly deleting all but the one from Reunion, he began to read. As he did, a cold smile spread across his face, puckering the burn scars on his cheek and neck.

"At last, little brother, you finally got some balls."

He fumbled for the remote and turned off the TV. There were things to do and arrangements to make. He rolled out of the bed, dragged his suitcase from the closet and began to pack.

It was almost over.

But Frank Wilson was due for some more delays. He caught a few hours sleep and by daylight was on his way to the airport. By the time he got to Chicago O'Hare, it was just before seven in the morning and the gentle rain of the night before had turned into violent storms. Planes were grounded until further notice, and the airport was a melee of angry and unruly travelers.

Cursing the weather and people in general, he bought himself a cup of coffee and a doughnut, then settled down to read his newspaper. Time was still on his side.

The small Canandaigua Airport was a madhouse of voices and people. David stood at the windows overlooking the runway, watching the big silver plane coming in for a landing. As the wheels touched down, his heart skipped a beat. His daughter was on that plane, and for the first time in his life, he was going to see her in person.

Shifting nervously, he watched the plane as it began to taxi toward the terminal. A voice over an intercom announced the arrival of flight 447 at gate 9, and people began gathering, anxious for that first sight of their loved ones. David wondered what it would be like to stand with those people—to see the look of recognition on Bethany's face and feel her arms around his neck as she greeted him with delight. But as he'd learned long ago, he kept his thoughts to himself, masking emotion behind an expressionless exterior.

A few minutes later, the first of the passengers appeared at the gate, then more and more, until a steady stream of travel-weary travelers straggled from the ramp into the terminal.

He shifted his position so that he could better see the faces, his anxiety growing as the line continued and still no sign of the woman he'd seen in Cara's pictures.

Then suddenly she was there, walking beside a tall, sandy-haired man who was carrying one sleeping child while Bethany held hands with the other. Her shoulder-length hair was dark and straight like his, and she was taller than he'd expected. She was slim and graceful and when she smiled, he could see the beginnings of a dimple in her left cheek.

Without thinking, he moved toward her, wanting to hear the sound of her voice. Although there were at least a dozen people between them, he could hear her talking to her husband about how good it was to be on firm ground and laughing at something her oldest daughter just said.

God in heaven, he didn't think this would be so hard.

He paused a few feet away and watched as they passed by. As they did, a small stuffed rabbit fell out of the oldest girl's backpack. He pushed through the passengers and snatched it from the floor, then caught up with them a few feet away.

"Excuse me," he said, and briefly touched Bethany's shoulder. "This fell out of her backpack."

Surprised, Bethany turned, saw the rabbit in the stranger's hands and smiled.

"Oh, my! Thank you so much, that's Rachel's favorite toy." Then she looked down at her daughter and lightly touched her on the head. "Rachel, would you like to thank the man for finding Henry?"

David felt himself smiling as the little girl nodded.

"So, his name is Henry?"

She nodded.

"Well, it's a good thing I saw him jump out, right?"

Her eyes widened appreciably as he handed her the toy.

"He jumped?"

Without breaking a smile, David nodded. "It looked like it to me. Better hold him tight."

The child clutched the rabbit against her chest.

"Thank you so much," Bethany repeated. "Losing Henry would have been nothing short of disastrous."

"You're welcome," David said. Resisting the urge to touch the children, he nodded a goodbye to her husband as well as Bethany and disappeared into the crowd.

Bethany looked at her husband. "That was fortunate, wasn't it?" she asked.

Her husband nodded, still looking in the direction that the man had gone.

"You know, he reminded me of someone, but I can't think who," he muttered.

Bethany shrugged. "Come on, Tom. I'm anxious to get home and check on Mother."

"Yes, you're right," he said, and then headed toward the baggage claim.

A short while later, they were on the road home, unaware that the man they'd just seen was on a plane of his own and bound for the nation's capital.

Chapter 11

All day, Cara found herself listening for the sound of David's voice, although she knew that he was gone. Never in the three years she'd been widowed had she felt so alone. A gut-wrenching fear had settled itself in the pit of her stomach, and she couldn't find a way to get past it. She could only imagine what he was going to have to face, but could not wrap her mind around the truth of it. His brother wanted him dead. Dear God, how much more was he destined to withstand?

She'd prayed for him until her mind was spinning and the words numb upon her lips. She had nothing left to do but wait, and it was the uncertainty that was driving her mad. In desperation, she cleaned her house from top to bottom, even preparing some extra food, knowing Bethany and her family would arrive before the day was out.

During the cleaning, she'd run across the envelope of pictures she'd taken on their day at the lake. It had almost been her undoing. Looking at the images of a happier time and wondering if they would be all she had left of him had sent her into another wave of weeping. Unwilling to put the pictures away, she searched out some empty frames and framed the best of the lot, adding them to the mantel with the others of her family. Only after she stepped back to look at them as a whole did the pain begin to subside. It was as if the pictures had given credence to his reappearance into her life.

Then she rubbed the diamond solitaire he'd put on her finger, shamed that her faith was so shallow. The pictures were wonderful, but she didn't need them, or the ring, or any tangible reminder that David Wilson was alive. As long as her heart beat, he would never be forgotten. With one last look at David laughing and holding up a very small fish, she blew him a kiss and walked away.

Four hours later, Bethany was at the door.

"Darling, how wonderful to see you again," Cara said, as she stepped aside to let her daughter in.

Bethany took one look at the spreading bruise on the side of her mother's face and burst into tears.

"Oh, Mother, your poor little face."

Cara quickly embraced her daughter. "Honey, it's not as bad as it seems, I promise."

Bethany was forty years old and almost a head taller than her mother, but at that moment, she felt like a child again. The horror of knowing how close she'd come to losing her was too horrible to contemplate.

"I can't believe that this has happened," she said, as her gaze searched the familiar contours of Cara's face. "Are you sure you're all right? Is there anything I can do?"

"Yes, I'm fine, and you can come inside and sit down with me. I want to hear all about your trip." Then she looked over Bethany's shoulder, suddenly realizing the rest of the family was nowhere in sight. "Where are Tom and the girls?"

"They'll be along later," Bethany said. "I left them at home unpacking." She traced the curve of her mother's cheek with her fingertip, barely grazing the purpling flesh. "I couldn't wait to see you."

Cara smiled and did a dainty pirouette.

"Well, you see me. How do I look?"

Bethany frowned. "Actually, except for that awful bruise, you look wonderful." Suddenly, she remembered the man named David and looked around. "Where is this David person? I want to meet him."

Cara's smile slipped, but she wouldn't give in. Not now. Not in front of Bethany.

"And you will, but not today," Cara said. "He was called away on business quite suddenly. Actually, he left very early this morning, so you've just missed him." Then she remembered the pictures she'd put on the mantel and took Bethany by the hand. "However, I can show you a picture. I took some when we went fishing the other day."

Bethany followed her mother into the living room and was startled to see that her mother had put up not one, but three snapshots of the man on the mantel—and right in the middle of the family grouping. For once, she kept her thoughts to herself and smiled as her mother handed her the first one.

"This was taken last Tuesday at the lake…or was it Wednesday?" Then Cara smiled. "Oh, I don't remember, but we had the most marvelous time."

Bethany scanned the image and then started to look at the others when something about the first one clicked. He hadn't been smiling when she'd seen him, but she would bet her best pair of earrings that she'd seen him before. She grabbed her mother's arm.

"Mom! You won't believe this, but I think we met this man!"

Cara turned. "When?"

"This morning. At the airport. Henry fell out of Rachel's backpack as we were getting off the plane and a man came out of the crowd and gave it back. I swear it was the same man, right down to those silver strands of hair over his ears."

Cara's heart started to pound. She should have known that David would find a way to look at his daughter's face—just in case he— She stifled a sob, unable to finish her own thought.

"Oh, Bethany, are you sure?"

Bethany looked intently at the other two snapshots, then nodded. "Positive." When she looked up, she knew something was wrong. "What?

Cara hesitated.

"Damn it, Mother, I knew something was wrong from the start. Talk to me. Who is he? What has he done to you to make you cry?"

"His name is David Wilson, and I'm crying because I'm scared. The first time he left me to fight a war." She inhaled on a shaky breath. "And he left again because...because for him, that war has never ended."

Bethany's heart started to pound. She heard her mother's words, but they didn't make sense. She knew the man who'd been staying with her mother was named David Wilson. She'd heard her mother call him David, and they'd heard his last name when the incident had made the news. Her biological father's name had been Wilson, but he died in Vietnam. Hadn't he? What had her mother just said about the first time he left her? She started to shake.

"Mother?"

Cara felt guilty for the confusion on Bethany's face and

when she heard the tremble in her voice, she reached for her hands, holding them close against her breast.

"That man...the man you saw in the airport...the man who saved my life...is your father."

Bethany's face crumpled and she staggered backward to a chair, her voice barely above a whisper.

"But you said he was dead."

"We all thought he was dead," Cara said.

"Where...why...?"

Cara sighed. "It's a long, terrible story, my darling, and it's not mine to tell. When David comes back, he will tell you himself."

Bethany looked up, the yearning there on her face for Cara to see.

"Will he come back?"

Cara smiled. "Yes, I believe he will."

"How can you be sure?" Bethany said.

Cara held out her hand. "Because he put this on my finger."

Bethany took one look at the diamond and burst into tears.

Cara knelt, cradling her daughter in her arms.

"Don't cry, darling. It's actually wonderful, you know. It's a miracle that David and I have been given a second chance for happiness."

"I'm not crying because I'm unhappy," Bethany sobbed. "I'm just crying, okay?" Then she clutched Cara a little tighter. "Oh, Mom, he has to come back."

Cara closed her eyes momentarily, refusing to give in to the fear.

"Yes, darling, I know just how you feel."

"Ladies and gentlemen, please fasten your seat belts and put your seats and tray tables in their upright positions. We will be landing in a few minutes and there will be personnel at the gate to help you with flight information should you be traveling on to other destinations. On another note, the time in our nation's capital is now one oh five p.m. The weather is hot and sunny, ninety-five degrees with a slight westerly breeze. Enjoy your stay and thank you for flying with us.''

Ignoring the flight attendant's spiel, David glanced out the window as the plane began its descent. From where he was sitting, he could pick out several landmarks, the most noticeable of which was the Washington Monument. The spire was like a finger pointing the way to heaven—or away from hell. In this city, it was always a toss-up as to which one was in power at the moment. A sense of timelessness hit him as he looked down at the great white dome of the nation's Capitol. Since its inception, so many people had dedicated their lives to making certain that the nation maintained itself as a democracy, while others had spent fortunes trying to manipulate and control it. David had seen both sides and right now wasn't too enamored with either. All he wanted was to enjoy what was left of his life—and he wanted to do it with Cara. God willing, it would happen.

By the time the plane touched down, he had the entire situation mapped out in his mind. He would send Frank another e-mail. The meeting would take place. And he knew just where it would happen. A little bit of Vietnam—the place where it all began.

The park surrounding the Vietnam War Memorial was spacious and at the right time of night fairly deserted. There was plenty of cover. Plenty of places where a man could stand without being detected. Frank's name was on the wall. He wondered if Frank had ever seen it, but he knew it was a hell of a feeling to know that the rest of the world had given up and forgotten you. It was the closest a living man could come to knowing what it was like to be a ghost—that the only tangible evidence of your life on this earth was a name engraved on black stone.

But David had something more now than he did the last time he'd come to this city. He had Cara again, and he was going to have his daughter. Almost a year ago he'd come to D.C. and left a rose at the wall beneath his brother's name. Now he was coming back to kill him. It was a nightmare of unspeakable proportions.

God help me.

He shuddered, and as he thought of what lay ahead amended the thought to, God help them both. If only Frank would have a change of heart. If by some miracle he would simply appear and turn himself in, David would be ecstatic. There was nothing he felt he needed to prove—to himself or to Frank—and he so desperately wanted to be free of the past.

"Sir?"

David looked up. The flight attendant had her hand on his shoulder, smiling down at him.

"Yes?"

"I have instructions to tell you that you will be met."

It didn't surprise him. The President was doing his part to help bring an end to this, too.

"Thank you," he said.

"You're welcome, sir. As soon as the plane lands, I will escort you to the door of the cockpit. You will be the first to exit."

He nodded again, ignoring the curious stares from the other first-class passengers.

She walked away, taking her seat at the front of the plane and preparing herself for the landing, as well.

A minute or so later, the plane was on the ground and taxiing toward the terminal. His flesh crawled, much in the same way it had in the jungles of Vietnam.

It was beginning.

As promised, the moment the Fasten Seat Belt sign went off, the attendant was at his seat. He stood, retrieved his bag from the overhead bin and moved toward the cockpit.

A short, heavyset man who'd been sitting across the aisle from David grumbled just loud enough to be heard about some people getting privileges when they'd all paid to fly first class. But when he met David's gaze, the grumble stilled.

For David, that man was nothing more than a fly in the ointment of his life. By the time his foot touched the exit ramp, he was forgotten. David emerged into the terminal with his bag on his shoulder and immediately found himself flanked by another duo of suited men. He didn't know their faces, but he knew who'd sent them.

"Sir, Federal Agent MaCauley. May I take your bag?"

He lifted it from David's shoulder without waiting for an answer.

"I'm Federal Agent Matthews. This way, sir," the other said. "We have a car waiting for you."

David nodded. There was no reason to chitchat. They didn't expect it and he wasn't in the mood.

The ride to the hotel was smooth and silent. Every now and then he would glance out the window from his seat in the back of the car, absently admiring the lush, green beauty of the surrounding forests. When they crossed the river, his pulse accelerated. The closer he came to the Wardman Park, the closer he came to his destiny.

A few minutes later they reached the hotel. Before he could get out, the agent on the passenger side was out and opening his door while the other agent took his bag from the trunk.

"This is as far as you go, men," David said. "I can handle it from here. Thank you."

"Yes, sir. You're welcome, sir," they said, and then disappeared as quickly as they had appeared.

David turned toward the hotel and started inside, only to be met at the doorway by another man, this time an employee of the hotel, who promptly relieved David of his bag again.

"Sir, you've already been checked in. If you'll follow me, I'll escort you to your suite."

David had been here before and barely glanced at the elegant lobby or the open bar beyond. As they turned left at the hallway to go toward the bank of elevators, a woman suddenly jumped up from a nearby chair and grabbed his arm.

"Hey! Long time no see," she said, and tried to give him a kiss.

David grabbed her arms, gently but forcefully preventing the move.

"I'm sorry. You have mistaken me for someone else," he said, and tried to walk away, but she persisted.

"No need to act like that," she said. "I kept our little secret."

David frowned. He wasn't in the mood for this.

"Lady, I don't know who are you, so if you will please excuse me, I'm on my way to my room."

"Come on, Larry, this isn't funny," she muttered.

"My name isn't Larry," he said and pulled out of her grasp.

She frowned and then furtively glanced around before pulling a pair of glasses from her shoulder bag. The moment she slid them up her nose, her expression changed.

"Oh, my! You're not Larry. Larry's eyes are brown." Then she giggled. "Sorry. My mistake."

David was already walking toward the elevator.

"Everything all right, sir?" the man asked.

David nodded. "A case of mistaken identity."

As the elevator doors slid shut, David realized the woman was nowhere in sight. He frowned as a warning went off in his head and then moments later shrugged it away.

At the moment David was entering his room, the woman was in a stall in the women's bathroom with her cell phone to her ear, waiting for her call to be answered.

"This is Sheila. He's here." She waited, listening intently to the man on the other end of the line, then she smiled. "You're welcome," she said. "If there's ever anything else I can do for you…well, let's just say…you know where to find me."

She hung up, strode out of the bathroom and out of the hotel, hailed a cab. Having done her part, she disappeared from David's life.

Frank Wilson shoved his cell phone in his pocket, silently cursing the weather for causing the delays. He was still at the Chicago airport and David was already in D.C. He bolted up from his seat and strode to the window. Outside, the black wall of thunderstorms still hovered overhead, while intermittent flashes of lightning continued to strike. As he watched, one bolt suddenly came out of nowhere, striking so close he was momentarily blinded by the flash.

Covering his face, he turned away, his gut in knots, his body shaking. It was too reminiscent of the fire that had nearly consumed him. When he started to return to his seat, he realized someone had taken it, which just added to the unsettled mood he was in.

Cursing beneath his breath, he headed for a newsstand a short distance away. He bought another paper and then ambled toward a restaurant, finally finding himself a seat at the bar.

"What'll it be?" the bartender asked, as Frank slid onto the bar stool.

"I'll have a dark lager and a hamburger."

"Coming up," the bartender said, and walked away.

Frank opened the paper and began to read. A short while later, his food arrived. He ate for sustenance, not pleasure, hardly noticing that the meat was dry and the bread too soft. When it began to fall apart in his hands, he shoved the plate aside and sat sipping his beer instead.

It wasn't until the man at his right laughed abruptly and made a comment to a friend about a real-life Dirty Harry that he began to listen. As he did, he realized they were discussing a recent incident in a small town in upstate New York. At that point, memory clicked, and he remembered hearing part of it on the news the night before. But it wasn't the incident itself that had captured his interest. It was the name of the man who had been credited with the rescues. He continued to eavesdrop.

"Yeah, it was a hell of a deal," the man was saying. "Walked into this supermarket with a handgun and took down three thugs who'd taken eleven people hostage."

His friend made a comment Frank couldn't hear, but when the man next to him answered, the hair suddenly rose on the back of his neck.

"Oh, hell, isn't that the truth," the man said. "I got the same name as him, but I sure don't have the balls to pull something like that. But here's the kicker, Joe. You know what my wife said? If she'd married that David Wilson instead of me, she probably wouldn't fall asleep during sex."

Both men laughed, but Frank's focus had moved past the joke. Granted, David Wilson was a very common name, yet he couldn't help wondering how many men with that name could pull off such an incident and walk away without a scratch. That kind of skill came from combat— and special forces training.

He dropped the newspaper and strode out of the bar, his mind racing. Could it be? Would David do something so brash as to call attention to himself in this way? And why would he resume using his real identity?

The moment he asked himself the question, he knew.

Of course.

David had walked away from SPEAR. He would have had to anyway since his identity had been compromised. But why upstate New York? What could he have possibly been doing there if he was so focused on their meeting? Frank's mind was racing. *What would I do if I thought I was going to die?*

I would want to see Martha.

The answer startled him. But David didn't have a Martha. He'd never married, and their parents were dead. To Frank's knowledge, he didn't have a personal tie on this earth.

At that point, he froze, then inhaled slowly. There was a flaw in that thought.

To his knowledge.

That's where Frank's mistake had begun. Just because he didn't know about any personal ties didn't mean they didn't exist. It occurred to him then that he'd never really explored that side of David's life. He'd been so busy trying to find him, then take him down from within SPEAR, that he'd never thought about investigating him from a personal angle.

He looked up, gazing blankly at the people passing by him and the others sitting glumly in their seats, as stranded by nature as he. Despite the fact that David had summoned him to D.C. and was already there waiting, Frank didn't want to pass up an opportunity to turn the knife after he'd plunged it into David's chest.

He turned, searching for a place where he could make some calls without being overheard, then realized there was no such place. Considering the small risk he would take in making the calls, he headed for a bank of pay phones, opting for one of the cubicles. He waited for one to vacate then slipped into the seat and took out his cell phone, pausing momentarily as he debated about who to call first. A few moments later, he punched in a series of numbers then waited for his call to be answered.

"Petroski Heating Oil, Pete speaking."

"I need a favor."

"Like what?" Pete asked warily.

"There was an incident in a small town in upstate New York yesterday. Something about a man rescuing a bunch of hostages from a supermarket."

"Oh, yeah, I heard about that. Some hotshot, huh?"

Frank frowned. "Maybe, but that's not the point. Is your brother-in-law still on the police force on Wykomis?"

"Yeah, but he ain't gonna go for—"

"Just shut up and listen to me," Frank said. "All I want is some information. I want to know the name of that town and what this David Wilson was doing there. I want to know how old he is, what he looks like, and was he just passing through or visiting. Get it?"

"Yeah, sure," Pete said. "I can do that. Give me an hour and I'll see what I can come up with. How can I reach you?"

"I'll call you back," Frank said, and disconnected.

He moved from the pay phones to a seat near his gate. This time when he sat down, his patience had taken itself to a new level. If there was a way to make David's life more miserable before he died, it would be Frank's pleasure.

Outside, the storms continued to hover over the city of Chicago, but it was the storm inside Frank Wilson's heart that was the most dangerous. Neither wind nor time was going to move it away. Only the sight of his brother's blood was going to put out the fire of his hate.

He sat without moving, his eye on a clock across from

where he was sitting. When the minute hand finally ticked over for the sixtieth time, Frank took his cell phone from his pocket and made the call.

Pete answered on the first ring. "This is Pete."

"Talk to me," Frank said.

"David Wilson, mid to late fifties. Dark hair with some gray at the temples. A little over six feet tall and physically fit. They're calling him Rambo or something like that. He was picking up this woman and when she didn't come out, he went in after her."

"What woman?" Frank asked.

"Her name is Cara Justice. Gossip has it that she had his kid way back when. He was staying at her house when the incident occurred."

A slow smile began to spread across Frank's face, crumpling the scars and pulling the flesh until the smile turned into a grimace.

"The name of the town, please."

"Chiltingham, in upstate New York. It's up by the Finger Lakes region. Nearest airport would be at Canandaigua."

"Your check is in the mail," Frank said softly, and disconnected.

Then he stood abruptly and strode to the check-in desk.

"I want to change my flight," he said.

"But sir, none of the planes are taking off now," the clerk said.

"I know that," he said softly. "But when they do…"

The clerk felt herself resisting the urge to shiver as the man thrust his ticket across the counter and continued.

"I need to reroute from D.C. to Canandaigua, New York."

"Yes, sir," she said. "You do know there will be an extra fee for—"

"Just do it," Frank said. "Money is no object."

Chapter 12

It was just after nine the next morning when Frank's plane landed at Canandaigua Airport. He disembarked without notice, just one of the twenty-three passengers to arrive, and proceeded through the terminal to rent a car. Within the hour, and armed with a map of the area, he drove out of the airport toward Chiltingham. He had no plans beyond finding Cara Justice's home. After that, he would let impulse lead him.

A couple of hours later, he entered the city limits and was surprised by the quaint New England charm of the small country town. Saltbox houses abounded, some painted a pure robin's-egg blue with white trim, others in varying shades of pastels and whites. Lawns and hedges were neatly trimmed and the flower boxes at the downstairs windows of the houses overflowed with splashes of color.

He tried to picture the man known as Jonah living in a nondescript place like this, but the image wouldn't come.

He reminded himself they'd grown up in a place not unlike this. He sneered. So little brother was trying to return to his roots. Too damned bad.

His stomach grumbled, a reminder that he hadn't eaten since yesterday afternoon, so he pulled in at the curb in front of a small café and went inside.

The scent of frying bacon and coffee only increased his hunger as he took a seat in a corner booth. Before he could reach for the menu resting between the napkin dispenser and the salt and pepper shakers, a waitress was at the booth with a pot of fresh coffee.

"Coffee, sir?" she asked.

He nodded and turned over the cup already at the place setting.

"Do you know what you want, or would you like a little time to look at the menu?"

"Bring me a couple of eggs over easy, bacon and hash browns and some whole wheat toast."

"Yes, sir. Would you care for juice?"

Frank looked up at her and smiled. "Sure, why not? How about grapefruit?"

The waitress nodded, although her attention had been transferred from the order she was taking to the mass of scars on the side of his face.

"It isn't catching," Frank said, taking some satisfaction in her embarrassment as she hurried away.

But the incident only served to remind him of why he'd come.

An hour later he drove out of town with a full belly and the directions to Cara Justice's home. It was relatively easy to find. His confirmation that he was at the right place was the name on the mailbox at the end of the drive.

Justice.

He smiled. How ironically perfect. That's what he'd come for—some justice. He paused at the mailbox to look at the house, making a quick assessment of the layout of the grounds. Since there was no need advertising his presence yet, he would come back after dark. As he put the car in gear to drive away, a woman came around the corner of the house with a garden hose in her hand. He hit the brakes, his eyes narrowing as he watched her watering the shrubs next to the house.

So, you take good care of what belongs to you. That's good. My Martha was a woman like that.

Suddenly angry with himself for even thinking of Martha and this woman in the same breath, he accelerated angrily and sped away.

At the sound of flying gravel, Cara turned, noticing a tan sedan as it sped past her house. She shook her head as she returned to her task, thinking that some people should never be allowed to drive.

As the water began to flow, a small fly buzzed at the corner of her eye and she turned to brush it away. When she saw her reflection in the windows above the shrubs, she couldn't help but flinch. The bruise on the side of her face was huge now, a dark, purplish-green. It was also the main reason she'd skipped going to church services this morning. If she'd gone, she would have had to talk about the incident at the supermarket and she wasn't in the mood. And there were bound to be questions as to why David wasn't with her, and where he had gone, and she darned sure wasn't in the mood to talk about him. So she was here, watering her plants and fussing at flies as if those were the only important things in her life, when in reality she wanted to scream. At least she would have Bethany and her family as dinner guests tonight. The vitality of their growing family should be enough to keep her mind off of what was happening with David, if only for a while.

A short while later, she went back inside and began making a strawberry tart for tonight's dessert.

* * *

Frank had always liked the dark. Even as a kid, he'd felt safe within the thick velvet shadows. It gave him a feeling similar to that of being cosseted beneath a warm comforter on a cold winter night. Tonight, he had the added adrenaline rush of a foray into new territory. He'd driven his car off the road into the woods about a quarter of a mile below Cara Justice's house and now he stood at the edge of the clearing, watching as she bid her company goodbye.

From the way they were all behaving, he took them to be family—a man, a woman and two young girls. He moved closer, staying within the tree line but wanting to hear what was being said. When he heard Cara Justice call the woman Bethany, he flinched. By God, two birds with one stone. If he had a rifle, he could fix it right now. David's woman. David's child. The perfect justice. If he popped both of them, he might just walk away from baby brother and let him live with the hell of knowing he was the cause of their deaths.

Then his flights of fancy settled. No need to make hasty decisions. The only certainty in his life was meting out a justice of his own. He leaned forward, listening intently as the people bid their goodbyes.

"Dinner was great, Mom," Bethany said.

"No, it was fantastic," Tom added, and Cara chuckled.

"I sent you the rest of the strawberry tart, so you don't have to keep bragging," she said.

Her son-in-law laughed. "You don't think I laid it on too thick?"

"Well, yes, but it was unnecessary. You were going to get the leftovers anyway."

Cara leaned in the back seat of the car and blew kisses to her two granddaughters.

"You're going to have to come spend the night with me at least one more time before school starts," she said.

"Oh, Nanny, don't even mention school," Rachel said.

"No school," her little sister, Kelly, echoed, although she wouldn't even attend preschool for another year.

Cara laughed and then stood back as they drove away, waving until the taillights of Tom's car disappeared.

Rubbing her arms with her hands and wishing David was here to hold her close, she took a deep breath and looked at the sky. The night was clear, the sky littered with stars.

"I'm here, darling, under the same sky, looking at the same stars. Just come home safely," she said softly, then dropped her head and said a brief, silent prayer.

An owl hooted from a nearby tree and she turned to look, hoping for a glimpse of the nighttime visitor, when something told her she was no longer alone. She turned abruptly, raking the area with a nervous gaze, but saw nothing to cause her alarm. Still the notion wouldn't go away. Uneasy, she hurried inside, locking the door behind her, then quickly moved throughout the rest of the house, making sure all the windows and doors were locked. Only after she'd set the security alarm did the hackles on her neck begin to settle. By the time she had turned out the lights and was moving toward her bedroom, she had almost convinced herself she'd been imagining things.

Almost—but not quite.

A short while later as she lay in bed, drifting between restlessness and sleep, the feeling came back. But it was too brief to hang on to. Exhaustion claimed her, and she slept.

Frank had the license number of Bethany's car. It would be simple enough to hack into the DMV and find her address. She would come later, after he'd dealt with her mother.

He waited until Cara had turned out the lights before making his move, still impressed by the fact that she'd sensed his presence. That wasn't something he'd expected. But then he thought of the man David had become and decided he wouldn't have settled for any ordinary woman. Jonah had to have a mate comparable to his talents.

A frisson of anticipation rippled through Frank's body. It stood to reason she would be perceptive enough to sense something amiss in her world. Would she sense him again—when he was standing at the foot of her bed?

When more than an hour had passed, Frank was satisfied that enough time had passed. He started toward her house, thankful that she didn't own a dog. He hated dogs.

For more than half an hour, he moved around outside, looking in windows, peering into the place where David had left his heart. From the little he could see, the house looked warm and inviting, and again he thought of Martha and ached. People lied when they claimed the passage of time made a loss easier to bear. For him, it was the opposite. The longer he was without her, the emptier his world became.

When he discovered the windows to Cara's bedroom, he ran his fingers along the edges, just to check and make sure they were locked, which they were. It didn't stop him from watching her through the part in the curtains. He watched for several long minutes until he was certain she was soundly asleep, then he headed for the electrical box he'd seen on the backside of the house. He knew the house was protected by a security alarm, but for a man who'd hacked into top secret computer files of the United States government, bypassing a personal security system was simple.

A few snips here, a couple of connections there and he

was in. After that, he picked the lock on her front door and walked inside.

Once in, he stood for a moment, letting his vision adjust to the absence of light, until he could easily make out shapes of furniture as well as a hall leading toward the back of the house.

As he began to move, he smiled at the thickness of the wall-to-wall carpeting. Perfect covering to mask his steps, should she be a light sleeper.

He took a small penlight from his pocket and raked the walls with the tiny beam, more out of curiosity than anything else. He'd seen what Cara Justice looked like. Now he wanted to know what turned her on. Did she like bright, vibrant colors, or was she as subdued as she appeared?

As the light fell on the mantel, he saw the pictures she'd displayed and moved closer. From what he could tell, she had three, not just one child as he'd first believed, and she'd obviously been married to someone other than David. Two of the children looked like the stocky blond man standing beside her in one of the pictures. But it was the tall, slender woman with dark hair that Frank was interested in—the one who looked like David.

Bethany.

Nice name. Probably a nice enough woman. Damned shame his brother's blood ran in her veins.

He moved the penlight along the mantel, and when it fell on the snapshot of David with the fish, he caught himself from grunting aloud. It was a kick in the gut feeling of déjà vu that made him sick to his stomach.

David was laughing, making fun of the size of the fish on his line, and before Frank thought, he was grinning, too.

Stupid little shrimp of a fish. Why the hell would he want to have his picture taken with something like that?

And then he jerked as if he'd been slapped, reminding

himself of why he was here. He was wondering about David when he should have been asking himself what the hell was wrong with him. He didn't give a damn about what David liked to do for recreation. It didn't even matter that David had looked so happy, or so at peace. He set the picture back on the mantel and turned away.

It, by God, does not matter.

Making himself focus on why he had come, he headed for the hall, remembering the direction of Cara's bedroom as he went. It should be the one at the far end of the house. Sure enough he was right.

He stood quietly just outside the doorway, listening to the soft, even sounds of her breathing, and checked his pocket for the knife that he carried. He favored knives over guns, two to one. They were swift and silent killers, much cleaner than a gun. Bullets always tore up the body. A knife, when used properly, could empty a body of blood within a minute, often less.

Confident that she was still asleep, he took two steps to the right and then one forward, then smiled.

He was inside her bedroom.

He could tell she was above average height and quite slender, although she lay on her side with her back to the door.

A dim glow from the outside security light pierced the gap in the curtains, highlighting the hair spilling across her pillow. From where he was standing, it looked like gossamer, and he had a sudden desire to see if it was as soft as it looked.

Resisting his carnal urges, he moved to the foot of her bed instead, and then slowed his breathing as he watched her sleep. Her breasts were full, her skin firm. She was a woman in every sense of the word. As he stood, watching her sleep, his palms began to sweat. It had been a long, long time since he'd lain with a woman like that.

She shifted in her sleep, quietly sighing and then rolling over onto her back.

He froze. Only when he was certain she was still asleep did he shift position again, this time moving slightly toward the doorway for a better view of her face.

God. She was beautiful.

He shivered with sudden anger, unable to believe that a woman other than Martha could awake any sort of emotion. His hands curled into fists and he tried to make himself move. In one single leap, he could be in her bed, lying on top of her, hearing her scream. He could have her with ease, savoring her panic as he whispered what he was going to do to her and her lover. It would be easy, so easy.

As a jealous lust for what was David's gained momentum, he leaned forward. Then he heard her take a deep breath and exhale on a sob. He paused again, frustrated by his hesitation.

So she's grieving. So what? So am I.

He took another step forward, his fists uncurling, his fingers itching to encircle the fragility of her neck.

Frank...I'll always love you.

He jerked as if he'd been slapped. Martha's voice was as loud in his head as if she was standing beside him.

His eyes narrowed. He wondered what she would think if she saw him now. Would she still love him, or would she look upon him with loathing for what he'd become?

As he watched, a tear rolled down the side of Cara's face then he heard her whisper a name.

David.

He cursed silently. Damn her. Damn her to hell. Fingering the blade of his knife, he started across the floor.

Bethany sat up in bed.

One moment she'd been sound asleep, and the next she was wide awake and cognizant. It was a skill she'd perfected after the birth of her first child, and it had yet to prove her wrong.

Glancing over at Tom, who was still sound asleep, she smiled to herself and then slipped out of bed. The roof could fall in and he wouldn't hear it. Out of habit, she reached for her robe as she left their bedroom.

As she entered her daughters' bedroom, she instinctively moved toward Kelly's bed first. As the youngest, she was still prone to more of the childhood illnesses than her sister, Rachel, who was almost ten.

But a quick check of her daughter's cool forehead eased her worries. Obviously, it wasn't Kelly who'd awakened her. She turned then, moving quietly to Rachel's bedside, but she, too, was resting quietly and fast asleep.

Frowning, she left their room, pausing momentarily in the hallway to listen. The house sounds were normal.

A clock ticking.

A tree branch scratching at the eaves of the house.

The intermittent sound of Tom's occasional snore.

Nothing that should have awakened her in such a manner.

Shivering now from nerves rather than cold, she wrapped her arms around herself and thought about waking Tom. But he had to go to work tomorrow and she resisted the notion. Telling herself that she must have been dreaming, she started toward their bedroom.

No sooner had she begun to move than she heard the faint sound of a board squeak, and when it did, her heart skipped a beat. There was a loose floorboard beneath the kitchen linoleum that squeaked just like that as she stood at the kitchen sink and another by the doorway leading into the living room.

Now she was scared.

Bolting into the bedroom, she shook Tom awake, then put her hand over his mouth and whispered in his ear.

"I think someone is in the house."

Tom's eyes widened. Without speaking, he rolled out of bed and hurried toward their closet. Taking a box down from the top shelf, he unlocked it, took out a loaded handgun and motioned for her to call 911.

"What about the girls?" she whispered.

"Call the police first and then get them," he mouthed back.

Bethany watched in horror as Tom slipped out of their bedroom, then bolted for the phone. Seconds later, the 911 dispatcher came on the line.

"Nine one one. What is your emergency?"

"I think someone is in our house," Bethany whispered.

"Ma'am, are you alone?"

"No, my husband, Tom, is here, too. He's gone into the front of the house to check. He has a gun."

"Is your address one oh seven Sunset Drive?"

"Yes. Please hurry."

"Yes, ma'am, please stay on the line while I dispatch the call."

Now Bethany's heart was pounding. She needed to be across the hall with her children.

"Hello? Hello?" she whispered.

"Yes, ma'am, I'm still here," the dispatcher said.

"I need to be across the hall with my girls," she whispered.

"Ma'am, I need you to stay on the line with me. There is a police unit in your area. It should be there in a couple of minutes."

"Oh, God," Bethany whispered. "That could be too late."

"Just stay calm and listen to me, please. What's your name?"

"Bethany Howell."

"Okay, Bethany, tell me what you hear."

"Nothing now. I don't even hear Tom."

She started to shake. What if something had happened to him? What if someone was already coming this way? She needed to get to the girls. She needed to get them out of the house.

"Please. I need to get my daughters. I need to get them out of the house."

"Ma'am. Please. I need you to stay calm and stay quiet. Your husband might hear you moving around and think you were the thief. We don't want any accidental shootings, all right?"

Lord. She hadn't thought of that.

"All right, but please hurry."

The moment the board squeaked, Frank flinched. Seconds later, he heard bedsprings give and then the soft pat-pat sounds of bare feet on tile. His fingers curled around the knife in his hand as he moved toward the doorway. Moments later, he saw the woman come out of the bedroom and walk down the hall into another room.

His eyes narrowed angrily. That woman was David's daughter—but she was also his niece.

A good mother always checks on the children first.

The thought came out of nowhere and then he realized it was something his mother used to say when she would come in to tell him and David good night.

Son of a bitch. Why am I dwelling on all of these people who are already dead? They don't matter anymore. I need payback, not a stroll down memory lane.

Moments later, the woman exited the bedroom and stopped in the hallway. Instinctively, he slid into the shadows, and as he did, another board squeaked. He rolled his eyes, wondering why the hell these people hadn't nailed down the floors like they should have done. He stood there in silence, well aware he'd been made. Should he run, or just finish what he came here to do?

When she bolted into the bedroom, he hesitated only moments before his decision was made.

Bethany stood at the window, the phone still at her ear, watching and praying for the police to arrive. At that moment, she got a glimpse of flashing lights topping the hill just beyond their house, then they disappeared behind the trees.

She started to cry softly.

"They're here. They're here," she whispered.

"Ma'am, are you saying the police are at your door?"

"No, but I saw their lights on the hill."

"Don't go to the door, ma'am. Wait for them to knock, okay? They'll search the outside of the house to check for signs of entry before they attempt to come inside."

"Yes, all right," she said, her heart a little lighter now that she knew help was here.

Seconds later, she heard the crunch of gravel as the car pulled in the drive.

"They're outside now," she said.

"Just stay with me, ma'am."

"Yes, all right," Bethany whispered. Then to her horror, she heard her oldest daughter call out.

"Mother! Mother!"

"My daughter is awake," Bethany said. "I've got to get her before she walks into danger. I won't hang up, but I'm going after them."

Without waiting for permission, she bolted out of the room and down the hall. Rachel was sitting up in bed, rubbing her eyes.

"Mother, there's a police car outside the house."

"Yes, I know," she said softly. "I'm going to get Kelly

and we're going to go to Mother and Daddy's room, understand?''

The confusion on her daughter's face turned to fear as her voice started to shake.

"Mommy...what's wrong?"

"Maybe nothing," she said. "Daddy's just checking the house." She scooped Kelly up in her arms and laid her across her shoulder and then grabbed Rachel's hand. "Come with me, baby, and don't talk anymore."

In seconds, she was across the hall and inside her bedroom. Quietly, she shut the door and then laid Kelly down on the bed, pulled Rachel into her lap and then picked up the phone.

"I'm back," she said.

"Are your children with you?" the dispatcher asked.

"Yes."

"Where is your husband?"

Bethany wanted to scream. Instead, she took a deep breath and made herself focus.

"I don't know."

"You're doing fine," the dispatcher said. "Tell me...what are your children's names?"

"Rachel and Kelly."

"Rachel Howell? Is she in the fourth grade?"

"She will be," Bethany said.

"I know her. My son, Billy, is her age. My name is Jenn Parker. My dad owns the bakery."

The image of a familiar face to go with the voice on the other end of the line was somehow encouraging.

"Jenn, I'm so scared."

"You're doing really good," the dispatcher said. "The police tell me they're going to your front door. Is there someone there to let them in?"

"Tom. Tom should be there."

"All right. Just stay with me a minute until I know they're inside."

Bethany could hear the faint but unmistakable sounds of someone knocking at the door. She caught herself holding her breath, praying that the sounds would stop, because that would mean that Tom had let them inside. They knocked again. Tears were rolling down her face.

Please God, don't let anything happen to my husband.

"No one is answering," the dispatcher said. "The police are asking me to tell you that they're going to come inside."

"The door is locked," Bethany said.

"They know. Just stay where you are, okay?"

"Yes," Bethany said, then dropped her head and started to sob. Something was terribly wrong.

David paced the floor of his room—from the bed to the windows and back again. He couldn't sleep. Every instinct he had told him something was wrong. What if Simon saw the broadcast of the robbery? What if he put two and two together and went looking for answers? Then he relaxed. No way! Simon never even knew about Cara, so he couldn't know about Bethany either.

Damn it to hell, but he hated being cooped up in this place. He was no better than a caged rat, waiting for someone to open a door so he could make a run for the cheese. Only the cheese in this maze was his brother, and his brother was taking his own sweet time about answering the e-mail that had been sent out.

Damn him, David thought. *Damn him to hell.*

He started for the phone, the need to talk to Cara uppermost in his mind, but then stopped. It was after three in the morning. Just because he couldn't sleep didn't mean he needed to disturb her rest. He hoped she'd taken a sedative to help her relax. The kidnapping and the assault were so recent, he knew she would still be suffering from the memories of the incident. Even worse, it galled him to know that just when she needed him most, he'd left her alone.

Damn Frank Wilson to hell and back. Why had he survived? What possible good had his existence proved?

Then he thought of Frank's daughter, Lise Meldrum, who by now was probably Mrs. Russell Devane. Her life was proof that there had still been some good left in Frank—that he'd at least been capable of loving a woman long enough to father a child. From what he knew, Frank's wife had been dead for years and Lise had been running their Australian cattle station in her father's absence. If Frank had died in that fire all those years ago, then Lise would never have been born.

David dropped onto the side of the bed, his shoulders slumped with fatigue. He glanced at the clock one more time and then rolled over onto his side. The least he could do was close his eyes and rest.

Within minutes, he was asleep.

Chapter 13

It started to rain just as Frank reached his car. Hurrying before his clothes got all wet, he opened the door and jumped inside. But he didn't bother looking back to see if he'd been followed. He'd already been out of the house and into the woods before the police cruiser had even pulled into the yard. As he locked the car door, he took a gun out of his pocket and laid it beside the knife he'd been carrying.

He paused a moment, resting his forehead against the steering wheel and letting the adrenaline rush settle as his heartbeat shifted into a normal rhythm. When he finally looked up, he was smiling. The gun he'd taken from Bethany's husband was out of habit. He'd never left a weapon on a victim before and he wasn't starting now, but as he'd been running through the woods, a thought had occurred. Now that he was on his way to D.C., how poetic would it be to kill David with his own daughter's gun?

He liked the idea. In fact, he loved it. But getting it on

a plane could be a problem. He started the car and quickly drove away. Considering what he'd left behind, lingering in the area wasn't wise, but as he drove, his mind was still sorting through the possibilities that would yield him what he wanted.

The streets were deserted as he entered Chiltingham on his way to the Canandaigua Airport. Even though no one was in sight, he still took great care not to speed or run any lights. The last thing he needed was to get caught with a stolen weapon.

On his way out of town, he passed a billboard advertising Fedex. About a half a mile later, the significance of that sign suddenly hit him, and a plan began to evolve. Now he knew how to get the gun to D.C. All he needed was a small box and some packing and the address of his hotel. With a little luck, it would be there waiting for him when he arrived.

It was mid-morning the next day when an envelope suddenly appeared beneath the door in David's room. Still in the shower and unaware of what had happened, he didn't notice until his breakfast arrived.

Later, as he was dressing, someone knocked on his door. Tucking a rugby shirt into the waistband of his slacks, he went to answer it, and as he did, he noticed the envelope and picked it up.

"Who is it?" David asked.

"Room service," a man answered.

Although he was expecting the food, he still looked through the peephole before opening the door. A bellhop smiled a good morning as he pushed a food-laden cart into the room.

"Where would you like this, sir?"

"On the table by the window will be fine," David said,

as he signed the check and handed it to the bellhop, along with a generous tip.

"Thank you, sir. When you've finished, ring guest services and we'll come and remove the dishes. Enjoy your meal."

When he was gone, David sat down before the food, surprised to find he was actually hungry. He laid the letter aside for the moment and spread some jelly on his toast before tackling the first bite of his eggs. When he had partially satiated his hunger, he took a drink of coffee and then picked up the letter. Curious, he leaned back in the chair as he slit the flap, unprepared for what was inside. Abruptly, he sat up with a thump and reached for the phone.

"Front desk. How may I help you, Mr. Wilson?"

"Someone left a note under my door this morning. I want to talk to who put it there."

"Let me connect you with the mail office."

A few seconds later a woman answered. David repeated his request. There was a slight pause, as if she was checking her records.

"I'm sorry, Mr. Wilson, but we have no record of a letter being sent to your room."

"Are you sure?"

"Yes, sir, I'm sure. I've been on duty since six this morning. I would have known."

"Thank you," David said, and hung up.

His food no longer appealed, his appetite completely gone. Damn it to hell. Frank had once again regained the upper hand. He'd found David, had some flunky deliver a message and walked away without notice. As he reread the letter, his stomach knotted.

O two hundred hours tonight, little brother. At the Wall.

David laid down the note, his gut in knots. How ironic that it was both their intentions to meet at the same place.

The Vietnam Memorial, otherwise known as the Wall, was fitting. A symbol of where it all began.

He stood abruptly, gathered his room key and wallet and then picked up his tray and set it in the hall. He would meet Frank at 2:00 a.m. as he'd requested, but he had some reconnoitering in the area that he wanted to do first and he needed to rent a car.

The day was hot, the wind brisk, and still they came. From the steps of the Lincoln Memorial where David was standing, hundreds of people could be seen milling about the grassy mall. Some were taking pictures, others laughing and talking, pointing with excitement at the surrounding monuments. Teenagers abounded in groups and he remembered that age—the awkwardness and lack of respect for anything or anyone older than themselves.

As for the veterans, they were easy to pick out. They were the ones who stood the longest, spoke the least and quite often left with tears in their eyes. And then there were their widows and families, tenderly stroking stone and marble that had been set in their loved one's honor because it was all they had left to touch.

The long, crystal-clear waters of the gazing pool that lay between the Lincoln and the Washington monuments reflected the surrounding treetops, as well as a clear, cloudless sky. At the north end of the pool, David watched a flock of circling pigeons as they landed on the greens and then proceeded to the water for a drink. The setting was idyllic—a picture-perfect day. It seemed obscene that before the night was over, either he or Frank would most likely die in this place.

Abruptly, he adjusted his sunglasses and took the steps downward, angling to the left as he went. He'd been at the Wall many times before, but never with the need to lay out an ambush.

As he approached it, a wave of guilt washed over him. That he was actually coming to this place with such a heinous plot in mind seemed sacrilegious, yet he'd been given no choice. Even if he'd been inclined to change the game plan, it was too late now. The wheels of his destiny had been set in motion. All he had to do was make sure he wasn't run over and killed in the process.

Anxious to get this over with, he sidestepped a couple pushing a stroller, then moved past a group of teenagers. As he neared the Wall, he came up behind an elderly couple trying to negotiate the downward incline. The old man was using a walker and his wife was trying to hold it upright, since it had a tendency to roll faster than either of them could walk.

At that moment, the last thing he wanted was personal contact with anyone, but his conscience wouldn't let him ignore them.

"Need some help, sir?" he asked, and then gripped the front of the walker and proceeded to slow it down so the old couple could keep up.

The woman's face was pink from exertion and the smile she gave David was enough to make him sorry he'd even hesitated to help.

"Oh, thank you, son. We didn't know this was so steep. Matthew's walker was about to take him for a ride."

Her youthful giggle surprised David, and he caught himself smiling back.

"Have you been here before?" he asked.

Her smile crumpled. "No. We always meant to, but we live so far away. We're from Idaho, you know. Our son Dennis's name is here. Matthew wanted to see it before—"

She didn't finish what she'd been going to say, but David knew what she meant.

"Got cancer," the old man suddenly offered, as he

scooted along under David's guidance. "I reckon I'll die of old age before I die of the cancer, though."

David didn't know what to say. Their optimism in the face of such adversity shamed him.

"We never know what life's going to hand us, do we?" he finally said, and then changed the subject. "Do you know what section your son's name is in?"

The old woman gave him a scrap of paper she'd been holding.

"The lady back at the information booth gave that to us."

He read the name, the section and row and then turned toward the Wall, checking to see how far along they'd come.

"It's a little bit farther down," he said. "Can you make it?"

"Me and Shirley made it this far. I reckon I can go a little farther," Matthew said.

A few yards down the slope, David stopped.

"Just a minute, sir. It should be right along here."

The old man turned his walker so it would no longer roll, and then stared at the Wall, suddenly overwhelmed by the expanse of names that seemed to go on forever.

"We sure weren't the only ones who grieved, were we, Shirley?"

His wife leaned her head against his shoulder, tears streaming down her face.

Then David turned. "Here. His name is here."

They stared at the name, as if trying to conjure up an image to go with it, but he could see their eyes were blurred by tears.

"It's been such a long time," Shirley said. "I thought I'd cried myself out years ago."

"Yes, ma'am," David said softly, and handed her his handkerchief. "I know what you mean."

Matthew looked at him then, judging him with all the wisdom of his eighty-plus years.

"You got kin on this wall, too?"

"Yes, sir."

"Damn shame, that's what it is," he muttered, and then took out his own handkerchief and blew his nose while his wife began fumbling in her handbag. When she pulled out a camera, David knew what she intended.

"Ma'am, if you would allow me, I'd be glad to take your picture."

"I want to stand beside my boy's name," Shirley said, as she patted at her hair, trying to smooth down the white, flyaway fluff that the breeze had disturbed.

"The names don't show up too well on photographs," David said. "But if Matthew will turn just a little bit this way," David said, easing the old man and the walker a little closer to the wall, "and if you'll stand on this side, you can put your hand on your son's name. That way it will be easier for you to see it when the picture is developed."

Shirley nodded, but as she reached toward the name, her gnarled fingers tracing the letters, her little face crumpled. David looked away, waiting for her to contain her emotions.

"I'm ready now," she announced.

He took a few steps backward and lifted the camera to his face.

The image caught within the parameters of the lens almost sent him to his knees.

A dying father.

A grieving mother.

And all that was left of their son was his name on a wall.

He made himself focus and then took a deep breath.

"On the count of three," he said. "One. Two."

He snapped the picture.

"Take one more," Shirley said. "Just in case."

He took the second one, and when he handed her the camera, she gave him back his handkerchief and then gave him a hug.

"Thank you, son," she said. "And we're sorry for your loss."

David nodded, but there wasn't anything he could say. His loss? For years, he believed that he'd lost much more than a brother. Until last week, when Cara Justice had taken him back into her life and her heart, he'd almost lost his faith in God.

David started to help them along when Matthew shook his head.

"It's uphill the rest of the way and I can push better than I can run. We'll make it from here."

They meandered away, talking with animation, delighted that their quest was complete, and as they walked, David noticed that when one of them faltered, the other was there on which to lean.

A knot rose in his throat, swelling and burning until he thought he would choke. When he turned back to the Wall, he found himself looking through a thick blur of tears. Instead of looking for Frank's name, he bowed his head and closed his eyes.

And so he stood within the silence of his own heart, absorbing the peace of the monument and giving homage to the men who'd fought, those who'd died and those who were forever lost. He lost all track of time, freeing his mind of everything and feeling a cleansing from within that he'd never known before.

Finally, he lifted his head and as he started to leave, the hair on the back of his neck suddenly crawled. The sensation was old but familiar. He knew he was being watched.

Remembering the letter he'd found under his door, he turned, eyeing everyone who passed, but saw no one who set off any internal alarms. Convinced he wasn't imagining things, he began scanning the surrounding area. Again, no one person stood out in the crowds that should cause this alarm.

Still uneasy, he began to walk toward the east, coming out of the walkway and up onto the sidewalk. At the crest of the hill, he paused again. The feeling was still there.

A woman screamed loudly off to his right, shrieking her disapproval at her children. Instinctively, David turned toward the sound, and as he did, he caught a flash of movement within a cluster of trees a couple of hundred yards to his left.

There. That's where it was coming from.

It had to be Frank.

He lifted his head, his chin thrust forward in a gesture of defiance.

Frank smiled derisively as he watched his little brother playing Boy Scout to the old man and woman. When they finally moved on and he saw David bowing his head, he sneered.

"Pray, you son of a bitch. You're going to need all the help you can get."

When David suddenly looked up and then turned in place, he realized something had spooked him, but what? Adjusting his binoculars, he began to scan the area, too, searching for answers. When he looked back, David was no longer in sight. A slight spurt of panic came and went as he stepped out from behind a cluster of trees for a closer look. A few seconds later, David emerged from the walkway, pausing at the crest of the hill. As he did, Frank breathed a sigh of relief. It wasn't as though he was going to do anything here—too damned many witnesses, but he liked being the one in control, and being the observer gave him a sense of power.

He moved a step backward, and as he did, he saw David's focus shift. Cursing his carelessness, he retreated behind the trees, then lifted the binoculars, adjusting the focus to make up for David's new location.

When his brother's face came into focus, he jerked as if he'd been shot. David was looking straight at him. His heart started to hammer. His hands started to shake.

"You bastard…you arrogant bastard."

Through the lens, David stood tall and straight, his chin thrust forward in a dare-to-take-me attitude—his feet slightly apart, as if bracing himself for battle. Frank knew that he should move, but he couldn't tear his gaze away. At that moment, the truth of who his brother had become finally hit. Intellectually, he'd known David had been the omnipotent Jonah for several years, but looking at him now, he realized what that entailed.

The man he saw was a modern-day warrior, broad-shouldered and lean, hardened by the years and by life. The word invincible came to mind, but he shoved it aside, because that meant unbeatable, and Frank Wilson wasn't a man who accepted defeat.

To his utter dismay, as he watched, David took off his sunglasses, smiled directly at him, then turned his back and walked away. For Frank, it was a slap-in-the-face gesture he couldn't ignore.

"You'll pay, little brother, and I'll be curious to see how wide you smile when you see your daughter's gun pointed at your head."

Seconds later, he was gone.

David was calmer now than he'd been since this hell began. By this time tomorrow, it would be over. Instead of ordering room service, he decided to go down to the hotel restaurant for dinner. He came out of the elevator and past the bar with nothing but a medium-rare steak on his mind when he suddenly flashed on Cara's face. He was seeing her as she'd looked on the morning he left her sleeping, her hair in gentle disarray, her hands cupped beneath her chin as if she was praying. He wanted to hear her voice—to say something witty that would elicit that throaty chuckle. But if he called her now, before this was over, she would take it as a defeated farewell, rather than the selfish gesture it actually was. So he told himself to suck it up and kept on walking.

A short while later, a hostess seated him at a table for one and laid food and wine menus on the table. He ordered a glass of wine and then opened the menu. A small note was attached at the top, with one word printed in bold, black ink. *Bang.* Anger followed shock as he bolted from his table and headed toward the door, grabbing the hostess by the arm and spinning her around. It wasn't the woman who had just seated him.

"Where is she?" he yelled.

"Sir?"

David saw the fear on her face and immediately regretted his actions as he turned her loose.

"I'm sorry. I didn't mean to frighten you, but I need to talk to the other hostess. Where did she go?"

"There is no other hostess, sir. I'm the only one on duty tonight."

David lowered his voice when all his instincts made him want to scream.

"Not two minutes ago, a woman was standing right where you're standing. She picked up the menus and took me to that table in the back near the windows."

She looked at David as if he'd gone mad.

"Two minutes ago, I was in the kitchen. There was no one else here."

David slapped his leg in frustration and bolted out of the restaurant, then stopped about ten feet from the door. There were at least four different directions she could have gone, and each one of them led outside. As he stood, a sense of calm began to settle. He shook his head and then almost smiled. That was so like Frank. Always wanting to have the last word.

Refusing to let Frank's antics psych him out, he turned and walked into the restaurant, sat down at his table and ordered his meal. When it came, he ate slowly and with relish. Words on paper were nothing but mind games that he wasn't going to play.

Afterward, he went to his room. Debating with himself about what he wanted to do, he hesitated twice and then said what the hell and made the calls, leaving messages at each one.

About fifteen minutes later, one of his calls was returned. He took down the information without comment then sat on the edge of the bed, staring at the numbers. Finally, he picked up the receiver and made one more call, leaving one brief message before hanging up.

He left a wake-up call for midnight, took off his clothes, then laid down and went to sleep.

Frank's confidence had slipped another notch after watching David ignore his latest stunt. Still in his disguise, he'd been at the bar across from the restaurant sipping a drink when David had come running out. He'd been pleased by the anger and confusion he'd seen on David's face. And then he'd seen his brother smile.

It had unnerved him to the point that he'd ordered a second drink. But he'd come to his senses before he drank it, tossed a handful of bills onto the table and left without looking back. He kept running through scenarios all the way to his hotel.

Should he shoot him in the back and get it over with, or follow his urge to confront him first by toying with his mind and watching him come undone?

He thought he would prefer the latter.

When he reached his room, there was a message light blinking on the phone. He frowned. No one knew he was here. He picked up the receiver and punched in the code to the mailbox, listening as the automated voice came on the line.

Mailbox 1077 has one new message. Message received at 8:05 p.m.

Frank's fingers clenched as a man's deep voice slid into his ear.

You missed.

His eyes widened in disbelief as he slammed the phone down. Damn it all to hell and back, how had David found him? He hadn't registered under his own name. He had not even shown his real face. He'd stayed in disguise from morning to night, removing the facial prosthetics only when he went to bed.

The son of a bitch!

Panic spread as he turned out the lights and then moved to the windows. Were they watching his room—just waiting for him to make his move? Was he going to be arrested before he even had a chance to pay David back for the hell he'd put him through?

He stood in the dark, peering into the streets below, trying to sort through the traffic for a sign of something suspicious.

There in the parking lot! Behind the wheel of that car on the end. Someone was sitting in the dark behind the wheel. He could see the end of their cigarette glowing in the dark.

But as he watched, a woman suddenly appeared within his vision, and as she did, the driver of the car emerged and went to meet her. They embraced briefly, then got in the car and drove away.

Frank cursed beneath his breath and moved his attention to some people on foot, certain that he was being watched. Yet each time he thought he'd zeroed in on a target, it would prove him false.

Every time he heard footsteps in the hallway, he expected a knock upon his door, and each time the footsteps went away, he went limp with relief. Finally, his nerves shot, he packed his bag, put on a new disguise and slipped out of the hotel, confident he had not been seen.

So he'd go to the meeting place early. There were plenty of places he could hide without being seen. He had yet to be beaten at his own game.

Even when he'd been shot.

Even when he'd been set on fire.

Even then, he had survived.

Tonight wasn't going to be any different.

Satisfied that he'd gotten away unobserved, Frank got in his car and drove away. He had Bethany's gun, his favorite knife, a one-way ticket to the Florida Keys and was already planning what kind of place he would buy. Something small but comfortable and close to the water. He liked the water. He liked to fish. That's what he would do. By the time he got to the area and parked, he was already planning what kind of furniture he would buy. He started to cross the greens and then paused and went back to the car. He opened the trunk, removed a bag and quickly removed his disguise. When he met David face to face, he wanted him to see the real damage that the fire had done. He needed to see the guilt and the shame on his baby brother's face—right before he killed him.

* * *

David rolled over and opened his eyes, wide awake and rested before his wake-up call came. When it did, he was already into the preparations for what lay ahead.

His pants were black and fit close to his body, leaving no loose fabric to catch on anything. A black shirt—lightweight but long-sleeved, to cover any white flesh that would show in the dark. Black, flat-heeled, rubber-soled shoes, soundless on any surface. In the bag that he carried was a handgun—the same one he'd used to free the hostages—a knife that he'd carried since Vietnam and a cell phone that was, for the moment, turned off. He tossed a small tin of camouflage face paint into the mix and then zipped the bag.

Exiting his room, he decided against the elevator and made his way to the stairs, taking the six floors down in less than a minute, retrieving his car from hotel parking without being observed, and was on the street within seconds—a true credit to being Jonah. He drove through the streets of D.C., parked on a side street beneath a broken streetlight and quickly disappeared into the night.

Although it had been a long time since he'd actually been on any missions, it felt normal, even comfortable to blend with the shadows. He'd learned long ago that darkness could be a friend, and in his business, he had few friends he could claim.

As he moved through the area, he felt the differences in the air out in the open as opposed to that beneath the trees. Even at night, there was a difference in temperature. It even felt thicker, although he knew that was a fanciful thought.

Once, he paused near a cluster of shrubs and glanced at the sky. What heavenly bodies had been visible were now all but obliterated by a growing bank of clouds.

On the horizon, he could see the faint threads of distant

lightning, although the storm was too far away to be heard. He glanced at the digital readout on his wristwatch and then resumed his trek.

It wouldn't be long now.

Would Frank be waiting where he'd said he'd be, or would he be lying in wait, waiting to shoot him in the back as he passed?

David couldn't assume that his brother would do anything honorable. Not at this point. He didn't know what to expect, but he did know that whatever it was Frank had planned, he would most likely have a slim-to-none chance of survival.

Although he didn't like the odds, it was the *slim* that he focused on, rather than the *none*. He'd survived a lot worse with a lot poorer odds, so he hastened his steps, moving quickly now, anxious to get there. Anxious to get it over with.

By the time he got within seeing distance of the Wall, he was moving with extreme caution—always staying within cover until he was confident of the area before him. Dressed like the shadows within which he moved, he got as close as he could.

David stood quietly for long, silent minutes as time continued to pass. The closer and closer it came to 2:00 a.m., the more certain he was that Frank was nearby. But there was no way he could get to the Wall without being seen, so he stood and he waited, praying for something to change. When it did, he took it as a positive sign that God might be on his side.

It started to rain, first a whisper of mist, and then, within seconds, a blinding downpour. He was instantly drenched, but it was the first time in his life he could ever remember being glad to be this wet. The heavy rainfall afforded him the best cover he could possibly have achieved. And, as though he was fairly certain at this point that he could have walked up on Frank without being seen, he wouldn't abandon all caution.

He dropped to his stomach and started to crawl.

Chapter 14

Despite the dark, overcast sky, the lights from the surrounding monuments kept the night at bay, and even though the hour was late, an occasional tourist could be seen meandering on the path leading to the Vietnam Memorial. Frank figured them as vets by their army surplus clothing and the way they lingered at the Wall, as if standing at attention. They didn't stay long, but the intermittent appearance of strangers kept him nervous. What if their presence kept David away?

With each passing hour, Frank felt himself coming unwound. This moment had been too long in coming. Instead of being tensed and focused, he felt weary and old. Hell, he was old in the ways that counted.

The fact that he'd been here at the monument far longer than he'd planned to be wasn't making things any easier. Within an hour of leaving the hotel, he knew that he'd overreacted, but it was too late to go back. So he had walked the area until midnight, searching for the best place to hide, finally settling among a thick stand of shrubs beneath a cluster of trees. Sheltered from most of the lighting and from any passersby, he began his watch.

Now he'd been here for hours. It was well after one in the morning, his knees were hurting, and the overcast sky had started to come undone. What had begun as a faint, drifting mist was escalating into an all-out thunderstorm, seriously diminishing his view. From where he was hiding, he could no longer see the Wall. If and when David showed, he wouldn't know it. If the rain didn't stop, he would have to move, well aware that when he did, he would give himself away. So he watched the time, hoping the storm would pass.

It didn't.

Thirty minutes later, the rain was still coming down and it was time to end that which had been left undone. He emerged from the bushes, completely soaked. Although the gesture was futile, he swiped his hands across his face to clear his vision, then checked his weapons.

His knife was still in his vest and the gun he'd taken from Bethany's husband was on his hip. The familiar shape of metal against his palm was comforting to a man who had lived his life by the sword.

Once more, he glanced at the digital readout on his watch. It was exactly 2:00 a.m. He straightened his shoulders and started to walk, no longer concerned about staying concealed. Face to face was how it had begun. Face to face was how it would end.

He moved past the statue of the nurses honoring the women who'd served in Vietnam, staying on the footpath that would bring him in at the east end of the Wall. Although the lights still burned, the Wall itself was a dark blur within the downpour. He felt the ground beginning to slope and knew he was moving downward on the right path. Every sensory nerve that he had was on overload as he listened, trying to decipher sounds that didn't belong to the storm. By the time he reached the apex of the memorial he was in knots, damning his brother and damning this rain.

It took David several seconds to realize that one of the shadows he'd been watching had started to move. Only after he blinked did he realize that it wasn't the shadow that was moving, but the man who was passing through.

His pulse jerked, but it was the only thing about his body in motion. He lay flat to the ground and watched, confident that Frank could pass right by him and never know he was there. He also knew that if he wanted, he could shoot Frank right now, without a word, without having to look at his face.

And it had to be said that he considered it. He wanted this over with in the very worst way, but he could also subdue and arrest him. It wouldn't be hard. That would leave the mess with Uncle Sam. It would, however, also endanger SPEAR, and that couldn't happen.

He knew Frank well enough by now to know that if he wound up in jail, there wasn't a cell in solitary strong enough to stop him from talking. With a few well-chosen words to the right—or wrong—people, SPEAR's benefit to the world would be null and void. And so David lay in the rain, struggling with his conscience and with what he knew he would have to do, all the while watching as Frank came closer and closer.

Frank was jumpy enough, but when a shaft of lightning suddenly struck nearby, shattering what was left of his control and striking close enough that he ducked, he hit the ground with a curse. Momentarily blinded by the flash, he covered his eyes. When he finally struggled to his feet,

David was standing less than ten feet away. Adrenaline kicked like a mule as he went into a crouch, grabbing the pistol, swinging it toward his brother's chest.

"Hello, Frank. Long time no see."

Frank was pissed. He was the only one holding a weapon and yet once again, his brother seemed to have taken the upper hand. He straightened, unwilling to be the one who'd first taken a defensive stance.

Rain pelted both men, running down their faces and onto the ground between them, culminating in an eddying swirl that disappeared into some underground drain.

"You son of a bitch," Frank snarled.

David stared, trying to find the brother he'd once known in the tangled flesh of that man's face.

"We came from the same woman, Frank. Be careful what you say."

Frank roared. The rage came up and out of him without warning, diluted by the rain and tempered by the power of the storm.

"You set me on fire! What kind of a brother would do something like that? Answer me!" he screamed. "I want to know! I need to know!"

"I didn't set you on fire to harm you. I was trying to hide the shame of what you'd done from everyone, including the military. Besides, I thought you were dead."

Forty years of anger overwhelmed whatever caution Frank Wilson had left.

"Bull!" he screamed, and started walking toward David, the gun aimed right at his face.

But David didn't move—didn't even back up. Instead, he extended his arms to his sides, and for a moment it looked to Frank as if David was offering himself up for crucifixion.

"So...you're going to shoot me again, are you, brother?"

Frank stumbled. "What the hell do you mean...again?"

David stared at him without moving, unflinching beneath the onslaught of the storm and the dark, ominous barrel of the gun in his brother's hand.

"You shot first, you sanctimonious bastard," David said. "The gunrunner's money was worth more to you than I was, remember?"

Frank's heart skipped a beat. His gut started to burn.

"Shut up," he yelled. "Just shut up and say your prayers."

"I've already said them earlier today," David said. "Don't you remember?"

"Yeah, I saw you playing Boy Scout for that old man," Frank yelled. "You cared more for him than you did for me. I had a good thing going there in Nam and you screwed it up. We would have both been set for life when the war was over. But no, you had to play Boy Scout then, too, didn't you?"

Anger pushed back at David, and he started to talk, raising his voice with every word until at the end he was shouting at Frank through the rain.

"You were selling our guns to the enemy, Frank. How do you justify that in your sleep? How many ghosts haunt your dreams every night? How many men did you put on this wall?"

Frank shook his head. "You're changing the subject. Stop changing the subject!"

"No," David shouted. "You *are* the subject. Your whole life has been selfish. No one ever mattered to you. No one ever counted but you. You've spent the last twelve months trying to bring me down, and still you couldn't do it. You didn't give a damn that you were ruining good people's lives, or that you had put our entire country in jeopardy. All you wanted was revenge. But it's not going to happen. It's over, Frank. Even if you kill me, you're finished. You'll never get away.''

Frank blinked, suddenly aware that his brother might not have come alone, after all. He glanced over David's shoulder into the darkness, waiting for the shadows to move. Desperate to get this over with, he took aim again.

"I will get away, just like I've always done.'' Then he smiled.

David hid a shudder when the scars on Frank's face twisted the smile into a demonic grimace.

But Frank didn't give a damn about how he looked and he wasn't through turning the knife in his brother's heart. If David loved Cara Justice as much as Frank thought he did, his little trump card would drive David insane. The idea was good. He wouldn't wait any longer to lay it down.

"She's pretty, you know. You always did have good taste in women.''

David's mind went blank. He couldn't think past the gut-wrenching fear and the smile on Frank's face.

"She's even pretty when she sleeps,'' Frank continued, and then laughed, a low, cunning chuckle that made David's flesh crawl.

Oh, God. Oh, Cara. "What the hell have you done?''

Frank's smile grew wider. The fear on David's face was what he'd been needing. Now he was back in control.

"Done? Why, nothing you wouldn't have done in my place,'' he said.

David flinched, his mind racing.

"As for your daughter, she's a fine-looking woman, too. This is her gun, you know. Consider it justice that your child's possession will be the thing that ends your life.''

Frank cocked the hammer on the pistol.

He never saw the knife David palmed until it was imbedded to the hilt in his chest. Oddly enough, there was no pain, only a rapidly spreading weakness. The gun slid from his fingers as he reached for the knife, trying to pull it out with both hands. Instead, his legs went out from under him and he fell backward and face up in the rain, his thoughts scattering as quickly as the blood ran out of his body.

This isn't fair. It wasn't supposed to happen this way.

David bolted, grabbing Frank by the shoulders and shaking him where he lay, the fear inside him so great, he could barely make himself heard.

"What did you do to Cara! Tell me, you son of a bitch. If you hurt her, I swear to God I'll follow you to hell."

Frank's eyes rolled back in his head. He wanted to laugh. He wanted to tell what he'd done, but words were beyond him. He sighed, and the sound came out in bloody bubbles. Like most of his life, it was a wasted effort as he died in David's hands.

David rocked on his knees and lifted his face to the storm.

"No!" he raged, and then pushed himself upright, fumbling in his pocket for a phone then punching in a quick code.

Seconds later, a voice answered. David's orders were painfully brief.

"This is Jonah. I need a cleanup crew at the Vietnam Memorial and I need it now."

"Yes, sir! In less than five."

David disconnected, then quickly dialed Cara's number.

It rang.

And it rang.

It rang while his heart began to shrivel.

It rang as he watched Frank's blood going down the drain with the rain.

It rang when he picked up Bethany's gun and put it in his belt.

It rang as he turned his face to the Wall and wanted to die.

He disconnected, then took a slow, sickening breath and dialed another number, unable to even pray.

It rang twice.

On the third ring, Bethany answered.

"Hello?"

The startled sound of her voice was a blessing. He took a deep breath and tried to speak, but the words wouldn't come.

"Hello? Is anyone there?"

"Bethany."

He heard a hesitation, and then a catch in her voice.

"Daddy…is that you?"

Suddenly blinded by more than the rain, he staggered away into the darkness, his chest swelling with a pain he couldn't ignore.

"Yes…it's me…your mother…I can't—"

"She's here," Bethany cried, and he heard her calling Cara's name, then she returned to the phone. "Someone broke into our home and injured my husband, Tom. He's in the hospital. It's only a mild concussion but they wanted him to stay. Mother's been here with the children so I could be with him during the day."

Ah, God…she was alive. They were both alive.

He started to cry, hot, burning tears that tore up his throat, leaving him both mute and blind.

"Are you coming home soon?" Bethany asked, unaware her voice had taken on the tone of a hesitant child.

He looked behind him and moved deeper into the shadows. Some of his agents were arriving on the scene. He was still struggling to be able to speak.

"Yes…I'll be home soon."

"I can't wait," Bethany said, and then she added, "Mother wouldn't tell me anything about where you've been. She said it was your story to tell." Then she added quickly, "Mother's here now. I'm glad you called."

"So am I," he said gruffly, then held his breath, waiting for the sound of Cara's voice.

"David?"

He felt weak. Just his name on her lips was all he needed to hear—to know that it was going to be all right after all.

"Yes, baby, it's me."

He heard a catch in her breath and then she whispered, as if she didn't want Bethany to hear.

"Is it over?"

He closed his eyes, wondering if the nightmares would ever go away.

"Yes, it's over."

"Are you all right? I was so worried."

"I was worried about you, too," he said softly. "Bethany said someone broke into her house. Do they know who it was?"

"Not a clue," Cara said. "We've been afraid to close our eyes for fear he would come back."

David hesitated, but leaving them in fear was unthinkable, especially when he knew all the answers.

"Tell her not to worry anymore. He won't be back."

"I don't understand," Cara said. "How could you possibly—"

He heard her gasp, then he heard a soft moan.

"David...my God...are you saying that it was—"

"He said you were beautiful when you slept."

There was a long, startled silence. He couldn't see, but he knew then that she was probably crying.

"He was here?"

"Is Tom missing his gun?"

"Yes."

"I think I have it. I'll bring it back when I come."

"Oh, my God."

"He didn't touch you? He didn't hurt you in any way?" David asked.

"No, my God, no! My security alarm didn't go off or anything."

"Have an electrician look at it tomorrow...or rather today," he said. "It was probably bypassed."

"I will. I will." Then she lowered her voice again, only this time not in fear. "When are you coming home?"

He almost managed to smile. "Soon, baby. Soon."

"You're not in any kind of trouble or anything...I mean because of—"

"No."

"You're sure?"

This time he did smile. "I'm sure. I have... clearance...for this kind of thing."

The hesitation was longer this time before she answered, and he knew she was absorbing the fact that the man she loved had a license to kill.

"David?"

"Yes."

"I love you very much."

He closed his eyes as the last of his anger washed away with the rain. She made this all worthwhile.

"I love you, too," he said softly. "Have you been picking out that wedding date like I asked you?"

"No."

"Why not?"

"Because you're part of this act, so we're going to do it together. Is that okay?"

"Yeah, that's okay."

"David?"

"Yes, baby?"

"I'm so sorry."

He looked back at the Wall. There was no one in sight. Nothing to prove that he or Frank Wilson had ever been there at all. And even if someone had seen what had happened, it wouldn't have really mattered. A man can't die twice. And Frank's name was already on the Wall.

"Yes, Cara...so am I."

It was after four in the morning when David walked into his hotel room, hanging the Do Not Disturb sign on the doorknob as he went. He walked straight to the bathroom, leaving behind a trail of water from his clothes. The moment he was inside, he began stripping them off, leaving them in a sodden pile on the floor as he got in the shower.

It might have seemed odd for a man who'd been so wet for so long to feel the need to wash, but he felt tainted to the soul by all that had transpired. The only saving grace had been in knowing that Frank would never be able to threaten or harm anyone again.

Bracing himself against the walls, David leaned into the spray, lifting his face and then bowing his head to the power of the jets. He stood that way for what seemed like an eternity before he reached for shampoo. Methodically pouring a dollop of the creamy liquid into his hand, he worked it into his hair and rinsed, then picked up the soap bar and did the same for the rest of his body. He scrubbed until his skin was tingling and the bar had dissolved. Weary in body and heart, he crawled out of the shower and grabbed a towel from the rack, halfheartedly drying as he went. With a bone-deep groan, he collapsed facedown in the middle of the bed and closed his eyes.

It was four-thirty in the morning.

At noon the next day, his phone rang. He rolled over on his back and reached for the receiver without opening his eyes.

"Hello."

"I'm calling to express my sympathies for the way things went last night."

David recognized the President's voice and sat up in bed, rubbing the sleep from his eyes.

"Thank you, sir. I'm sorry I didn't call you right after it—"

"Not necessary. I got the word. I'm also wondering if it would be possible for you to come to my office...say around four?"

"Today?"

A soft chuckle sounded in his ear. "Yes, if you don't mind."

David scooted to the side of the bed. "Of course not, sir. I will be there."

"Thank you." Then he added, "It's almost over, isn't it, son?"

David slumped, his head dropping between his shoulders.

"Is it ever, sir?"

"Look at it this way. We all have crosses to bear. He *was* yours, but he's in God's hands now."

Oddly enough, hearing someone else verbalize what he'd been trying to convince himself of made it a little easier to accept.

"Yes, sir. You're right."

"Of course I am." He chuckled. "I'm the President. Now you go have yourself a good meal and think about that pretty woman who's waiting for you back home."

David smiled, and in that moment, he knew that whatever else had yet to happen, he was going to be okay.

"Yes, sir."

The line went dead in his ear.

David replaced the receiver then pushed himself off the bed. There were things to do before he went home to Cara. He had to arrange for his personal belongings to be shipped to Chiltingham and buy some presents for his family.

And then he suddenly stopped in the middle of the room and just smiled.

Family.

He had family.

There was a woman who loved him and a daughter who was willing to give him a chance. He even had a son-in-law and granddaughters to formally meet. Granted, they'd seen each other in the airport, but this time it would be different. He would be able to touch them and hold them, and if God was merciful, they would learn to love him.

He took a suit off the hanger, laid it on the bed and went to get a fresh shirt from the drawer. The least he could do was look respectable when he turned in his resignation.

"Sir...the President will see you now."

At the secretary's bidding, David stood abruptly and walked into the Oval Office. The President rose as David entered, and circled his desk, coming toward David with an outstretched hand.

"Glad you could come," the President said, and led him into an adjoining room. "I thought we would be more comfortable in here," he said. "Please sit down. Would you care for something to drink? Coffee? A cola?"

"No, thank you, sir," David said, and unbuttoned the jacket of his suit as he took a seat in a wing chair opposite the one the President had chosen.

For a few moments, David bore the President's silent scrutiny and then someone knocked on the door and the President looked up.

"Catherine, would you hold all my calls for a while. I don't want to be disturbed."

David knew the precision it took to keep a country running as smoothly as this man had done. He owed him a lot for keeping the faith during the security crisis that Frank had caused, yet he waited for him to speak first.

The President cleared his throat and then leaned forward, resting his elbows on his knees and reducing the meeting to that of one man to another.

"You probably deserve a medal for what you've done," the President said. "At the least a commendation." Then he sighed. "You know you'll get neither."

"This job was never about notoriety, sir."

The President nodded and then leaned back in his chair.

"Are you going to be all right?"

"Yes."

"Have you been debriefed since the incident?"

"Yes, sir. I finished about an hour ago."

"That's fine, just fine."

"Sir...if I may speak freely?" David said.

"Yes, of course. What's on your mind?"

"If I had ever been hired, this is where I would hand you my resignation."

The President grinned, amused by David's wry brand of humor.

"Yes, anonymity is a bitch to tackle, isn't it?"

David smiled back. "Yes, sir, considerably so. And...considering the damage that Frank has done to SPEAR's security, you and I both know my effectiveness is over. Besides, it's time I stepped down."

The President nodded. "You're going to be a hard man to replace."

"But you've already done it, haven't you, sir?"

Again surprised by David's intuitive humor, he laughed aloud.

"Actually, yes."

"And he can take control immediately, I hope?"

"He's already in flight."

An amazing weight lifted from David's shoulders. Surprised by how wonderful it felt, he leaned back in his chair and briefly closed his eyes.

"You did an amazing job for us," the President said.

"It was my honor, sir."

"I assume you've taken care of your personal belongings."

"Yes, sir."

"Again, I'm so sorry that I cannot publically acknowledge your unselfish contributions to this country's safety and security, both here and abroad, but there is a tidy little severance package in your name that I hope will soften the blow."

David smiled. He'd already received the paperwork that would net him more retirement money annually than he could have imagined.

"Let's just say it didn't hurt my feelings," David said.

Again, the President laughed, then stood, signaling an end to their conversation.

David stood as well, readying himself to leave.

"Is there anything I can do for you?" the President asked. "Anything at all?"

David hesitated, and then thought, *What the hell. The man asked. All he can do is tell me no.*

"Yes, actually there is," David said.

"Name it."

"If there are any military planes heading toward the state of New York, I'd like a fast ride home."

The President beamed. "I can do you one better than that," he said, and reached for a phone.

Chapter 15

Cara ran a brush through her hair one last time and then did a quick turn in front of the mirror.

"You look beautiful, Mom."

Cara turned. Bethany was standing in the doorway, smiling.

"Except for this lovely bruise, which isn't quite so vivid thanks to pancake makeup, I'll do. As for looking beautiful, so, my dear, do you."

Bethany fidgeted with the neckline of her dress.

"I feel a little bit like I did the first time I went on a date," she said, and then smoothed her hands down the front of her pink summer sheath. "I want him to like me and I want to like him, but I don't really know him."

Cara thought of what David had gone through with Frank, and with the last forty years of his life.

"But you will, darling, in time. Right now, all he is asking for is a chance to get to know you. He isn't trying to take Ray's place in your life, or anything like that."

"I know...but Mom...he's my father. My real father."

Cara stared, a little surprised by the tone in Bethany's voice.

"Why, honey, I never knew you felt anything less from Ray."

"It had nothing to do with the way I was treated, Mom. Please don't believe that. But think about it. Tyler and Valerie are shorter and blond like Ray. I'm taller than everyone in the family, including you. My hair is dark. My eyes are brown. In the family pictures, I looked like the cuckoo's child."

Cara felt like crying. To think Bethany had kept this to herself all these years was heartbreaking.

"I'm so sorry," she said, and hugged her daughter close. "I wish you'd said something to me."

Bethany smiled and shrugged. "What could you have done?"

Cara sighed. "Nothing, I guess, but it might have helped if you'd just talked about it."

"I wasn't sad. Just accepting," Bethany said. "It wasn't like I was the only kid whose father was dead." Then her eyes widened. "That's what makes this so special! It's nothing short of a miracle that he's back in our lives, and as for you marrying him..."

"So you're happy about that, too?"

"No. Ecstatic would be a better word."

Cara sighed. "I called Valerie and Tyler yesterday and told them a little about David."

Bethany frowned. "Surely they weren't upset?"

"I suppose a more accurate description would be puzzled. I'm not the impulsive type, you know, but here I am, engaged within a week to a man I hadn't seen in forty years. I think Tyler wanted to hire a private detective to investigate David's background."

Bethany chuckled. "It would be interesting to see what they came up with, wouldn't it?"

Cara smiled. All Bethany knew was that her dad had worked in a high-level branch of the government that dealt with security. She had no idea of the scope of David's duties or the life that he'd led, and in Cara's opinion, the less said the better. All she wanted was for David to have the life with them that he'd never had.

She wanted him to be able to make new friends and go fishing whenever he wanted. To look forward to rainy days and lazy mornings, and holidays with big family dinners. She wanted to know that, with time, the nightmares he lived with would fade. That's what she wanted for him and for her. God willing, it would happen.

"Where are Tom and the girls?" Cara asked, suddenly realizing the house was too quiet.

"He took them out back for a walk in the woods. I think he wanted to keep them occupied so that we'd have a little time alone together."

"Is he up to that?" Cara asked.

"Yes, I think he'll be all right. I don't know who was happier that he was released yesterday, him or me."

"I knew there was a reason I loved that man," Cara said.

They both laughed.

Suddenly, the back door slammed and they could hear both children shrieking at the top of their lungs. Bethany was out of the room first, with Cara close behind.

"Mommy! Mommy! Come look! Come look! There's a big hepacopter up in the sky."

"Helicopter," Bethany corrected, as she let Kelly lead her outside by the hand. Then she turned toward Cara, smiling. "I can't imagine why all this fuss. You'd think she's never seen a helicopter before."

Cara could hear it, too, and followed them out.

Tom was standing on the porch, shading his eyes from the sun with his hand. He looked a little lopsided with the hair they'd cut away from his wound, but Cara thought he was a hero for standing between his family and a killer and had told him so more than once.

"It's a military chopper," Tom said. "And I think it's going to land."

Cara started to smile. There was only one reason a military helicopter would be landing in her back yard—and he was getting out right now.

She walked off the steps, unwilling to wait a moment longer to feel his arms around her. About ten feet from the back yard fence, the chopper lifted off in a swirl of leaves and grass, leaving the man who'd disembarked to make his own way to the house in the distance.

The distance between Cara's steps increased, and by the time she cleared the gate, she was running.

David ducked his head and closed his eyes as the chopper lifted off. When he turned around, he saw Cara running toward him. The last of his old fears took wing, following the chopper's ascent. He dropped his suitcase and started toward her. Moments later, he was swinging her off her feet and into his arms. This felt so good—so right—and when he thought of how close he'd come to losing both her and Bethany, it made him sick. To this day, he didn't know what had stopped Frank from killing them, and he wasn't going to try to second-guess a man who'd lost his mind.

"I missed you," he whispered, and buried his face in the curve of her neck.

She laughed aloud and then kissed him soundly without care for the quartet who was watching.

"There's someone else who needs a welcome hug," she said softly.

David looked over her shoulder, then put her down.

Cara heard his breath catch and saw the fear in his eyes as Bethany came toward them.

"It will be all right," she said, and gave him a gentle push in the middle of his back.

He went to meet her—this daughter he'd never known—and when they were so close he could see his reflection in the color of her eyes, he reached toward her hair, fingering the dark, silky texture that was so like his own.

"My mother...your grandmother...had hair this color."

For Bethany, he couldn't have said a more perfect thing. This man who was her father was giving her roots to a family she'd never known.

"Was she pretty?" Bethany asked.

David smiled. "Not as pretty as you." Then he held out his hand. "Bethany, I'm really glad to meet you."

Her chin quivered. "I'm really glad to meet you, too." Then, ignoring the handshake he offered, she wrapped her arms around his neck and started to cry.

Two weeks ago, holding a crying woman might have undone him, but not anymore. He had a whole new set of responsibilities, and with so many females in his new family, he suspected that getting used to tears should be first on the list.

Cara came up behind them and put her arms around them both, willing herself not to cry.

David felt her presence and reached for her, pulling her into the family embrace.

Up on the steps a distance away, Bethany's two daughters stared intently at their mother and grandmother being hugged by the stranger. Finally, it was Rachel who spoke.

"Daddy, who's the man hugging Mommy?"

"Honey... it's her daddy."

"I thought Grandpa Ray was her daddy."

Tom sighed. "It's complicated to explain, but trust me, he's her daddy, too."

Rachel frowned. "I think she's crying."

Tom smiled. "Probably."

"Is he hurting her?" she asked.

Tom shook his head and then cupped the back of both his daughters' heads, unable to imagine what David must be feeling, to be holding his own daughter for the very first time.

"No, she's not hurting, she's happy. See how she and Grandma are smiling and talking."

Rachel leaned against her father, uncertain of all this grown-up stuff and even more uncertain where she fit into the mess.

"Is he going to hug me and Kelly, too?"

"I don't think so—at least not yet," Tom said. "But one of these days, I think you're going to want him to."

"Why?"

"Because he's also your grandfather, and grandfathers are really good things."

Rachel looked interested now. She loved Grandpa Joe. He always did lots of stuff with them, like riding bikes and playing tennis with them. She thought of the picture they'd shown her of this man—the one Nanny had on her mantel.

"Do you think he might take us fishing sometime?"

Tom grinned. No matter how young the woman, they always seemed to feel the need to plan a man's life.

"You'll just have to ask him, okay?"

"Okay."

Rachel stood, watching as they started toward the house—her mother, her nanny—and that grandfather she didn't know. And the nearer they came, the quieter she got, almost holding her breath and waiting for that first moment of eye contact between them.

David nodded at Tom and then they shook hands before he turned his attention to the girls.

Granddaughters. Lord in heaven, he had granddaughters. And they were so beautiful—and they looked so confused. He squatted, putting himself at their level.

"Are you Kelly?" he asked, as the little one leaned against her father's leg.

She nodded and then smiled as only an innocent child could.

David's heart melted. He reached behind her ear and pulled out a gold-colored coin.

"You better be careful about washing behind your ears," he teased. "Look what I found back there."

She laughed aloud as he handed her a newly minted dollar.

Rachel held her breath, wondering what he was going to do next. Curious, she tested behind her ears just in case, but there was nothing there.

David saw what she did and stifled a laugh.

"And you're Rachel, aren't you?"

She nodded.

"I remember your rabbit, Henry. I trust he hasn't hopped away anymore?"

Her eyes widened. This was the man who'd found Henry at the airport!

"I know you, don't I!" she cried.

He hesitated briefly, then knowing he was courting rejection, still held out his hand.

"You will, honey. You will."

Rachel glanced at her mother, who nodded an okay. Slowly, she laid her hand in the middle of David's palm, thinking as she did that he was bigger than her daddy and that his eyes were brown like Mom's.

David was a goner, and he knew it. All the ugliness of

the past forty-eight hours withered and died in this little girl's eyes.

"I saw your picture on Nanny's mantel," Rachel said.

"You did? What did you think?" David asked.

She frowned in deliberation, wanting to be fair without actually asking the favor.

"I think you can fish."

He smiled. "Yes, I can. Do you like to fish?"

It was the opening she'd been waiting for.

"Oh, yes, I do. And if you will take me sometime, I will show you how to catch a much bigger fish."

David rocked back on his heels and burst into laughter.

Rachel looked a little startled, not quite sure what everyone thought was so funny, but glad they were happy.

David stood and wrapped his arms around Cara.

"Thank you, darling," he said softly.

"For what?" she asked.

"For letting me know what it feels like to come home."

Epilogue

July 4, 2001

The day was hot and still. In the distance, the United States Marine Band was tuning up as people continued gathering on the mall between the Lincoln Memorial and the Washington Monument. In a few moments, David would join his family for the festivities, but there was something he'd left undone. Something he'd done at the Wall every Fourth of July since its inception.

He started down the pathway in front of the memorial, trying not to think of what had happened here only a few short days before. With the sun beaming down on his bare arms, he should have been sweltering, but his mind was locked into a storm, and the rain pouring down—and his brother pointing a gun at his chest.

Dozens and dozens of people lined the path along the Wall, each paying their own tribute to a loved one on this day of independence. The rose he was carrying felt heavy in his hand—a burden he didn't want to bear. Unconsciously, his fingers clenched, and as they did, a thorn pricked. He winced, but considered the pain as no less than he deserved.

Ten, maybe twelve steps more and he would be there— at the place where Frank had died. He couldn't look down—wouldn't look down—yet when he got there, his gaze automatically fell to the place where Frank had fallen.

He paused, staring at the concrete until his eyes began to burn. Finally he sighed.

Nothing.

They'd left nothing behind—not even a bloodstain marred the place where he had died.

He turned, searching the Wall for Frank's name and then moving through the crowd to touch it, tracing each letter with his fingertip, as if the simple act might resurrect and save a man who'd most likely gone to hell.

"Family?"

He turned. A stately, gray-haired woman dressed in black was standing at his side.

He nodded.

She pointed with a long, perfectly manicured fingertip. "That's my husband's name right below."

He looked. "Anthony C. DeFranco," he read, only afterward realizing that he'd read it aloud.

"I called him Tony," she said, and then dabbed a handkerchief beneath the lenses of her sunglasses. "We'd been married six weeks when he got drafted." She sighed. "I never saw him again."

"I'm very sorry," David said.

She sighed. "Yes, I know. We're all sorry, aren't we? But it happened and all I could do was go on." She shrugged, as if to indicate it was out of her hands. "What could I do? I was still alive, wasn't I?"

Then she walked away, leaving David with her simple truth.

He turned again, this time looking at Frank's name with new emotion. The woman was right. Even though Frank had died only days ago, technically, he'd been dead for forty years and God knows, David had grieved for him more than most.

It was time to move on.

After all, he was still alive.

He laid the red rose at the base of the wall, touched Frank's name one last time and then turned, looking back up the path at the way that he'd come.

Cara was there, as were all of her children. They'd taken to him in spite of themselves, and God willing, they had years and years left to learn to love.

He started to walk, moving against the stream of people who were still filing down—through a group of teenage girls, past a couple arm in arm, then behind a solitary man in an outdated uniform—until Cara was in his arms.

He held her there without speaking beneath the heat of the sun, cherishing the beat of her heart against his chest.

"Okay?" she asked quietly.

He made himself smile, and as he did, realized that for the first time in years it felt right.

"Yes, okay."

"Then let's go home."

They walked away, losing themselves and the past in the gathering crowd.

* * * * *

Coming soon, you won't want to miss this bestselling author's exciting new novel from MIRA books!

Look for SNOWFALL by Sharon Sala in November 2001.

Author Note

I was born during a war, grew up within another, and raised my children during the tragedy that became Vietnam. When I saw a grandchild being born during a war called Desert Storm, I wondered if it would always be so—that we seemed destined to annihilate our youngest and best at least once in every generation.

I lost family and loved ones during the first three wars and watched in horror as the last one was played out on television for all the world to see.

It doesn't seem enough to be dedicating this simple book to them, to all the men and women who have fought over these past one hundred years to keep our country free, but I'm doing it just the same. I'm doing it because I can, and because, after all the time that has passed—other than remember that they lived—it's all I can do.

For my father, Master Sergeant Herman A. Smith, and for all the ones who came before and after, I offer you my heartfelt thanks.

Daddy, I wish you were still alive to read this.

a Year of loving dangerously

If you missed any of the riveting,
romantic Intimate Moments stories from
A Year of Loving Dangerously, here's
a chance to order your copies today!

#1016	**MISSION: IRRESISTIBLE** by Sharon Sala	$4.50 U.S.☐	$5.25 CAN.☐
#1022	**UNDERCOVER BRIDE** by Kylie Brant	$4.50 U.S.☐	$5.25 CAN.☐
#1028	**NIGHT OF NO RETURN** by Eileen Wilks	$4.50 U.S.☐	$5.25 CAN.☐
#1034	**HER SECRET WEAPON** by Beverly Barton	$4.50 U.S.☐	$5.25 CAN.☐
#1040	**HERO AT LARGE** by Robyn Amos	$4.50 U.S.☐	$5.25 CAN.☐
#1046	**STRANGERS WHEN WE MARRIED** by Carla Cassidy	$4.50 U.S.☐	$5.25 CAN.☐
#1052	**THE SPY WHO LOVED HIM** by Merline Lovelace	$4.50 U.S.☐	$5.25 CAN.☐
#1058	**SOMEONE TO WATCH OVER HER** by Margaret Watson	$4.50 U.S.☐	$5.25 CAN.☐
#1064	**THE ENEMY'S DAUGHTER** by Linda Turner	$4.50 U.S.☐	$5.25 CAN.☐
#1070	**THE WAY WE WED** by Pat Warren	$4.50 U.S.☐	$5.25 CAN.☐
#1076	**CINDERELLA'S SECRET AGENT** by Ingrid Weaver	$4.50 U.S.☐	$5.25 CAN.☐
#1082	**FAMILIAR STRANGER** by Sharon Sala	$4.50 U.S.☐	$5.25 CAN.☐

(limited quantities available)

TOTAL AMOUNT	$ _____
POSTAGE & HANDLING	
($1.00 each book, 50¢ each additional book)	$ _____
APPLICABLE TAXES*	$ _____
TOTAL PAYABLE	$ _____
(check or money order—please do not send cash)	

To order, send the completed form, along with a check or money order for the total above, payable to **A YEAR OF LOVING DANGEROUSLY** to: **In the U.S.:** 3010 Walden Avenue, P.O. Box 9077, Buffalo, NY 14269-9077 **In Canada:** P.O. Box 636, Fort Erie, Ontario L2A 5X3.

Name: _____

Address: _____ City: _____

State/Prov.: _____ Zip/Postal Code: _____

Account # (if applicable): _____ 075 CSAS

*New York residents remit applicable sales taxes.
 Canadian residents remit applicable
 GST and provincial taxes.

Silhouette

Visit Silhouette at www.eHarlequin.com

AYOLD-BL11

Feel like a star with Silhouette.

We will fly you and a guest to New York City for an exciting weekend stay at a glamorous 5-star hotel. Experience a refreshing day at one of New York's trendiest spas and have your photo taken by a professional. Plus, receive $1,000 U.S. spending money!

**Flowers...long walks...dinner for two...
how does Silhouette Books
make romance come alive for you?**

Send us a script, with 500 words or less, along with visuals (only drawings, magazine cutouts or photographs or combination thereof). Show us how Silhouette Makes Your Love Come Alive. Be creative and have fun. No purchase necessary. All entries must be clearly marked with your name, address and telephone number. All entries will become property of Silhouette and are not returnable. **Contest closes September 28, 2001.**

Please send your entry to: **Silhouette Makes You a Star!**

In U.S.A.
P.O. Box 9069
Buffalo, NY, 14269-9069

In Canada
P.O. Box 637
Fort Erie, ON, L2A 5X3

Look for contest details on the next page, by visiting www.eHarlequin.com or request a copy by sending a self-addressed envelope to the applicable address above. Contest open to Canadian and U.S. residents who are 18 or over. Void where prohibited.

Silhouette®
Where love comes alive™

Our lucky winner's photo will appear in a Silhouette ad. Join the fun!

SRMYAS1

HARLEQUIN "SILHOUETTE MAKES YOU A STAR!" CONTEST 1308
OFFICIAL RULES
NO PURCHASE NECESSARY TO ENTER

1. To enter, follow directions published in the offer to which you are responding. Contest begins June 1, 2001, and ends on September 28, 2001. Entries must be postmarked by September 28, 2001, and received by October 5, 2001. Enter by hand-printing (or typing) on an 8 ½" x 11" piece of paper your name, address (including zip code), contest number/name and attaching a script containing <u>500 words</u> or less, <u>along with drawings, photographs or magazine cutouts, or combinations thereof</u> (i.e., collage) on no larger than <u>9" x 12"</u> piece of paper, describing how the <u>Silhouette books make romance come alive for you.</u> Mail via first-class mail to: Harlequin "Silhouette Makes You a Star!" Contest 1308, (in the U.S.) P.O. Box 9069, Buffalo, NY 14269-9069, (in Canada) P.O. Box 637, Fort Erie, Ontario, Canada L2A 5X3. Limit one entry per person, household or organization.

2. Contests will be judged by a panel of members of the Harlequin editorial, marketing and public relations staff. Fifty percent of criteria will be judged against script and fifty percent will be judged against drawing, photographs and/or magazine cutouts. Judging criteria will be based on the following:

   - Sincerity—25%
   - Originality and Creativity—50%
   - Emotionally Compelling—25%

   In the event of a tie, duplicate prizes will be awarded. Decisions of the judges are final.

3. All entries become the property of Torstar Corp. and may be used for future promotional purposes. Entries will not be returned. No responsibility is assumed for lost, late, illegible, incomplete, inaccurate, nondelivered or misdirected mail.

4. Contest open only to residents of the U.S. <u>(except Puerto Rico)</u> and Canada who are 18 years of age or older, and is void wherever prohibited by law; all applicable laws and regulations apply. Any litigation within the Province of Quebec respecting the conduct or organization of a publicity contest may be submitted to the Régie des alcools, des courses et des jeux for a ruling. Any litigation respecting the awarding of a prize may be submitted to the Régie des alcools, des courses et des jeux only for the purpose of helping the parties reach a settlement. Employees and immediate family members of Torstar Corp. and D. L. Blair, Inc., their affiliates, subsidiaries and all other agencies, entities and persons connected with the use, marketing or conduct of this contest are not eligible to enter. Taxes on prizes are the sole responsibility of the winner. Acceptance of any prize offered constitutes permission to use winner's name, photograph or other likeness for the purposes of advertising, trade and promotion on behalf of Torstar Corp., its affiliates and subsidiaries without further compensation to the winner, unless prohibited by law.

5. Winner will be determined no later than November 30, 2001, and will be notified by mail. Winner will be required to sign and return an Affidavit of Eligibility/Release of Liability/Publicity Release form within 15 days after winner notification. Noncompliance within that time period may result in disqualification and an alternative winner may be selected. All travelers must execute a Release of Liability prior to ticketing and must possess required travel documents (e.g., passport, photo ID) where applicable. Trip must be booked by December 31, 2001, and completed within one year of notification. No substitution of prize permitted by winner. Torstar Corp. and D. L. Blair, Inc., their parents, affiliates and subsidiaries are not responsible for errors in printing of contest, entries and/or game pieces. In the event of printing or other errors that may result in unintended prize values or duplication of prizes, all affected game pieces or entries shall be null and void. **Purchase or acceptance of a product offer does not improve your chances of winning.**

6. Prizes: (1) Grand Prize—A 2-night/3-day trip for two (2) to New York City, including round-trip coach air transportation nearest winner's home and hotel accommodations (double occupancy) at The Plaza Hotel, a glamorous afternoon makeover at <u>a trendy New York spa</u>, $1,000 in U.S. spending money and an opportunity to <u>have a professional photo taken and appear in a Silhouette advertisement</u> (approximate retail value: $7,000). (10) Ten Runner-Up Prizes of gift packages (retail value $50 ea.). Prizes consist of only those items listed as part of the prize. Limit one prize per person. Prize is valued in U.S. currency.

7. For the name of the winner (available after December 31, 2001) send a self-addressed, stamped envelope to: Harlequin "Silhouette Makes You a Star!" Contest 1197 Winners, P.O. Box 4200 Blair, NE 68009-4200 or you may access the www.eHarlequin.com Web site through February 28, 2002.

Contest sponsored by Torstar Corp., P.O Box 9042, Buffalo, NY 14269-9042.

SRMYAS